DREAM OF FAIR
to middling
WOMEN

Other Works by Samuel Beckett

Novels:
MURPHY	THE UNNAMABLE
WATT	HOW IT IS
FIRST LOVE	COMPANY
MERCIER AND CAMIER	ILL SEEN ILL SAID
MOLLOY	WORSTWORD HO
MALONE DIES	

Short Prose:
MORE PRICKS THAN KICKS	SIX RESIDUA
FOUR NOVELLAS	FOR TO END YET AGAIN
TEXTS FOR NOTHING	and other Fizzles
ALL STRANGE AWAY	COLLECTED SHORTER PROSE
IMAGINATION DEAD IMAGINE	1945–1988
NO'S KNIFE	STIRRINGS STILL

Poems:
AN ANTHOLOGY OF MEXICAN POETRY (translation)
ZONE (translation)
COLLECTED POEMS 1930–1989

Criticism:
PROUST and THREE DIALOGUES WITH GEORGES DUTHUIT
DISJECTA

Plays:
WAITING FOR GODOT	ENDS AND ODDS
ENDGAME	*Ends*
ACT WITHOUT WORDS I	NOT I
ACT WITHOUT WORDS II	THAT TIME
ALL THAT FALL	FOOTFALLS
KRAPP'S LAST TAPE	GHOST TRIP (TV play in *Journal*
EMBERS	*of Beckett Studies: I)*
HAPPY DAYS	. . . but the clouds . . . (TV play)
CASCANDO	*Odds*
WORDS AND MUSIC	4 ROUGHS (2 Radio, 2 Theatre)
PLAY	OHIO IMPROMPTU
COME AND GO	ROCKABY
EH JOE	CATASTROPHE
BREATH	PEACE OF MONOLOGUE
	WHAT WHERE

Film Scenario:
FILM

Samuel Beckett

DREAM OF FAIR
to middling
WOMEN

Edited by
Eoin O'Brien and Edith Fournier

Foreword by
Eoin O'Brien

ARCADE PUBLISHING • NEW YORK
in association with Riverrun Press

First North American Edition 1993

Library of Congress Cataloging-in-Publication Data

Beckett, Samuel, 1906–1989
    Dream of fair to middling women / Samuel Beckett ; edited by Eoin O'Brien and Edith Fournier ; foreword by Eoin O'Brien. —1st North American ed.
      p. cm.
    ISBN 1-55970-217-6
    I. O'Brien, Eoin. II. Fournier, Edith. III. Title.
    PR6003.E282D74   1993
    823'.912—dc20   92-56275

Published in the United States by Arcade Publishing, Inc., New York, in association with Riverrun Press

Distributed by Little, Brown and Company

10 9 8 7 6 5 4 3 2 1

Printed in the United States of America

PUBLISHER'S NOTE

The publication of Samuel Beckett's *Dream of Fair to middling Women* is an important event, both in itself and because, at long last, it brings to the public an essential text that has too long been available only to scholars.

Much will be made of the fact that Beckett did not allow the work to be published during his lifetime, and that when he referred to it, it was generally in derogatory terms. But those of us who knew Beckett for a long time—in my case roughly forty years—are well aware that he was prone to deprecate most, if not all, of his earlier work. Even *Waiting for Godot* did not go unscathed. In the 1970s when my wife and I were invited to see the revival of *Godot*, which was staged at the Odéon theater in Paris, we met the author after the play at a café in Montparnasse. Beckett was nursing a drink, and when we arrived he stood and greeted us warmly, as always, but then sat down and resumed communing for what seemed to us a very long time with the drink. Finally he asked us what we had thought of the play. We waxed enthusiastic, our reaction sincere, as he listened in silence. He knew that we had seen the original production some twenty years before at the tiny Théâtre de Babylone. "The stage is too big," he said, "far too big," referring

v

to the generous proportions of the Odéon. We agreed that perhaps the play had lost a smidgen of its intimacy, but none of its power. He shook his head. "The text," he said, "it doesn't stand up. . . ." His voice trailed off. Would he have liked to go back and change it? No, he couldn't do that. It was what it was. But, on an evening that, from our viewpoint, should have been a celebration—for bringing *Godot* to the Odéon, a national theater, was a consecration—there was a definite undertone of wake on the part of the author. He, who was constantly honing, paring away the words that seemed either excessive or imprecise, moving ineluctably toward the silence that had always been so important to him, could see nothing but the flaws. Despite that, we eventually repaired, with the play's designer, Alberto Giacometti—whose stark set at the Odéon Beckett did fully appreciate—to a *boîte* a block or two away where, late in the evening, Beckett actually accepted an invitation to get up and dance.

All this is to say that if he was harsh about *Waiting for Godot*, a play that had revolutionized contemporary theater, was universally hailed as a masterpiece, and was constantly being performed around the world, one can readily imagine how unremitting his judgment could be of his earlier work. It took years and years of cajoling to get him to allow publication of *Mercier and Camier*, or the reissue of works long out of print such as *More Pricks than Kicks* or *Whoroscope*. The fact is that when he wrote *Dream of Fair to middling Women*, he ardently desired to see it published. He wrote it in the summer of 1932, after having abruptly resigned his teaching post at Trinity College, Dublin, finding teaching to be anathema to him, and he wrote it in what has been described as a "white heat," finishing it before the end of summer. Having given up his two hundred pounds per annum stipend from Trinity, and with only symbolic monetary help from his parents, he felt the urgent need to earn some money from his writing. He knew that the book—which among other things contained incidents of sexual congress and masturbation, or what could very well be taken for such—could not be published in his native country, for reasons of censorship, which the editors of the present volume describe. He also knew it was impossible for any French publisher to take on and translate the novel, with its puns and wordplay, its word inventions and intentional misspellings. Most of his literary connections were in Paris, but the little magazines there were not in a position to publish more than an extract or two.

That left London. Beckett took the manuscript to England and sent it around to various British publishers. Chatto and Windus, who the previous year had published Beckett's perceptive essay on Proust to critical praise and considerable commercial success, seemed a likely prospect, as did the young, literary-oriented houses, Jonathan Cape and the Hogarth Press. But by early autumn 1932, he had found no takers and was down to his last five-pound note. One publisher's reader noted: "Beckett's probably a clever fellow . . . but I wouldn't touch this with a barge-pole." Another commented that it was "a slavish imitation of Joyce." Its erotic content was also duly noted, needless to say negatively, and the word *indecent* was prominent in the evaluation. On October 8, 1932, Beckett wrote from Dublin, to which he was forced to retreat after his London debacle, to his close friend and fellow poet George Reavey:

The novel doesn't go. Shatton and Windup thought it was wonderful, but they couldn't, they simply could not. The Hogarth Private Lunatic Asylum rejected it the way Punch would. Cape was écoeueré [*sic*] in pipe and cardigan and his aberdeen terrier agreed with it. Grayson has lost it or cleaned himself with it. Kick his balls off. They are all over 66 Curzon St. W.l.

I'll be here till I die, creeping along genteel roads on a stranger's bike.

Subsequently, Beckett sent the novel to other British publishers, but to no avail. That he wanted it published and was sorely disappointed when it was not is uncontestable.

Twenty years after this first effort at publication, another opportunity arose for the book, at long last, to see the light of day. In 1951, a young group of us living in Paris began publishing a literary magazine reminiscent in many ways of those that flowered when Beckett first came to Paris. In the second issue of that magazine I wrote an essay on Beckett in which, with fairly little to go on—*Murphy, Molloy*, and *Malone Dies*—I proclaimed Beckett a writer of major importance "to anyone interested in contemporary literature." Subsequently, *Merlin* featured something by Beckett in virtually every issue of the magazine. When, the following year, the *Merlin* group began to publish an occasional book and, having heard that Beckett—who by then was writing and publishing in French—had one, possibly two, unpublished manuscripts in English, I wrote the author through the intermediary of his French publisher, Jérôme Lindon, asking if *Merlin* could see it/them, with a view toward publication. The two were, *Dream of Fair to middling Women* and *Watt*, the second of which Beckett had written in the Vaucluse during the war. Eventually

Beckett brought by the manuscript of *Watt*, which "Collection Merlin" duly published in 1953 in an edition of 1,125 copies, of which 25 were a limited edition signed by the author and 1,100 intended for "general circulation." Beckett again wrote his old friend George Reavey, who after World War II had made a valiant effort to place *Watt* with a British publisher, without success:

> Also, (tiens-toi bien) our old misery, Watt [is due out] with the Merlin juveniles, who are beginning a publishing house.

Two months later, after the book appeared, Beckett wrote Reavey again:

> Watt is just out in an awful magenta cover from the Merlin Press.

Subsequently, we approached him with the idea of publishing the "other novel in English," but Beckett politely declined. Whether his attitude was the result of the "awful magenta" cover of *Watt* or his reluctance to see *Dream* in print at that time will forever remain a mystery.

There was a final possibility the novel might be published in Beckett's lifetime. In 1986, when Beckett's long-time friend, American publisher Barney Rosset, was unceremoniously deposed from Grove Press, the publishing house he had founded, Beckett, quite characteristically, looked for ways to help. The best way would be to give him an unpublished work, and *Dream* came immediately to mind. Beckett discussed the idea with the future editor of the work, Eoin O'Brien, who had recently published the monumental *The Beckett Country*, which the author greatly admired, but eventually Beckett decided he could not face the pain—O'Brien's words—of going back to the manuscript. But, as O'Brien relates in his Foreword, Beckett did recognize that the book should indeed be published, but not until "some little time after my death."

There is doubtless a kind of ironic, if belated, justice in the fact that, after all, *Dream of Fair to middling Women* was first published in Ireland, the only one of his works to be so honored, under the aegis of the Black Cat Press, of which Eoin O'Brien is a principal. I suspect, too, that Beckett would have been pleased to know that this first, simultaneous American and U.K. edition of "the chest into which [he] threw [his] wild thoughts" has been a collaborative effort between two of his oldest friends and publishing colleagues, his British publisher John Calder and me, and that Barney Rosset's advice and counsel on many key aspects of the publishing process of the work were cogent and perceptive.

—Richard Seaver

FOREWORD

"The chest into which I threw my wild thoughts."

Dream of Fair to middling Women, Samuel Beckett's first novel which has remained unpublished for sixty years, was written at the Trianon Hotel, on the Rue de Vaugirard in Paris, during the summer of 1932 when the author was twenty-six years old.

At the time Samuel Beckett's published writings consisted of a prize-winning poem *Whoroscope* published in 1930, two essays of criticism: "Dante . . . Bruno . Vico . . Joyce" published in 1929 in the collective work *Our Exagmination Round His Factification for Incamination of Work in Progress*, and his *Proust*, published in 1931. Some eight poems and several of his short prose texts had also been published in reviews among which were, a piece of satire "Che Sciagura" (1929), four short prose pieces, "Assumption", "The Possessed", "Text" and "Sedendo et Quiescendo"; the latter two were to be included in *Dream* along with some of the poems in prose form. In essence, therefore, this work of fiction reaches back to the author's deeper roots in earlier days and forward to future writings in that it foretells much of what was to follow in poetry, prose and drama. Indeed many aspects of Samuel Beckett's philosophy are enunciated in *Dream: "Doubt, Despair and Scrounging, shall I hitch my bath chair to the greatest of these?"* Some semi-autobiographical elements are prevalent in the portrait of Belacqua, the main character of the book, yet they are not to be overrated. The timeless span, later to become so characteristic of Beckett's work, gives to *Dream* a universal value for the reader to assess, fathom and enjoy.

Dream was submitted by Samuel Beckett to a number of publishers without success. He knew that Ireland offered no hope given the anti-intellectualism of Irish Catholicism at the time and the lack of any rational objectivity in the unrelenting attitude of the Irish Censorship Board, which certainly would not have brooked such a novel as *Dream of Fair to middling Women*. He later castigated the Board in a witty essay, "Censorship in the Saorstat" (1935), by which time he himself was a victim with the banning of *More Pricks than Kicks*. London publishers were to prove no more audacious when he went there in 1933, hoping to find one sympathetic to *Dream*.

Rather than pursue the fruitless fight for publication, Samuel Beckett decided to assemble some of the stories from *Dream* with others, including "Dante and the Lobster" which had been published in the Paris review *This Quarter* in December 1932. This collection of stories was published in London in 1934 as *More Pricks than Kicks*. That he had not at this time resigned himself to the rejection of *Dream* and that he intended, moreover, to have *Dream* published, albeit at some future unspecified date, is announced in *More Pricks than Kicks*:

*The powers of evocation of this Italianate Irishman
were simply immense, and if his Dream of Fair to
Middling Women, held up in the limæ labor stage for
the past ten or fifteen years, ever reaches the public,
and Walter says it is bound to, we ought all be sure to
get it and have a look at it anyway.*

In much later years, Samuel Beckett would express his
strong doubts and misgivings about the creation of more
youthful days, as indeed about much of his published work
("my other writings are no sooner dry than they revolt
me"), including *More Pricks than Kicks* which he forbade
to have reprinted for many years. Alert to these misgivings, while aware also that his deep feelings about *Dream*
were not so clear-cut and hostile as he may have let appear,
the decision to publish *Dream* has not been taken lightly.
Indeed, if today *Dream* reaches the public as it was "bound
to", it is at Samuel Beckett's own behest, expressed to me
in talks on the subject between 1975 and 1989.

When I began writing *The Beckett Country: Samuel
Beckett's Ireland* in 1975, I realised how deficient a book
purporting to illustrate the origins of much of Samuel Beckett's writing would be if *Dream*, a novel which ranks as one
of his most Irish writings, was not referred to. He agreed to
my quoting whatever I wished to take from *Dream* for *The
Beckett Country*. My reading of the transcribed copy of the
manuscript of *Dream* at the Beckett Archive in Reading
University was, of necessity, perfunctory at the time, but it
led to many discussions with Samuel Beckett about the
work. In particular, I recall, he was interested in the reaction of a man more than thirty years his junior to *Dream*
or, as he called it, *"the chest into which I threw my wild
thoughts"*. His interest was all the more acute, I think, because he had forgotten much of the detail of *Dream* and it

allowed us to wallow gently in the nostalgia of his Dublin. We discussed, during those meetings in Paris, his having "pilfered" the "chest" and whether or not anything worthwhile remained. Such discussions were a means of fond recollection, yet he could not tolerate memories of times past if the pain became too acute. When, for example, I showed him the photograph I had found of Bill Shannon, the postman of *Dream*—and later of *Watt*—who whistled "The roses are blooming in Picardy", his face, first alight with joy, disassembled into anguish and he knew I appreciated the need for us to part so that he could be alone.

In 1986, Samuel Beckett asked me to visit him in Paris to discuss *Dream*. He was considering, he told me, how best to help a friend to whom he wished to give a text for publication, and he asked me if it should be *Dream*. We did not reach, nor attempt to reach, a decision that evening, but merely bandied about the pros and cons. When I returned to see him shortly afterwards, he had made up his mind. He could not face the pain of going back to the "chest" where, whether they had been happy or fraught with sorrow, the wild thoughts of his youth-days were so vividly stored.

Shortly afterwards, he told me *Dream* should be published, but he did not want this to happen until he was gone "for some little time". He asked me to hold the "key" to the "chest" until I thought fit.

The original typed manuscript of *Dream* had remained in Samuel Beckett's possession until 1961 when he gave it, with other texts, to Lawrence E. Harvey to assist him in writing his critical monograph *Samuel Beckett: Poet & Critic* which remains the finest biographical study published on Beckett. Harvey gave the manuscript to Dartmouth College, New Hampshire in 1971, stating in so doing that he regarded *Dream* as "valuable for the insights it provides into the temperament, intellect, talent, and interests of the young Beckett and constitutes the necessary point of departure in assessing his development as a writer".

Dream is indeed such and very much more besides. It is a major literary achievement and this consideration, together with Samuel Beckett's wishes in regard to publication, led his literary executor and long-time friend, Jérôme Lindon, to grant permission for me to edit *Dream* for publication.

Up to now *Dream* has been available only to scholars and researchers who could peruse the original manuscript in the Dartmouth archives, or, later on, a typed transcription of it in the Beckett Archive at Reading University. This has led inevitably to an unsatisfactory state of affairs whereby much of *Dream* has been quoted and published, with more or less appropriate comments, in substantial extracts which deny the reader an objective, unbiased and personal appreciation of the whole novel. Moreover, such extracts can but dangerously misrepresent the entire work.

Samuel Beckett himself, as I have pointed out, "pilfered the chest" which served as a point of commencement for many later works—*Happy Days* and *Krapp's Last Tape* spring to mind. It was also a depository for some earlier writings—the poems "Enueg I", "Dortmunder", "Alba" and "Casket of Pralinen for a Daughter of a Dissipated Mandarin" being examples. Substantial parts of *Dream* appear almost verbatim in *More Pricks than Kicks*, notable examples being "The Smeraldina's Billet Doux", "Ding-Dong" and "A Wet Night". Here again such extracts can but give a restricted and pale idea of the whole novel. *More Pricks than Kicks* is a collection of vignettes of Dublin life; *Dream of Fair to middling Women* has the wealth of the complete form and full structure of a novel about a young man, his loves and travels in Europe.

Thus *Dream* provides us with some precious, almost *archaeological*, insights into the developing aesthetics of a remarkable mind, demonstrating the path that the later works were to follow. For example, we see the artist in turmoil with himself and with art:

The mind suddenly entombed, then active in an anger and a rhapsody of energy, in scurrying and plunging towards exitus, such is the ultimate mode and factor of the creative integrity, its proton, incommunicable; but there, insistent, invisible rat, fidgeting behind the astral incoherence of the art surface.

As Samuel Beckett struggles with the essence of the artistic experience, solutions become apparent:

. . . we do declare and maintain stiffly (at least for the purposes of this paragraph) that the object that becomes invisible before your eyes is, so to speak, the brightest and best.

The future form of writing, if not yet apparent in the exuberance of *Dream*, may be seen, nonetheless, clearly taking shape:

I was speaking of something of which you have and can have no knowledge, the incoherent continuum as expressed by, say, Rimbaud and Beethoven. Their names occur to me. The terms of whose statements serve merely to delimit the reality of insane areas of silence.

Indeed, the expression of his unique vision was only to be fully realised later, when he returned spiritually to the "chest" to find once again the way forward:

The experience of my reader shall be between the phrases, in the silence, communicated by the intervals, not the terms, of the statement, between the flowers that cannot coexist, the antithetical (nothing so simple as antithetical) seasons of words, his experience shall be the menace, the miracle, the memory, of an unspeakable trajectory.

Dream should not, however, be considered only with a backward glance from the vantage point Samuel Beckett's completed *œuvre* provides us with today. Whatever its progeny may have been in the author's later writings, it stands on its own, imposing itself on us with its exuberant wealth, a full-blown "rhapsody of energy", indeed, as Belacqua says. Harvey, most appropriately, alludes to the "verbal exuberance", the "undisciplined fantasy" and the "intellectual virtuosity" to be found in *Dream*. The young Beckett delights in words, he is exhilarated by the use of several languages, inebriated by the sheer joy of inventing new words and coining new phrases which abound "scurrying and plunging towards exitus". Much of the very lively wealth of *Dream* lies in that turmoil of language, in that inventiveness which is far from being merely clever intellectual gymnastics, but much more essentially the expression and deep imprint of Samuel Beckett's vital sense of humour. *Dream* is a book of humour—of "laffing and laffing"—which, like so much of his later work, already belies the serious misconception that his work is only of the dark and gloomy side.

A few words need here be said about the editing of *Dream*. The first is to express the debt I owe my co-editor, Edith Fournier, a life-long friend of Samuel Beckett who has translated some of his works from English to French. Without her help I would have been unable to complete the task of editing which became a much more complex assignment than I had originally envisaged. Precisely on account of the verbal exuberance and inventiveness of *Dream*, we had not only to be obsessional in proofreading—not as straightforward a task as might usually be the case—but, more importantly, we had to discuss nuances that might have been typographical errors made by Samuel Beckett or intentional word-playing and wordcoining, precious "margaritas", not to be lost in the proceedings. In *Dream*, Samuel Beckett crossed the barriers of language from English—and English as used by the Irish—to French, from German to Italian and Spanish, and he resorted quite often to Latin. He also experimented with words and deliberately flaunted grammatical convention at times outrageously so that in truth there were occasions when only he could have said what was intended. In such instances we had to rely as much on our knowledge and understanding of Samuel Beckett, the man, as of his writing. If we have failed him, the responsibility is ours.

We were faced with a decision to delete short pieces of text only twice, when of two almost identical passages, one was obviously the weaker preliminary draft of a later improved version. This replication served no purpose and Samuel Beckett, we believe, would have done as we did had he been reading the proofs. First, the passage on pp. 68–70 ("Ne suis-je point pâle?" down to "helmet of salvation") was retained in preference to a shortened, but essentially similar passage which had followed the paragraph ending with: ". . . she was the living spit of Madonna Lucrezia del Fede" on p. 15. Secondly, the Dartmouth manuscript contains two versions of the novel's ending, the final part of the subsequent version being hand-written by Samuel Beckett. We have chosen the latter, which does not differ in meaning but is so much better in expression than the earlier version.

We have also been careful not to distort through correction Samuel Beckett's idiosyncrasies of punctuation and spacing. In his typescript, he emphasised intervals of time, interludes, and changes of mood by varying the conventional line-spacing and indents. The subtlety of this contrivance might easily be overlooked but we believe it important that it be retained, unusual though it may seem at times. *Dream*, after all, is an unusual book.

In the same way we have been faithful to his use of italics, none where none intended. Wisely, because of the profusion of various languages, Samuel Beckett desisted from applying to foreign words the usual italics which he reserved solely for the purpose of emphasis.

The manuscript we relied upon was the original one in Dartmouth College, which had been typed and corrected by Samuel Beckett, though the Reading copy, which was not transcribed by him and differs from the Dartmouth original in minor respects, was also consulted.

Whatever the scholastic merits or demerits of *Dream* are judged to be, in introducing the book sixty years after it was written, we do so knowing that it will bring considerable wealth to many, perhaps especially to youth, for the book has not aged and it is a book of humour and sensitivity, of hope and music, much music. *Dream* can be read at two levels at least. Continuing the musical analogy, the reader can simply hum the tune and the air is a catching one, or he can, if he has the mind to do it, study the music and fail not to be enthralled. It is also a book of colour, pervaded by Samuel Beckett's technique of invoking colour to heighten mood with a unique chromatic intensity.

A special word of thanks to Jérôme Lindon who made this undertaking possible, to Paul Bennett who patiently withstood our numerous typesetting changes, to the Board of Black Cat Press, most especially Ted and Ursula O'Brien, and Tona, each of whom understood the importance of *Dream*. I am also indebted to Kevin and Kate Cahill, Caroline Murphy and Edward Beckett, John Calder, the Dartmouth College Library, New Hampshire and the Beckett Archive, Reading University. In their different ways all participated in bringing this prodigal novel to awakefulness.

Eoin O'Brien,
Seapoint,
June 1992

DREAM OF FAIR
to middling
WOMEN

A thousand sythes have I herd men telle,
That ther is joye in heven, and peyne in helle;
But —

ONE

Behold Belacqua an overfed child pedalling, faster and faster, his mouth ajar and his nostrils dilated, down a frieze of hawthorn after Findlater's van, faster and faster till he cruise alongside of the hoss, the black fat wet rump of the hoss. Whip him up, vanman, flickem, flapem, collopwallop fat Sambo. Stiffly, like a perturbation of feathers, the tail arches for a gush of mard. Ah . . . !

And what is more he is to be surprised some years later climbing the trees in the country and in the town sliding down the rope in the gymnasium.

TWO

Belacqua sat on the stanchion at the end of the Carlyle Pier in the mizzle in love from the girdle up with a slob of a girl called Smeraldina-Rima whom he had encountered one evening when as luck would have it he happened to be tired and her face more beautiful than stupid. His fatigue on that fatal occasion making him attentive to her face only, and that part of her shining as far as he could make out with an unearthly radiance, he had so far forgotten himself as to cast all over and moor in the calm curds of her bosom which he had rashly deduced from her features that left nothing but death to be desired as one that in default of Abraham's would do very nicely to be going on with in this frail world that is all temptation and knighthood. Then ere he could see through his feeling for her she mentioned that she cared for nothing in heaven above or the earth beneath or the waters under the earth so much as the music of Bach and that she was taking herself off almost at once and for good and all to Vienna to study the pianoforte. The result of this was that the curds put forth suckers of sargasso, and enmeshed him.

So now he sagged on the stanchion in the grateful mizzle after the supreme adieu, his hands in a jelly in his

3

lap, his head drooped over his hands, pumping up the little blirt. He sat working himself up to the little gush of tears that would exonerate him. When he felt them coming he switched off his mind and let them settle. First the cautious gyring of her in his mind till it thudded and spun with the thought of her, then not a second too soon the violent voiding and blanking of his mind so that the gush was quelled, it was balked and driven back for a da capo. He found that the best way to turn over the piston in the first instance was to think of the béret that she had snatched off to wave when the ship began to draw clear. The sun had bleached it from green to a very poignant reseda and it had always, from the very first moment he clapped eyes on it, affected him as being a most shabby, hopeless and moving article. It might have been a tuft of grass growing the way she ripped it off her little head and began to wave it with an idiotic clockwork movement of her arm, up and down, not to flutter it like a handkerchief, but grasping it in the middle to raise it and lower it with a stiff arm as though she were doing an exercise with a dumb-bell. The least reference of his thought now to these valedictory jerks, the monstrous grief in the hand clutching the livid béret like a pestle and pounding up and down, so that every stroke of the stiff arm seemed to bray his heart and propel her out of his sight, was enough to churn his mind into the requisite strom of misery. He found this out after a few false starts. So, having fixed the technique, he sat on working himself up to the little teary ejaculation, choking it back in the very act of emission, waiting with his mind blank for it to subside, and then when everything was in order switching on the tragic béret and the semaphore vale and starting all over again. He sat hunched on the stanchion in the evening mizzle, forcing and foiling the ebullition in this curious

4

way, and his hands were two clammy cadaverous slabs of cod in his lap. Until to his annoyance the fetish of her waving the béret in the manner we (concensus, here and hereafter, of me) have been at such pains to describe, refused to work. He switched on as usual, after the throttling and expunction, and nothing happened. The cylinders of his mind abode serene. That was a nasty one for him if you like, a complete break down of the works like that. He cast round in a kind of panic for some image that would do to start things moving again: a Rasima look in her sunken eyes towards the end of the evening, the dim fanlight of the brow under the black hair growing low and thickly athwart the temples, the dell at the root of the nose that she used to allow him to palp and probe with his forefinger pad and nail. And all to no purpose. His mind abode serene and the well of tears dry.

No sooner had he admitted to himself that there was nothing to be done, that he had dried himself quite with this chamber-work of sublimation, than he was seized with a pang of the darkest dye, and his Smeraldinalgia was swallowed up immediately in the much greater affliction of being a son of Adam and cursed with an insubordinate mind. His mind instructed his hands now to stop being clammy and flabby in his lap and to try a little fit of convulsions, and they obeyed instanter; but when it instructed itself to pump up a few tears in respect of the girl who had left him behind her, then it resisted. That was a very dark pang. Still on the stanchion in the mizzle that would not abate until everybody had gone home, wringing his hands faute de mieux, mindless of the Smeraldina-Rima, he pored over this new sorrow.

Meanwhile a cobalt devil of a very much less light and airy high and mighty description was biding its time

5

until the Adam grievance should have shot its bolt as all Belacqua's grievances did, leaving him in a disarmed condition that was most disagreeable. For him the Great Dereliction was the silver lining and its impertinent interventions. For the mind to pore over a woe or in deference to a woe be blacked out was all right; and of course for the mind to be enwombed and entombed in the very special manner that we will have more than one occasion to consider was better still, a real pleasure. But this impudent interpolation of the world's ghastly backside, dismantling his machinery of despond and hauling him high and dry out of his comfortable trough, was a solution of continuity that he objected to particularly.

Not that he could complain that the texture of the current dejection had been seriously faulted in this respect. There had been no lull of any consequence between the break down of the love-ache and the onset of the pang. Indeed whatever little interspace there was had been filled by an ergo, the two terms had been chained together beautifully. And now in the very process of his distress at being a son of Adam and afflicted in consequence with a mind that would not obey its own behests was being concocted a gloom to crown his meditation in a style that had never graced the climax of any similar series in his previous experience of melancholy. A positively transcendental gloom was brewing that would incorporate the best and choicest elements in all that had gone before and made its way straight in what at first sight would have the appearance of a conclusive proposition. Needless to say it would be nothing of the kind. But considered in the penumbra of a clause on which to toss and turn and whinge himself to sleep it could scarcely have been improved on.

He was still grinding away at No. 2, with the hands

back in the lap in a pulp, when suddenly the impression that there was a rough gritty man standing before him and stating what sounded unpleasantly like an ultimatum caused him to look up. It was only too true. It was the wharfinger, seeking whom he might devour. Belacqua gave heed to what was being said to him, and elicited in the end from an exuberance of coprolalia that the man was requiring him to go.

"Get off my pier" said the wharfinger rudely "and let me get home to my tea." This seemed fair enough. It even seemed natural enough to Belacqua that the man should speak of the pier as his. In a sense it was his pier. He was responsible for it. That was what he was there for. That was what he was paid for. And it was very natural that he should want to get home to his tea after his day's work.

"To be sure" said Belacqua, rising from the stanchion, "how thoughtless of me. May I . . ." He felt in his trouser pocket for a sixpenny bit or failing that a shilling, and pulled out all that he had left—twopence. Belacqua stood hatless in the mizzle before his adversary, the foreskirt of his reefer flung back, and the discoloured lining of the pocket protruded like we cannot think what. It was a very embarrassing moment.

"May you what?" said the wharfinger.

Belacqua blushed. He did not know where to look. He took off his glasses in his confusion. But of course it was a case of locking the stable-door after the steed had flown. Dare he offer such a heated man twopence?

"I can only apologise" he stammered "for having put you to this inconvenience. Believe me, I had no idea . . ."

The wharfinger spat. No smoking was allowed on the pier but spitting was different.

"Be off my pier" he said with finality "before that spit dries."

Belacqua thought what an extraordinary expression for a man in his station to use. The phrase was misapplied, he thought, surely something was wrong with the phrase somewhere. And in such weather it was like inviting him to postpone his going till the Greek Kalends. These conceits passed through his mind as he walked rapidly landward down the wharf with his oppressor hard on his heels. When the gate had slammed safely behind him he turned round and wished the wharfinger a courteous good-evening. To his surprise the man touched his cap and replied with quite a courteous little good-evening. Belacqua's heart gave a great leap of pleasure.

"Oh" he cried "good-evening to you and forgive me, my good man, won't you, I meant no harm."

But to acknowledge an obvious gentleman's courtly greeting was one thing and to pooh-pooh offhand a flagrant act of trespass was quite another. So the wharfinger hardened his heart and disappeared into his hut and Belacqua had no choice but to hobble away on his ruined feet without indulgence, absolution or remission.

God bless dear Daddy, he prayed vaguely that night for no particular reason before getting into bed, *Mummy Johnny Bibby* (quondam Nanny, now mother of thousands by a gardener) *and all that I love and make me a good boy for Jesus Christ sake Armen.*

That was the catastasis their Mammy had taught them, first John, then Bel, at her knee, when they were tiny. That was their prayer. What came after that was the Lord's. Their prayer was a nice little box and the Lord's was a dull big box. You went down in a lift and your only stomach rose up into your craw. Oooaaah.

He got up and got into bed and the blue devil that had been waiting for just such an opportunity got in beside him and represented to him there and then and in the most insidious terms that it was a nice state of affairs when the son of Adam could quash the lover of the Smeraldina-Rima or any other girl for that matter and if that was all being in love with a girl from the girdle up meant to him the sooner he came off it the better. Thus he was crowned in gloom and he had a wonderful night. He groped, as one that walks by moonshine in a wood, through the grateful night to the impertinent champaign of the morning. Sin is behovable but all shall be well and all shall be well and all manner of thing shall be well. *Inquit Grock* . . .

A low capital in the crypt of the Basilica Saint-Sernin in the most beautiful city of Toulouse is carved to represent a rat gnawing its way into a globe. The Dutch cheese of La Fontaine's fable of the catawampus that withdrew from the cares of this world? We think not.

The fact of the matter is we do not quite know where we are in this story. It is possible that some of our creatures will do their dope all right and give no trouble. And it is certain that others will not. Let us suppose that Nemo is one of those that will not. John, most of the parents, the Smeraldina-Rima, the Syra-Cusa, the Alba, the Mandarin, the Polar Bear, Lucien, Chas, are a few of those that will, that stand, that is, for something or can be made to stand for something. It is to be hoped that we can make them stand for something. Whereas it is almost certain that

9

Nemo cannot be made, at least not by us, stand for anything. *He simply is not that kind of person.*

Supposing we told now a little story about China in
order to orchestrate what we mean. Yes? Lîng-Liûn then,
let us say, went to the confines of the West, to Bamboo
Valley, and having cut there a stem between two knots and
blown into same was charmed to constate that it gave forth
the sound of his own voice when he spoke, as he mostly
did, without passion. From this the phœnix male had the
kindness to sing six notes and the phœnix female six other
notes and Lîng-Liûn the minister cut yet eleven stems to
correspond with all that he had heard. Then he remitted
the twelve liŭ-liŭ to his master, the six liŭ male phœnix and
the six liŭ female phœnix: the Yellow Bell, let us say, the
Great Liŭ, the Great Steepleiron, the Stifled Bell, the Ancient Purification, the Young Liŭ, the Beneficient Fecundity, the Bell of the Woods, the Equable Rule, the
Southern Liŭ, the Imperfect, the Echo Bell.

Now the point is that it is most devoutly to be hoped
that some at least of our characters can be cast for parts in
a liŭ-liŭ. For example, John might be the Yellow Bell and
the Smeraldina-Rima the Young Liŭ and the Syra-Cusa the
Stifled Bell and the Mandarin the Ancient Purification and
Belacqua himself the Beneficient Fecundity or the Imperfect, and so on. Then it would only be a question of jug-
gling like Confucius on cubes of jade and playing a tune. If
all our characters were like that—liŭ-liŭ-minded—we
could write a little book that would be purely melodic,
think how nice that would be, linear, a lovely Pythagorean
chain-chant solo of cause and effect, a one-figured teleo-
phony that would be a pleasure to hear. (Which is more or
less, if we may say so, what one gets from one's favourite
novelist.) But what can you do with a person like Nemo

who will not for any consideration be condensed into a liŭ, who is not a note at all but the most regrettable simultaneity of notes. Were it possible to oralise say half-a-dozen Lîng-Liûn phœnix arising as one immortal purple bird from the ashes of a common pyre and crying simultaneously, as each one saw fit, a cry of satisfaction or of disappointment, a rough idea of the status of this Nemo might be obtained: a symphonic, not a melodic, unit. Our line bulges every time he appears. Now that is a thing that we do not like to happen, and the less so as we are rather keenly aware of the infrequency of one without two. Dare we count on the Alba? Dare we count on Chas. Indeed we tend, on second thoughts, to smell the symphonic rat in our principal boy. He might just manage, semel et simul, the Beneficient Fecundity and the Imperfect; or, better still, furnish a bisexual bulge with a Great Iron of the Woods. But ping! a mere liŭ! We take leave to doubt it.

Anyhow the next thing was a tiff with a lady, oh a proper lady, who told Belacqua to his brazen face that he was treating her like dirt and behaving like a cad, taking everything and giving nothing; and he said behind her back that she was jealous of the Smeraldina-Rima. This lady, whom we propose to polish off now once and for all, had a great deal of the predatory masochism of the passionate Quaker. She felt that going through hell was all my eye unless some peeping Nightingale got a thrill out of it. She wouldn't allow you to do anything for her, but it was a real pleasure, if you see what we mean, to refuse. Now of course he was too ecstatic a spectator altogether to come down to the mark from that point of view. Miranda was not in his class at all. He might conceivably have suffered mildly with those whose sufferings he saw reported in the continental press. But sonst, in the words of the song, gar nix.

11

The real presence was a pest because it did not give the imagination a break. Without going as far as Stendhal, who said—or repeated after somebody—that the best music (what did he know about music anyway?) was the music that became inaudible after a few bars, we do declare and maintain stiffly (at least for the purposes of this paragraph) that the object that becomes invisible before your eyes is, so to speak, the brightest and best. This is not to suggest that the lady in question did that. We simply mean that at the time we are referring to she was not an object at all, no, not an object in any sense of the word. Is that what we mean? What do we mean? Anyway, what it boils down to in the end is this: that he did not want to be slavered and slabbered on by her, he thought it would be nice to be slavered and slabbered on elsewhere for a change. So he packed a bag and made to depart. His Father said "tant pis, good-luck", lifted his shoulders and paid for his ticket. His Mother put her head into the taxi and before she broke down (the Mother, not the taxi) breathed "be happy", as if to insinuate: "again and again I request you to be merry". Long John Silver, the Polar Bear and a dear friend, on whom we are inclined to count to put a stop to this chronicle, waved a Mallarmean farewell from the Carlyle Pier. At Ostend he secured a corner seat in a through horsebox to Wien and defended it for 29 hours against all comers. The last 599 kilometres on beer (terrible stuff!), and in a horsebox, not a corridor coach, which explains why he stepped hastily out of the train at the Westbahnhof and looked feverishly up and down the platform.

The effect or concert of effects, unimportant as it seems to us and dull as ditchwater as we happen to know, that elicited the Smeraldina-Rima, shall not, for those and other reasons that need not be gone into, be stated. Milieu, race, family, structure, temperament, past and present and consequent and antecedent back to the first combination and the papas and mammas and paramours and cicisbei and the morals of Nanny and the nursery wallpapers and the third and fourth generation snuffles . . . That tires us. As though the gentle reader could be nothing but an insurance broker or a professional punter. The background pushed up as a guarantee . . . that tires us. The only perspective worth stating is the site of the unknotting that could be, landscape of a dream of integration, prospective, that of Franciabigio's young Florentine in the Louvre, into which it is pleasant to believe he may, gladly or sadly, no matter, recede, from which he has not necessarily emerged. We never set any store by the creased pants of the confidence trickster. The Smeraldina-Rima is not demonstrable. She has to be taken or left. Belacqua did a little of both. She obliged him to.

She had an idea she was studying music and eurhythmics in the very vanguardful Schule Dunkelbrau, ten miles out of town, on the fringe of the wild old grand old park of Mödelberg. This park was more beautiful and tangled far than the Bois de Boulogne or any other multis latebra opportuna that it is possible to imagine, quieter and fresher, except on Sundays when the swells used to drive out from town to take the air and perhaps even catch a glimpse of the Evites. The Dunkelbrau gals were very Evite and nudist and shocked even the Mödelbergers when they went in their Harlequin pantalettes, or just culotte and sweater and uncontrollable cloak, to the local Kino. All very callisthenic and cerebro-hygienic and promotive of great strength and beauty. In the summer they lay on the roof and bronzed their bottoms and impudenda. And all day it was dancing and singing and music and douches and frictions and bending and stretching and classes—Harmonie, Anatomie, Psychologie, Improvisation, with a powerful ictus on the last syllable in each case. *Friendly* intercourse between teacher and student was encouraged and Apfelmus was the staple of diet and sometimes a group would dart up to town for a concert or an Abknutschen. In the middle, the thick and the heat and the stress, of all this, the Smeraldina-Rima was everybody's darling, she was so young and had such a lovely face and amused the gals with foul stories and improvised so well. Behold Herr Arschlochweh, Swiss and melancholy and highbrow and the Improvisationslehrer. The Smeraldina-Rima stimulated this gentleman to certain velleities of desire, or so at least she allowed it to be understood, and sure enough that was Belacqua's own impression when he saw them together, which, let it be said forthwith, was not often. The Smeraldina never looked like being able to play the piano, but she had a curious talent for improvisation, which came up in her conversation. When she was in form, launched, she could be extremely amusing, with a strange feverish eloquence, the words flooding and streaming out like a conjuror's coloured paper. She could keep a whole group, even her family, convulsed with the ropes and ropes of logorrhœa streaming out in a gush. Her own Mammy used to foam at the mouth and the Mandarin was forgotten.

"Oh" coughed Mammy on these occasions "she ought to be on the halls" and the Smeraldina would broach another bobbin.

She liked Arschlochweh and adored Improvisation; but the Anatomiestunde and the bending and stretching she did not like. "Pfui!" she was disgusted, lifting her shoulders and spreading her hands like the Mandarin, "pfui! the old body!"; and that raised the hopes of Belacqua until she

14

made it clear, which she did in many ways, that she did not mean at all what he had hoped rather she might.

Because her body was all wrong, the peacock's claws. Yes, even at that early stage, definitely all wrong. Poppata, big breech, Botticelli thighs, knock-knees, ankles all fat nodules, wobbly, mammose, slobbery-blubbery, bubbub-bubbub, a real button-bursting Weib, ripe. Then, perched aloft on top of this porpoise prism, the loveliest little pale firm cameo of a birdface he ever clapped his blazing blue eyes on. By God but he often thought she was the living spit of Madonna Lucrezia del Fede.

On the fringe of the village, empty, invested with dilapidation, squatted the big blue Hof, four-square about a court-yard of weeds. There he lived, in a high dark room smelling of damp coverlets, with a glass door opening on to the park. To get to his room he could enter the Hof from the last village street and walk across the court-yard, or better still make the circuit of the corridors, or again he could come at it deliberately from the other side, from the park. As far as he knew, as he could hear, he had the whole of this side, the park aspect, to himself. At night, to be sure, the rats, galavanting and cataracting behind the sweating wall-paper, just behind the wall-paper, slashing the close invisible plane with ghastlily muted slithers and somersaults. Coming back after kissing the Madonna good-night under the arch of the school buildings, ten minutes' walk through the park away, and arranging at what time they could see one another (see one another!) next morning, he thought of the rank dark room, quiet, *quieted*, when he would enter, then the first stir behind the paper, the first discreet slithers.

He is in a great open place. On his right hand, his blind side, a tall palissade of trees; on his left, the low village dwellings and the splayed embouchure of the last village street; behind, the Dunkelbrau sanctuary into which she has passed; ahead, the clump of bushes where he makes water and the narrow breach in the hedge. Past the breach he shall see, apex of the avenue in the long crouch of the Blockhof, the distant lit room. But his impression is that he had extinguished before ushering her out into the sharp October night! That is definitely his impression. Every night when he squeezes through the breach and is absorbed by the avenue, that is his impression. But now, before that happens, before he regains his boxful of obsidional insanity, he stands well out in the dark arena, his head cocked up uncomfortably at the starfield, like Mr Ruskin in the Sistine, looking for Vega.

The night firmament is abstract density of music, symphony without end, illumination without end, yet emptier, more sparsely lit, than the most succinct constellations of genius. Now seen merely, a depthless lining of hemisphere, its crazy stippling of stars, it is the passional movements of the mind charted in light and darkness. The tense passional intelligence, when arithmetic abates, tunnels, skymole, surely and blindly (if we only thought so!) through the interstellar coalsacks of its firmament in genesis, it twists through the stars of its creation in a network of loci that shall never be co-ordinate. The inviolable criterion of poetry and music, the non-principle of their punctuation, is figured in the demented perforation of the night colander. The ecstatic mind, the mind achieving creation, take ours for example, rises to the shaftheads of its statement, its recondite relations of emergal, from a labour and a weariness of deep castings that brook no schema. The mind suddenly entombed, then active in an anger and a rhapsody of energy, in a scurrying and plunging towards

16

exitus, such is the ultimate mode and factor of the creative integrity, its proton, incommunicable; but there, insistent, invisible rat, fidgeting behind the astral incoherence of the art surface. That was the circular movement of the mind flowering up and up through darkness to an apex, dear to Dionysius the Areopagite, beside which all other modes, all the polite obliquities, are the clockwork of rond-de-cuirdom.

Nothing whatever of the kind of course occupied his fetid head nor was there room in his gravid heart for such strange feeling as he shuffles uneasily in the deeps of the desert place, peeping up like a fool at his dear little sweet little Fünkelein, green, bright and in the Lyre, on his poutlip the grip of the two of hers where she had fastened on and clipped it in the peculiar way she had, in the old heart something getting ready to give a great leap when he would be through with the privacies of his toilet and heave into view of the rat-trap, and the tilted brain flooded no doubt with radiance come streaming down from the all-transcending hiddenness of the all-transcending super-essentially superexisting super-Deity. Sonst, in the words of the song, gar nix.

Thus it was, evening after evening, without variety, and how, subsequently, he breasted the tides of the night and came through is more than we can tell you. But in the morning, not too bright or early, she would skip in in a most rudimentary woollen gymnasium sheath, the plump bright bare fleshstilts warmed up ad rudorem, and make tea to be drunk with a lemon. For weeks, until what we are about to relate to you came to pass, that was the best hour of the day: the night over, lying half asleep in the expectation of the desired footfall, opening the door on the clear keen park as soon as it declared itself, skimming through the variations of her oyster kiss against the boiling of the water, drinking buckets of weak tea mitigated with lemon-juice, smoking Macedonia. From that high hour the day slid down to the pit of the evening, night again, the crawl back from the school, the anguish before the beacon, the rats, the musty trap and the tides.

Until she raped him.

Then everything went kaputt.

The implacable, the insatiate, warmed up this time by her morning jerks to a sexy sudorem, she violated him after tea. When it was his express intention, made clear in a hundred and one subtle and delicate ways, to keep the whole thing pewer and above-bawd. So utterly did she queer his pitch that he was moved to quote "le soleil est mort" in petto, and his time of the lilies shifted over to the night hours, sitting vigilant among the rats, alla fioca lucerna leggendo Meredith. The tiffs started. He followed her into the tiny Lebensmittel store where their habit it was to buy eggs and tomatoes later to be flogged up to-gether in a kind of steaming Marie Laurencin polenta. She whirled round on him:

"Make the door to" she cried, with an exaggerated shiver.

"Make it to yourself" he said rudely.

That kind of thing. Another time she kept him waiting and the supper he had made was spoiling, it was cooling rapidly. He heard her plunging down the avenue. Well you may run, he thought. She was all apologies.

"Oh" she gasped "I met Arschlochweh and I had to get him to finger me a bit in my Brahms."

Brahms! That old piddler! Pizzicatoing himself off in the best of all possible worlds. Brahms! She started to coax and wheedle. Such a cat she could be.

"Don't be cross with me Bel don't be so böse" stretching out the vowel in a moan.

Brahms!

"You don't love me" he said bitterly "or you wouldn't keep me waiting for such Quatsch."

Still, bitched and all as the whole thing was from that sacrificial morning on, they kept it going in a kind of way, he doing his poor best to oblige her and she hers to be obliged, in a gehenna of sweats and fiascos and tears and an absence of all douceness. We confess we are so attached to our principal boy that we cannot but hope that she has since had cause to regret that first assault on his privities. Though it would scarcely occur to her, we believe, to relate the slow tawdry boggling of the entire unhappy affair, two nouns and four adjectives, to that lesion of Platonic tissue all of a frosty October morning. Yet it was always on that issue that they tended to break and did break. Looking babies in his eyes, the ---, that was her game, making his amorosi sospiri sound ridiculous. So that one day he forgot his manners and exhorted her:

"For the love of God will you not take a loiny cavalier servente and make me hornmad ante rem and get some ease of the old pruritus and leave me in peace to my own penny death and my own penny rapture."

No no no no, she would not let a man near her unless she loved him dearly, furchtbar lieb. And she was right and he was wrong and that was that—and would you be so kind as to take up position, my sad beautiful beloved? So. A man knows but a woman knows better.

Next he is called on to sustain the letter, really a rather unpleasant letter, with more spleen in it than appears on a first reading:

19

"Cher, (it ran)

Ce qu'on dit du style, et je veux dire, à coup sûr, ce que ce cochon de Marcel en dit, me plaît, je crois, si j'ose accepter, en ce moment, les hauts-de-petit-coeur-de-neige. Je te fais l'honneur, n'est-il pas vrai, de te parler, quoi, sans réserve. Donc : me trouvant couché, hier, auprès de l'inénarrable Liebert, j'ai proposé à sa puissante lucidité une phrase—pourquoi te le cacherais-je—de ta lettre qui n'a pas été, je te l'avoue, sans me faire de la peine: *P. se paye de mots. Il ne sait jamais résister à l'extase du décollage. Il réalise (et avec une morgue !) des loopings verbaux. Si loin, oh dégoût !, du réel dermique qui le fait tant trembler et transpirer.* Liebert, négligemment étendu à côté de moi, beau sans blague comme un rêve d'eau, lâche: "tunnel !" "Hein ?" "Il est si beau, ton ami, si franchement casse-poitrinaire, que je suis prêt à l'aimer. Est-il maigre et potelé là et là où il faut ? Vulgaire ? Lippu ? Ah ! vulgaire lippue chaude chair ! Gratte-moi" vociféra-t-il, en nage pour toi, "ardente cantharide, gratte, je te l'ordonne !" Je gratte, je caresse, je me dis : ce jugement est par trop indigne de cet esprit, vu que P. ne s'arrache à nul moment de l'axe glaireux de son réel. Il y reste enfoncé, il tord les bras, il se démène, il souffre d'être si platement compromis, il n'exécute nul looping, il s'est engagé trop profondément dans le marais, il atteint du bout de son orteil au noeud de son univers.

L. se lève d'un bond, se déshabille, fait son poème, fuit de tous les côtés. Devant moi, croisée tennysonienne, ta belle face carrée bouge, bat comme un coeur. L'intérêt de l'état de l'orient s'affirme. Il n'y a que lui, me dis-je, qui sache avoir honte, laisser percer une honte frivole, rougir. Les tiraillements du bas ciel cassent les carreaux. Du matin le tiroir s'entr-ouvre, crache le bébé, Polichinelle, sanguinolent à en mourir. En attendant que monte le thé simple que par conséquent je viens de commander, au fond des yeux clos le poème se fait:

> C'n'est au Pélican
> pas si pitoyable
> ni à l'Egyptienne
> pas si pure
> mais à ma Lucie
> opticienne oui et peaussière aussi
> qui n'm'a pas guéri
> mais qui aurait pu
> et à Jude
> dont j'ai adororé la dépouille
> qu'j'adresse la cause désespérée
> qui a l'air d'être la mienne

Je me penche, dominando l'orgasmo comme un pilote, par la fenêtre pour halener seulement un peu le placenta de l'aurorore. Il est inodore.

Oh et tu sais tu serais infiniment aimable de me faire savoir, dès que cela se pourra, à quel moment précis et du bord de quel rapide exact tu te proposes à te jeter sur Paris fumant. Je tiens à être le premier à t'étreindre à ton arrivée.

Quel intérêt aurais-je à te cacher que je suis, en ce moment, et ceci durera, MOROSE ? que physique-ment je dégringole à tombeau ouvert et qu'intellec-tuellement c'est plutôt et le plus souvent le calme plat ponctué, il est vrai, de vertigineuses éjaculations d'écume et de clarté. Il fait un temps notable—cette lumière pulpeuse à l'aube que tu aimes tellement à invoquer.

Ton petit flirt—hé ! hé ! touche donc à sa fin ?

"Ma surérogatoire et frêle furibonde !"

Ne t'amertume pas. C'est toi qui l'as dit.

Donc, tu viendras, piqué des accidences de cette fraîche Jungfrau . . . Je tendrai les doigts, comme pour frôler une surface peinte, et en t'effleurant comme ce papillon de mai que chante qui tu sais je saurai, n'en doute pas, tout ce qui a dû échapper à ses plus suaves et juteuses embrassades. Toutefois, si cela t'est préférable, j'amortirai le geste, je le calmerai, oui, je ferai cela. Tu sais, et ceci va te suffoquer, quand tu sentiras à quel Everest je suis à ta disposition . . . ! C'est plus fort, gros couillon, que

ton
Lucien"

That seemed to Belacqua a dark and rather disagreeable letter for one man to get from another and moreover unworthy of Lucien who was a young æsthetician for whom there was much to be said. He has no call, thought Belacqua, to throw his demented Liebert at me, and he need not crook his fingers at Smerry, whether fresh or frail or Jungfrau or none of the three. He saw in a vision the hands lifted, plucking and poking at the air in a futility of slow heavy stabs, then lowered on to a support, placed tentatively on his knees or a table and held there, stiff and self-conscious. Belacqua declined to be impounded like that, he declined to be strained against anything or anybody. And thinking of the little bare hands and the threat of the gesture stilled he was nearly taken with a vomiting.

22

Ah solitude, when a man at last and with love can occupy himself in his nose! He looked at his face in the glass and felt no desire to wipe it off. It is not beautiful, he thought, but it is not square. Bitterly he filed the letter in the jakes, promising himself to read it again in the morning if all went well, when perhaps he would find himself in a more tolerant frame of mind and apt to discover some gracious sentiment in what now, to him vigilant, for she was coming, there was her step, was merely an insipid salmagundi of vulgarities.

She looked very droopy and after the usual sat down in a heap on the edge of the bed. He enquired what the matter was, that she looked so jaded and depressed.

"You look as though you had lost something of great value and found something of no value at all, or next to none."

"Oh, this and that" she said weakly "this and that. Such a life" and she sighed.

In the silence that ensued he took stock of his Smerry. She was pale, pale as Plutus, and bowed towards the earth. She sat there, huddled on the bed, the legs broken at the knees, the bigness of thighs and belly assuaged by the droop of the trunk, her lap full of hands. Posta sola soletta, like the leonine spirit of the troubadour of great renown, tutta a se romita. So she had been, sad and still, without limbs or paps in a great stillness of body, that summer evening in the green isle when first she heaved his soul from its hinges; as quiet as a tree, column of quiet. Pinus puella quondam fuit. Alas fuit! So he would always have her be, rapt, like the spirit of a troubadour, casting no shade, herself shade. Instead of which of course it was only a question of seconds before she would surge up at him, blithe and buxom and young and lusty, a lascivious

23

petulant virgin, a generous mare neighing after a great horse, caterwauling after a great stallion, and amorously lay open the double-jug dugs. She could not hold it. Nobody can hold it. Nobody can live here and hold it. Only the spirit of the troubadour, rapt in a niche of rock, huddled and withdrawn forever if no prayers go up for him, raccolta a se, like a lion. And without anger. It is a poor anger that rises when the stillness is broken, our anger, the poor anger of the world that life cannot be still, the live things cannot be active quietly, that the neighbour is not a moon, slow wax and wane of phases, changeless in a tranquility of changes. But without measure, all anyhow. I, he thought, and she and the neighbour are cities bereft of light, where the citizen carries his torch. I shall separate myself and the neighbour from the moon, and the lurid place that he is from the lurid place that I am; then I need not go to the trouble of hating the neighbour. I shall extinguish also, by banning the torchlight procession in the city that is I, the fatiguing lust for self-emotion. Then we shall all be on the poor sow's back.

After a little conversation obiter she certainly did seem to look up, and again he appealed to her to confide in him and tell him what the matter could be, what it could be that had distressed her into such a dead calm. That was the expression he used: dead calm.

"You're going away" she vouchsafed to begin with "and then I won't see you for months and months. What'll I do?"

"Oh" he replied lightly "the time will be no time slipping over. I'll write every day, and think how wunnerful it'll be meeting again."

"Men don't feel these things" she complained "the way women do."

"No indeed" he said "I suppose not indeed. Do you

remember—of course she does!—the conversation, or rather, perhaps I should say, monologue . . ."

"Monologue?" She was hostile all of a sudden. "What's that? Something to eat?"

"Oh" he said "words that don't do any work and don't much want to. A salivation of words after the banquet."

"You use such long ones Bel." It was always the same passage, from the flashing eye and heaving bosom to the simpering pinafore. He thought it was a good thing and a thing to be thankful for that he had something long to use.

"Well" he said "I remember saying, or rather repeating after some one, and you seeming to hear and understand and agree, that it was not when he . . . er . . . held her in his arms, nor yet when he remained remote and shared, so to speak, her air and sensed her essence, but only when he sat down to himself in an approximate silence and had a vision on the strength of her or let fly a poem at her, anyhow felt some reality that somehow was she fidgeting in the catacombs of his spirit, that he had her truly and totally, according to his God. So that in a sense I suppose you might say, if you still acquiesce in that view of the matter, that I leave you now in a day or two in order that I may have you, in three days or four or even next month, according to my God."

"Besten Dank" she said.

"But Smerry" he appealed to her sense of equity "don't you see what I mean? Didn't you agree with me when I said all that before?"

"I don't know" she said roughly "what you are talking about, I never agreed with anything, you never said such horrid things to me."

"Oh well" he hastened to mend matters "I apologise, I beg your pardon. Don't let's talk about it any more."

"But I will talk about it. What do you mean, that you go away so as to have me. Don't you have me here? Such a thing to say!" she exploded "bist Du verrückt geworden?"

"It's the little poet speaking" he explained "don't mind him."

"But I will mind him" she moaned, on the verge, yes the marble verge, of tears. "Nobody ever said such things to me!" Then the belly-flopper: "Bel, you don't love me any more!"

Is it not the mercy of God that even a mediocre athlete seems able to console them?

Wien, biding her time, and the terrible Wiener-wald, the fields receding like a brow in sleep to the dark fringe of trees, crowded in upon him now and dehuman-ised the last days. He was no longer detached, nor ever almost at one with the girl, but an item in the Hof's invis-ible garrison, going siege-crazy. There was the jungle of stone and the other jungle, crowding in to invest them, soaking up the frivolous wild life of the park. He fidgeted by night in the dark room and the rats were with him, now he was one of them. He was anxious with their anxiety, shuffling and darting about in the room. Outside the bat-talions were massing, a heavy disorder of thicket and stone. He would not go out, though the girl still came, unscathed, from without. He stood in the courtyard, doomed. The fragile dykes were caving in on him, he would be drowned, stones and thickets would flood over him and over the land, a nightmare strom of timber and leaves and tendrils and bergs of stone. He stood amidst the weeds and the shell of the Hof, braced against the dense masses, strained out away from him. Over the rim of the funnel, when he looked up, the night sky was stretched like a skin. He would scale the inner wall, his head would tear a great rip in the taut sky, he would climb out above the deluge, into a quiet zone above the nightmare.

While he was making his usual moan about one thing and another, love, art and a mineral Dunsinane on the grand scale, his family, he was glad to hear, it was like a distant dog in the evening barking to hear it, was as he had left it, calm, blue-eyed, clean and gentle. The Polar Bear wrote and alluded fiercely to the "bitches and bastards"—an indivisible dumb-bell phrase for the P.B., like "verily and verily"—and demonstrating that no matter what modus vivendi might be reached by sensitive lovers it was bound to be a come down and a striking of the flag, since sensitive love, by definition, transcended the life interest. That was a good one and Belacqua noted it down. But by whose definition? Already even he preferred the old one: God or Devil or passion of the mind, or partly God, partly Devil, partly passion. The hyphen of passion between Shilly and Shally, the old bridge over the river. He scurried backwards and forwards like an excited merchant, and he was too busy altogether to pause at the crown beside Cellini and look down the royal stream. That was the modus vivendi, poised between God and Devil, Justine and Juliette, at the dead point, in a tranquil living at the neutral point, a living dead to love-God and love-Devil, poised without love above the fact of the royal flux westering headlong. Suicides jump from the bridge, not from the bank. For me, he prattles on, he means no harm, for me the one real thing is to be found in the relation: the dumb-bell's bar, the silence between my eyes, between you and me, all the silences between you and me. I can only know the real poise at the crest of the relation rooted in the unreal postulates, God-Devil, Masoch-Sade (he might have spared us that hoary old binary), Me-You, One-minus One. On the crown of the passional relation I live, dead to one-ness, non-entity and unalone, untouched by the pulls of the solitudes, at rest above the deep green central flowing falling away on either hand to the spectral margins, the red solitude and the violet solitude, the red oneness and the violet oneness; at the summit of the bow, indifferent to the fake integrities, the silence between my eyes, between you and me, the body between the wings.

Ain't he advanced for his age!

Here they had killed the lyrical October days, the magic film of light. And there, in its neutral sleep, the landscape was spending a slow phase. A man, a burly man, Nemo to be precise, paused on O'Connell Bridge and raised his face to the tulips of the evening, the green tulips, shining round the corner like an anthrax, shining on Guinness's barges. Behind him, spouting and spouting from the grey sea, the battalions of night, devouring the sky, soaking up the tattered sky like an ink of pestilence. The city would be hooded, dusk would be harried from the city.

From the Bridge, then, along the right bank, at that hour, it was Ronsard as far as the Park Gates. Magic, or, Deliverance from Love. At Island Bridge, a pang of light in the whore's garret. At Chapelizod, after the long journey, the long hour when darkness fills the streets, it was Homer. He spews, and we lick it up. The snug chez Isolde was a great perturbation of sweaty heroes come hastening down from watching the hurlers above in Kilmainham in time for a pint of nepenthe or moly or half-and-half. There he would have one or two and then he would tram back and go to the pictures, he would slip into the womb of the Grand Central burning on the waterside, and then he would crawl back home across the cobbles and his heart is a stone.

Confidence : on va déménager . . . gaz ! électricité ! salle de bains ! ascenseur ! vide-ordures ! . . . Ah, que la vie est belle !

He drew himself up to his full height, he had to, and named the day, and in the bitter morning handed her forth through the glass door and locked it behind them and put the key in her pocket and they set off for the station. Unspeakably lovely he thought she was in her coarse tweed mantle and the pale green casque reducing the fanlight of the forehead to an absurd white fin. Before them marched briskly a stout little local tart, his little laundress, pushing his effects in a frail hand-truck. The Smeraldina-Rima bought the tickets, for herself a return and for him a single. He was getting happier and happier—a mixture of rum and Reisefieber; he felt drawn to the plump little washerwoman when she blushed over the tip he gave her and waved, apparently moved, as the train drew out. Tears to his eyes. The Smeraldina was very still and silent, wringing her hands, bowed towards the floor in her corner seat. He waxed more and more excited. He crossed over and sat down beside her and played with the dimple between her brows, at the root of the nose. He prodded it gently with the yellowed nail of his index-finger, a nail bitten so close that the dimple got more of the pad than of it, and he knuckled it too with his swollen knuckle. At school he used to crack his fingers and had never been able to shake off the habit. She snatched off the casque, she extirpated it, it sailed in a diagonal across the compartment, her head fell back on his fairly manly shoulder and with her right arm taking a purchase on his neck, heedless of the baby anthrax that he always wore just above his collar, she slewed herself round on top of him.

"There there" he hushabied "there there. Nicht küssen" he said slyly "bevor der Zug hält."

Now she moaned, pianissimissima, and cold-bloodedly so, we regret to suspect. But he, be that as it may, was so lucid and fresh and gay, lit with rum and his temperature up, that to attempt any form of consolation was not to be thought of. Till Wien he held it, in a vision of ice-floes and stars and diamonds and steel and mica and feldspar and gulfs and brasiers and foam, and she lay there inert, surely uncomfortable, on top of him, muttering her German lament: "Dich haben! Ihn haben! Dich haben! Ihn haben!" They flew off in a taxi to a jeweller's where he bought her an exquisite silver powder-box, cockled, flat almost, ribbed and chased, a fragile silver conk, for her vanity bag. Very fine. Then to a Friseur for powder to fill it many times over. Then to a café. Then to the station. They whipped round and round the Stefanskirch, regardless, enlaced in the spacious open Wagen, through the scarifying morning. In the café he shed the last ballast and went aloft and talked and talked, and she crooned over the gift. Her eyes sped from her wrist-watch to his flaming face and back again from his flaming face to the wrist-watch and then settled in an ecstasy and an agony on the gift. She was like a bird, the eyes darting this way and that, then the little chirrup, the muted twitter, like an incantation, over the gift. Like a bird and like a child, with something bright and pretty to play with and someone to love and a Viennese Schokolade with lashings of cream to eat. The platform absquatulation was very mild, vaguely disagreeable, like an introduction. For him, lit with rum and fever and the erotico-mystic French highballs that her horse-sense found horrid, it was the most natural thing in the world to sustain with sang-froid the act of severance that to a man of say Mallarmé's complexion, high-mettled and viveur, communicated an anguish of such strength as to cause an azure mist to condense on his glasses. The Smeraldina bit her lip with great skill and did the brave girl until the Platznehmen of the porters became final. Then her tears fell fast and furious. A hiccup convulsed the train. Off flew the green helmet . . .

She assured him in a letter that she walked the streets as one demented, only returning to Dunkelbrau by the midnight train. And the squall caught him just beyond the frontier, shortly after the visit of the customs-officers, and with such violence that he envied the manhood of Toussaint l'Ouverture and heard the hooves of the wheels stating all night a dark thesis:

> Whoso hath with his good-will
> lost what he ought to love
> shall with sorrow lose
> what he hath loved

Driving through the dark that precedes the dawn to his room beyond the river on the Montagne Ste-Geneviève he was greatly distressed in the head. All night the parrots had swung roosting from his palate. His feet were in hot pulp. His body was foul and so were his clothes. He stank after the journey. As they coursed unimpaired down into the well of the city a magic dust lapsed from the desolate hour, from the disastrous expulsion of the morning, livid

31

strands in the east of placenta prævia, dust of his dove's heart, and covered him. Douceurs . . . There are souls that must be saved and there are souls that must not be saved. The magic, the Homer dust of the dawn-dusk. But it was only a dim impression, no more than the tumultuous cœnæsthesis (bravo!) of the degenerate subject. The facts— let us have facts, facts, plenty of facts—were: his feet, that they were in treacle, his fetid head, a swoon of halitosis, his altogether too tainted conditions. Lucien's shoulder was against his, he was thoroughly ashamed of himself, of the offensive state he was in.

"My dear man" he said, careful not to turn his head, "you really ought not to have given yourself the trouble of getting up at this unearthly hour merely in order that you might greet me a little earlier than you would have done in the ordinary course of events. You see I am so exhausted and stupefied after that abominable journey that I am incapable of the least movement of intelligent camaraderie. I can scarcely forgive myself for having been the cause of your putting yourself out so, because I know that you are no more of an early bird than I am myself, for nothing. 'Ad I had the least suspicion that I was to be so lamentable on arrival I would indeed have written to beg you to forego your kind arrangement and give me instead rends-toi for the afternoon in one of the cafés of the quartier. But it did not occur to me that a railway-carriage, a mere railway-carriage, could work such a prodigious alteration. I left Vienne, you know, as spruce and as keen as a new-ground hatchet. Then again I suppose it is wrong of me to suggest that the railway-carriage, and it alone, is responsible, when it was doubtless only one of a multitude of circumstances, no more, no doubt, than the sympathetic site of my disaggregation. Algia for the dear girl, the rum fairies taking wing in

a fume, a nameless dejection, a collapse into the deep sub-
normal slough to compensate the exaltation and the fever of
departure, that old bastard of Augustin strumming his blues
all night—these and innumerable other inchoate liminal
presentations clubbed together to destroy me."

They arrived. Vigorously the chauffeur hoisted down the
bag and placed it on the glimmering pavement.

"Can you pay this man" said Belacqua "because I spent
my last Groschen on a bottle."

Lucien payed the man off.

"I can only express my appreciation" said Belacqua by
way of conclusion, as the taxi faded away into the gloaming,
"of your charming gesture by apologising for myself, by
asking your pardon for the fact of myself."

Lucien's arms began to flutter.

"My dear friend" he said in a low, earnest tone, "please,
I implore you, do not, do not apologise. I spent the night
up with Liebert, who by the way asks most anxiously after
you. We dine together this evening—provided of course"
he added in a little gush, cocking up his bright eye, "that
that is agreeable to you?"

The Syra-Cusa: her body more perfect than dream
creek, amaranth lagoon. She flowed along in a nervous
swagger, swinging a thin arm amply. The sinewy fetlock
sprang, Brancusi bird, from the shod foot, blue arch of
veins and small bones, rose like a Lied to the firm wrist of
the reins, the Bilitis breasts. Her neck was scraggy and her
head was null. Faciem, Phœbe, cacantis habes. She was
prone, when brought to dine out, to puke, but into her
serviette, with decorum, because, supposedly, the craving
of her viscera was not for food and drink. To take her arm,
to flow together, out of step, down the asphalt bed, was a

33

foundering in music, the slow ineffable flight of a dream-dive, a launching and terrible foundering in a rich rape of water. Her grace was supplejack, it was cuttystool and cavaletto, he trembled as on a springboard, jutting out, doomed, high over dream-water. Would she sink or swim in Diana's well? That depends what we mean by a maiden.

In the young thought of Belacqua, stocked now against its own interests, confused in a way that was not native to it, the Smeraldina-Rima and the Syra-Cusa were related and compared, just as Lucien may later enter the scales with Chas. The burden of his argument was:

here, in a given category (skirts), are two independent items: on my right, the powerfully constructed Smeraldina-Rima: on my left, the more lightly built Syra-Cusa. Beautiful both, in so far as before the one as before the other I find myself waxing pagan and static, I am held up. If it be not beauty, the common attribute here that dynamises, or, perhaps better, inhibits me, then it is something else. That is a hair not worth splitting. The important thing is that I may, may I not, suppose that these two dear measures of discrete quantity could be coaxed into yielding a lowest common one of the most impassioning interest in the sense that in it might be expected to reside the quintessential kernel and pure embodiment of the occult force that holds me up, makes me wax pagan and static, the kernel of beauty if beauty it be, at least in this category (skirts).

But, poor Belacqua, do you not realise that the essence of beauty is predicateless, transcending categories?

It had indeed occurred to poor Belacqua that such was the case.

But I would like very much to know, he proceeds, how I can handle heterogeneous entities. Kindred items, cognate ones, like in kind, these I fancy can be reduced to a deep common point of divergence. Somewhere is the magic point where skirted beauty forks, giving me and all that have eyes to see, on the one hand, the Smeraldina-Rima, the heavy brune, on the other, the Syra-Cusa, the welter brunette. But to relate, say, volume to line, a beautiful hen, say, to a beautiful dry-point . . . Get along with you! No node can branch, here to the beauty of a bird, there to the beauty of a dry-point. (If indeed a dry-point can ever be said to be beautiful.) I cannot establish on a base Aa, where A is hen and a dry-point, a triangle with the desired apex, because, and you will appreciate this disability, I am unable to imagine the base Aa.

Unfortunate Belacqua, you miss our point, *the* point: that beauty, in the final analysis, is not subject to categories, is beyond categories. There is only one category, yours, that furnished by your stases. As all mystics, independent of creed and colour and sex, are transelemented into the creedless, colourless, sexless Christ, so all categories of beauty must be transelemented into yours. Take it, deary, from us: beauty is one and beauties uni generis, immanent and transcendent, totum intra omnia, deary, et totum extra, with a centre everywhere and a circumference nowhere. Put that into your pipe, dear fellow, and smoke it slowly.

But in the young thought of Belacqua, stocked, as we have said, and confused in a way that was opposed to its real interests, a pullulation of Neue Sachlichkeit maggots, the two girls simply had to be compared, as, at a later stage, Lucien and Chas may have to be.

35

Suddenly it did not matter a curse, not a tinker's curse, all these people, Smerry, Syra, Lucien, Chas, such names!, lonely grit. All egal. The wombs that bear me, he thought, and the wombs that bore me and the arces formæ and the arses formæ. Egal. EGAL. A scurry of grit in the mistral. (His thought was young and there was no Alba, only the name, magic name, incantation, abracadabra, two slithers, th, th, dactyl trochee, dactyl trochee, for ever and ever.) They took a good pull on their features, on the precious little eager clothed pudibond body, they pumped up an opinion, they let it come, through a nozzle of fake modesty and fair breeding: "it seems to me . . ." You were spattered all over. Then you reorganised yourself, the brisk homunculus, you pursed up your mouth like a bud, pompier, cul de coq, out oozed the phrase, cack: "I think I agree with you . . .", "I think I don't altogether agree with you . . ." That was when they were not too busy doing something to you, raping you, pumping your hand, frôling you like a cat in rut, clapping you on the shoulder, smelling at you and rubbing up against you like a dog or a cat, committing every variety of nuisance on you, or making you do something, eat or go for a walk or get into bed or get out of bed or hold on or move on, too busy committing nuisance on you or chivvying you into committing nuisance on yourself to have occasion to turn on the nozzle of fake modesty and fair breeding. Quatsch quatsch quatsch. Grit in the mistral, tattered starlings in the devil's blizzard, and all bursting with hope, faith, charity and good works, so pleased that they could do this and so proud that they could say that, sniffing at you and snatching at you and committing decorous nuisance with the nozzle.

Vuolsi così colà, dove si puote
ciò che si vuole, e più non dimandare . . .

Colà? And where might that be, if it is not a rude question?
Behind the gas-works, deary, behind the gas-works.

Money came from the blue eyes of home, and he
spent it on concerts, cinemas, cocktails, theatres, apéri-
tifs, notably these, the potent unpleasant Mandarin-
Curaçao, the ubiquitous Fernet-Branca that went to your
head and settled your stomach and was like a short story
by Mauriac to look at, oxygéné and Real-Porto, yes, Real-
Porto. But not on opera, never under any circumstances
on opera, unless he was dragged, nor, after a bit, on
brothels. Liebert forced him to see the . . . the Valkyrie
à demi-tarif. Une merveille ! Only to be turned away.
Belacqua laffed and laffed.
"Go home" they said gently "and get out of your cyclist's
breeches."
Liebert tore aside his coat.
"My plus fours" he cried "my beautiful plus fours!"
"Your friend" they explained, approving the drab trou-
sers of Belacqua, "is convenable. You—no. You must go
away."
Belacqua sprained the rim of his belly. The perfect Wag-
nerite in half-hose, turned away from the chevauchée!
"You take mine" he begged "and I'll take yours. We'll go
across to the Biard and change. I'm not keen."
He stood in the vestibule of the National Academy of
Music and pressed his respectable trousers on the suf-
focating Liebert. He implored him in vain to take his

trousers, they were at his entire disposal for the rest of the evening, they were his to do what he liked with. But no, not on any account. Who was Wagner anyhow?

"Who is Wagner?" said Belacqua.

"Yes" said Liebert testily "who is he anyhow?"

"He is a roaring Meg" said Belacqua "against melancholy."

Nor on brothels . . .

Which carries us forward into a very tender zone indeed, to a clarification that cannot be dodged and is of a most difficult and delicate nature. Prima facie, it is shocking. We set our principal boy down in this gay place and at the same time insist that he eschewed its bawdy houses. That is shocking to begin with. And we tremble lest the whole conduct of his life during this period, when we shall have gone into it and placed before you in as discreet and mildly worded a relation as is compatible with franchise the considerations that compelled him to certain conclusions and the course of action that enabled him to carry on very well, oh very well and quite nicely, without recourse to such excellent institutions of pleasure and hygiene, we tremble, we said so so far back that we had better say it again, lest it should appear that his conduct was not merely shocking, but positively *choquant.*

Quickly now, and bravely, and with a quick prayer to you to be just for a few moments grave, we quaver a very shaky proposition:

Love condones . . . narcissism.

We pause, we beseech you not to mind the terminology, nor allow yourselves to be angered by the terminology, and we raise, in fear and trembling we do it, the proposition a notch.

Love demands narcissism.

Do not take us up too fast, hear us out. Forbid the terms to heat you. No one knows better than we do that stated so barely they are very nasty. Therefore we place ourselves on all our knees, beginning with the right, we bend our body profoundly, and beseech you out of the midst of this respectful posture of multiple genuflexion to hold your horses before you condemn us. In fact we pray for gravity all round. We take it that a grave climate surrounds us. What we want to do is not at all to convince you, but to persuade you. And what gravity, with the best will in the world, is proof against the generalisation, the western bull and his final bellow? If you could manage provisionally, until after the operation, a deliberate: *credo quia absurdum, ut intelligam,* our cheeks would be saved such a blushing, you have no idea, and our lips an insidious speaking. If we can rely on you (and you) to suspend hostilities for the space of just one paragraph (one in a bookful, is that exorbitant?) and abdicate your right to be entertained, then we can disarm too and say what we have to say, for said it must be, per fas et nefas, how we have no idea, we dare not think, urbanely at least, and, so far as in us lies, without style. This is a humiliating exordium, but we feel as nervous as a cat in a bag. And just one more request: believe us when we say that when we said, brusquely, screwing up our courage, not to the sticking point, but to the plunge: *Love demands narcissism,* we meant that in a certain case, his, possibly, by all means, an isolated case, a certain quality of loving (as understood and practised by him, by him alone of all lovers if it pleases you to think so, it would not

39

be in our interest to deny it) imports a certain system of narcissistic manœuvres. That is all we meant. Just that. That is the writhing proposition that we would more than willingly refrain from bringing cautiously forward, the umble proposition that will out, that we beg now, if you will be so kind as to lower the lights, to introduce.

Consider him, loving the Smeraldina-Rima, and half the continent removed from smell and sound of her breathing. Ay, notwithstanding the Dunkelbrau defloration, loving the Smeraldina-Rima. Absence makes the heart grow fonder is a true saying. In his own way, having her according to his God, as he threatened he would. Hoc posito, how could a reasonable use of the brothel, measured by his system of reference, which of course is the one we are obliged to refer to for this passage, have constituted the least outrage to the sentiment he entertained for his distant bloom, the light, melody, fragrance, meat and embracement of his inner man? But: the inner man, its hunger, darkness and silence, was it left entirely outside the brothel, did it not participate at all in the shady communion of the brothel? It was not and it did. Again: it was not and it did. Inwardly, after the act, into the sanctuary whose provision depended on her or on thought of her, whose assuaging belonged to her or the passional thought, the vision, of her, there entered peace and radiance, the banquet of music. That was so. She ceased to be bride of his soul. She simply faded away. Because his soul, by implication, had as many brides as his body. The rare miracle of fulfilment that had been ascribed and referred to her, exclusively to her, with which she in his mind had been identified, the gift of magic from her, real and ideal, to the soul, about which his entire preoccupation with her was organised, whose collapse as an imminent recurrence, had

40

that been thinkable, would have involved automatically the collapse of that preoccupation, this miracle and this magic, divorced from her and from thought of her, were on tap in the nearest red-lamp. That was so. Beatrice lurked in every brothel. The usual over, its purveyor null as before, there began the other outpour, streaming into the parched sanctuary, a gracious strength and virtue, a flow of bounty. Always and only after the usual and the purveyor of the usual, conditioned by them and flooding over them, over the garbage of the usual and the cabbage-stalks of sex, obliterating them, only then at the end, when it was time to rise and go, was dispensed the inward spilling. And not only over the garbage of the usual and the cabbage-stalks, but over the Smeraldina-Rima herself, over her impermeable oneness and her monopoly as his donator. That was the position. The bloom—not that in his mind or in her person she was ever floral, but merely for the sake of the antithesis—in virtue of this strange emanation issuing finally from the garbage and flowing back upon it to submerge it, was each time identified and obliterated with the cabbage-stalks. That was not nice. So he refrained, during this period, from entering houses of ill-fame. It was intolerable that she should break up into a series of whores simply because he, cursed by some displaced faculty of assimilation, by this demented hydraulic that was beyond control, found himself obliged to extract from the whore that which was not whorish, but, on the contrary, the fee-simple of the Smeraldina-Rima, who, as it seemed then to him, had either to remain one and indivisible, or else disappear altogether, become a negligible person. And the more intolerable as he was already braced against her disintegration, if not into the multiple whore, at least into the simple whore. One and indivisible. The booby would insist

41

on that. Incorruptible, uninjurable, unchangeable. She is, she exists in one and the same way, she is everyway like her herself, in no way can she be injured or changed, she is not subject to time, she cannot at one time be other than at another. That or—nullity. Whore and parade of whores. He plastered the poor girl with the complete pleroma. And then he had all the trouble in the world getting them to stick. He hauled her thus adorned, in spite of himself, into the brothel; and there, as explained, all the fine feathers came off. There, as one and as spirit, as spirit of his spirit, she was abolished.

Whereas in the other mansion, the mansion of him whose shoe was loosed, the process was reversed. He committed fraud—but had her, her in spirit, her according to his God, in place of that terrible anachronism of inward flowing that dethroned and dishonoured her in his mind. Her by fraud, but in spirit and with finality, alone in that other mansion. (At least that was his impression, he was satisfied, God help him, in that impression.) In the brothel, from the insignificance that was not she, of course not, he elicited (sua culpa and sua culpa) the reality that could only be she, dared only be she—and was not. There, in the brothel, suddenly at one with the inward rapture, the horrible confusion between the gift and the giver of the gift. The carnal frivolity, broached in the first place in order that the real spirit might never be degraded to the rank of succubus, yielded the real spirit. That was an abominable confusion, a fragmentation of the realities of her and him, of the reality in which she and he were related. Whereas now, alone, by fraud, he forced her to play the whore, he exploited her unreal and arbitrary to the end that he might annex her real and unique, to the end that the gift, when it came pouring in, assuaging like an overtone, might also be the giver, to the end that he might be spared Beethoven stated through a bagpipe. When he excluded her carnally, broaching without scruple this and that carnal detail on the understanding, she being not flesh, but spirit, that no real issue was thereby involved, then she was denied to him in spirit (getting tired of that word), she was abolished as spirit. Now, when she was first glibly postulated as flesh, wilfully distorted by him into the carnal detail, then she was conferred upon him in spirit, as spirit she was affirmed. Adopting a fraudulent system of Platonic manualisation, chiroplatonism, he postulated the physical encounter and proved the spiritual intercourse. Fearful of being assumed alone, without her, or, worse still, with the carnal detail, into the champaign of the morning, he compelled her to have a share in his darkness.

Such were the dreadful manœuvers required of him at this period by the nature of his sentiment for the Smeraldina-Rima. They had to be discovered. They constituted, given his youth, his salad days, a forced move.

Da questo passo vinti ci concediamo . . .

The labour of nesting in a strange place is properly extenuating. The first week and more went to throwing up a ring of earthworks; this to break not so much the flow of people and things to him as the ebb of him to people and things. It was his instinct to make himself captive, and that instinct, as never before or since, served him well and prepared a great period of beatitude stretching from mid-October to Xmas, when deliberately he escaladed the cup so scooped out of the world and scuttled back to the glare of her flesh, deserting his ways of peace and his country of quiet. But for two months and more he lay stretched in the cup, sheltered from the winds and sheltered from the waters, knowing that his own velleities of radiation would never scale the high rim that he had contrived all around and about, that they would trickle back and replenish his rumination as marriage the earth and virginity paradise, that he could release the boomerangs of his fantasy on all sides unanxiously, that one by one they would return with the trophy of an echo. He lay lapped in a beatitude of indolence that was smoother than oil and softer than a pumpkin, dead to the dark pangs of the sons of Adam, asking nothing of the insubordinate mind. He moved with the shades of the dead and the dead-born and the unborn and the never-to-be-born, in a Limbo purged of desire. They moved gravely, men and women and children, neither sad nor joyful. They were dark, and they gave a dawn light to the darker place where they moved. They were a silent rabble, a press of much that was and was not and was to be and was never to be, a pulsing and shifting as of a heart beating in sand, and they cast a dark light.

If that is what is meant by going back into one's heart, could anything be better, in this world or the next? The mind, dim and hushed like a sick-room, like a chapelle ardente, thronged with shades; the mind at last its own asylum, disinterested, indifferent, its miserable erethisms and discriminations and futile sallies suppressed; the mind suddenly reprieved, ceasing to be an annex of the restless body, the glare of understanding switched off. The lids of the hard aching mind close, there is suddenly gloom in the mind; not sleep, not yet, nor dream, with its sweats and terrors, but a waking ultra-cerebral obscurity, thronged with grey angels; there is nothing of him left but the umbra of grave and womb where it is fitting that the spirits of his dead and his unborn should come abroad.

44

He understood then, when he came out of the tunnel, that that was the real business, the Simon Pure of this frail life that has already been described as being all temptation and knighthood, fake temptations and sham squabbles, highly delightful underclothes (dessous de femme "Mystère") and boy-scouts, patrol-leader Charlie chasing the barley. Torture by thought and trial by living, because it was fake thought and false living, stayed outside the tunnel. But in the umbra, the tunnel, when the mind went wombtomb, then it was real thought and real living, living thought. Thought not skivvying for living nor living chivvying thought up to the six-and-eightpenny conviction, but live cerebration that drew no wages and emptied no slops. In the tunnel he was a grave paroxysm of gratuitous thoughts, his thoughts, free and unprofessional, non-salaried, living as only spirits are free to live. And the fuss that went on about the monologue and dialogue and polylogue and catalogue, all exclusively intérieur. Oh the belle blague ! That did make him tired. And the Gedankenflucht! The Pons Asinorum was a Gedankenflucht. In the umbra and the tunnel no exchanges, no flight and flow, no Bachkrankheit, but thought moving alive in the darkened mind gone wombtomb. Le train ne peut partir que les paupières fermées. Hee! Hee! The prurient heat and the glare of living consumed away, the bloomers and the boy-scouts abolished, the demireps and the Saint-Preux and the baci saporiti and other abolished, he was in the gloom, the thicket, he was wholly a gloom of ghostly comfort, a Limbo from which the mistral of desire had been withdrawn. He was not proud, he was not a bird of the air, passing off into outermost things, casting out his innermost parts, his soul at stool, per fæcula fæculorum, setting his neb in the heavens. He was not curious, he was not a fish

45

of the sea, prowling through the paths of the sea, darting and coiling through the deeps of the world and the ordures of time that perish behind. He is a great, big, inward man, continent, sustenant, versus internus. Jawohl.

We find we have written *he is* when of course we meant *he was*. For a postpicassian man with a pen in his fist, doomed to a literature of saving clauses, it is frankly out of the question, it would seem to be an impertinence— perhaps we should rather say an excess, an indiscretion— stolidly to conjugate *to be* without a shudder. What we meant of course was that he *was* a great, big, inward man, etc., then. Now he is once more a mere outside, façade, penetrated, if we may pilfer to reapply the creditable phrase of Monsieur Gide, by his façade, delighting, as you can see, in swine's draff for all he is fit. But during the two months odd spent in the cup, the umbra, the tunnel, punctuation from the alien shaft was infrequent and then, thanks to his ramparts, mild. Even so they used to drive him crazy, the way a crab would be that was hauled out of its dim pool into the pestiferous sunlight, yanked forth from its lair of moss and stone and green water and set to fry in the sun. *They:* Lucien, Liebert, the Syra-Cusa. Lucien was the least noxious. He did not flounce in with a bright gay swagger and clang like the Syra-Cusa, and he was not to be heard bouncing and scuttling up the stairs and along the passage, bursting with the very latest and love and ideas (God forgive him, yes, ideas) like Liebert. Lucien oozed in, he crept up to the door and slid in on a muted tap-tap. Then his conversation was choice, he spoke slowly and quietly, with great distinction, he was intelligent, he had a fine depressed intelligence, damped in a way that was a pleasure. Nor did he lay himself out to persuade, à la Liebert, nor titillate and arouse, à la Syra-Cusa, he did not talk *at* a person, he just balladed around at his own sweet aboulia, and—oh douceurs !—he kept on the mute.

"A passage in Leibnitz" he said "where he compares matter to a garden of flowers or a pool of fish, and every flower another garden of flowers and every corpuscle of every fish another pool of fish . . ." he essayed the gesture and smiled, a drowned smile, "gave me the impression that Æsthetics were a branch of philosophy."

"Ah" said Belacqua.

"Whereas, of course," he sighed "they are not."

"No?"

"No no" he said "there is no relation between the two subjects."

The smile was terrible, as though seen through water. Belacqua wanted to sponge it away. And he would not abandon the gesture that had broken down and now could never be made to mean anything. It was horrible, like artificial respiration on a fœtus still-born.

Another day, catching sight of his hand in a glass, he began to whinge. That was more in Belacqua's own line and did not discompose him in the same way. Lucien did not know how to deal with his hands.

He used to tell stories—mostly of his own invention— about the grouch of Descartes against Galileo. Then he would laugh over them like a girl, a profuse giggle. "Idiot, idiot" he would giggle.

It was he who one day let fall nonchalantly, à propos of what we don't happen to know, so nonchalantly that it must have been his and not another's: "Black diamond of pessimism." Belacqua thought that was a nice example, in the domain of words, of the little sparkle hid in ashes, the precious margaret and hid from many, and the thing that the conversationalist, with his contempt of the tag and the ready-made, can't give you; because the lift to the high spot is precisely from the tag and the ready-made. The same with the stylist. You couldn't experience a margarita in d'Annunzio because he denies you the pebbles and flints that reveal it. The uniform, horizontal writing, flowing without accidence, of the man with a style, never gives you the margarita. But the writing of, say, Racine or Malherbe, perpendicular, diamanté, is pitted, is it not, and sprigged with sparkles; the flints and pebbles are there, no end of humble tags and commonplaces. They have no style, they write without style, do they not, they give you the phrase, the sparkle, the precious margaret. Perhaps only the French can do it. Perhaps only the French language can give you the thing you want.

Don't be too hard on him, he was studying to be a professor.

But Liebert and the Syra-Cusa were a cursed nuisance. How can we bring ourselves to speak of Liebert? Oh he was a miserable man. He was a persecution. He would come in in the morning, at the first weals of dawn, and drag the bedclothes off the innocent Belacqua. What did he want? That is what is so hard to understand. Nothing would do him but to elucidate Valéry. He declaimed Valerian abominations of his own.

"He is the illegitimate cretin" said Belacqua, worn out, behind his back one fine day to the scandalised Lucien, "of Mrs. Beeton and Philippus Bombastus von Hohenheim."

Lucien recoiled. Because every one that knew the man thought he was wonderful. He appeared one night with a portable gramaphone and put on the . . . the Kleine Nachtmusik and then Tristan and *insisted on turning out the light.* That was the end of that. Belacqua could not be expected to see him any more after that. But ill will was a thing that Liebert could not bear. Malevolent he could not bear to be. So when he went to England he quoted Belacqua as his bosom butty, ami unique and all the rest. And he picked up a slick English universitaire (hockey and Verlaine) in the provinces somewhere, she was a she-woman to her finger-tips, and by heaven he had to marry her. Belacqua laffed and laffed. He remembered how Liebert used to visit Musset in the Père Lachaise and sitting by the tomb make notes for a meditation and then come home in the bus and pull out photographs of the current pucelle who was so wonderful (elle est adorable, oh elle est formidable, oh elle est tout à fait sidérante) and who drove him so crazy and had such a powerful effect on him and gave him such a lift. He detailed the powerful effect, he set forth the lift, with piscatorial pantomime. A truly miserable man.

Why we want to drag in the Syra-Cusa at this juncture it passes our persimmon to say. She belongs to another story, a short one, a far far better one. She might even go into a postil. Still we might screw a period out of her, and every period counts. But she remains, whatever way we choose to envisage her, hors d'oeuvre. We could chain her up with the Smeraldina-Rima and the little Alba, our capital divas, and make it look like a sonata, with recurrence of themes, key signatures, plagal finale and all. From the extreme Smeraldina and the mean Syra you could work out the Alba for yourselves, you could control our treatment of the little Alba. She might even, at a stretch, be persuaded to ravish Lucien, play the Smeraldina to Lucien's Belacqua. She could be coaxed into most anything. Ça n'existe pas. Except to keep us in Paris for another couple of hundred words. The hour of the German letter is not yet come. A paragraph ought to fix her. Then she can skip off and strangle a bath attendant in her garters.

49

The Great Devil had her, she stood in dire need of a heavyweight afternoon-man. What we mean is she was never even lassata, let alone satiata; very uterine; Lucrezia, Clytemnestra, Semiramide, a saturation of inappeasable countesses. An endless treaclemoon at the Porte de la Villette with a chesty Valmont in crimson sweater, tweed casquette and bicycle clips—her tastes lay in that direction. Her eyes were wanton, they rolled and stravagued, they were laskivious and lickerish, the brokers of her zeal, basilisk eyes, the fowlers and hooks of Amourrr, burning glasses. Strong piercing black eyes. Otherwise we think the face ought to have been in togs. But from throat to toe she was lethal, pyrogenous, Scylla and the Sphinx. The fine round firm pap she had, the little mamelons, gave her an excellent grace. And the hips, the bony basin, coming after the Smeraldina-Rima's Primavera buttocks ascream for a fusillade of spanners, fessades, chiappate and verberations, the hips were a song and a very powerful battery. Eyes—less good, to be frank, than we make out, our pen carried us away—and the body like a coiled spring, and a springe, too, to catch woodcocks. And hollow. Nothing behind it. She shone like a jewel in her conditions, like the cinnamon-tree and the rich-furred cony and Æsop's jay and Pliny's kantharis. Another of the many that glare. She was always on the job, the job of being jewelly.

"She lives" said Belacqua, altogether extenuated, one day behind her back to Lucien, "between a comb and a glass."

The best of the joke was she thought she had a lech on Belacqua, *she gave him to understand as much*. She was as impotently besotted on Belacqua babylan, fiasco incarnate, Limbese, as the moon on Endymion. When it was patent, and increasingly so, that he was more Octave of Malivert than Valmont and more of a Limbo barnacle than either, mollecone, as they say on the banks of the Mugnone, honing after the dark.

One calamitous night Belacqua, on fire, it is only fair to say, with Ruffino, was affected by her person with such force that he pressed upon her, as a gift and a mark of esteem (mark of esteem!) a beautiful book, one that he loved, that he had stolen from shelves at great personal risk; with pertinent dedication drawn by the short hairs from the text. The crass man. His lovely book! Now he has only the Florentia edition in the ignoble Salani collection, horrid, beslubbered with grotesque notes, looking like a bank-book in white cardboard and a pale gold title, very distasteful. Not indeed that there is a great deal to be said in favour of Papa Isodoro, with his primos and secundos and apple-dumpling readings. But the book itself was nice, bound well, with a bad reproduction of the Santa Maria del Fiore prestidigitator, printed well on paper that was choice, with notes that knew their place, keeping themselves to themselves. He pressed this treasure upon her. Lit with drink he forced her to take it. She did not want it, she said she did not. It was no good to her, she would never read it, thank you very much all the same. Now if he happened to have such a thing as a Sadie Blackeyes . . . But he pestered and plagued her till she gave in to get rid of him and took it. Then she left it in a bar and he dragged her back from the Batignolles to near the Gobelins to retrieve it.

Now we seem to have got the substance of the Syra-Cusa. She was a cursed nuisance. Be off, puttanina, and joy be with you and a bottle of moss.

51

Toutes êtes, serez ou fûtes,
De fait ou de volonté, putes,
Et qui bien vous chercheroit
Toutes putes vous trouveroit . . .

Quoted by Chas, many a long day later, on a painful
occasion, by his dear friend Jean du Chas, who came to a
bad end.

There, until the light of the day should be gone, he
lay on his back on the bed, in the maw of the tunnel. The
head lay in the cup of the palms clasped behind it, the
thumb-nails scratched together rythmically the little boss
of amativeness, the spread flexed arms were the transepts
of a cross on the bolster, the knees were drawn up and
parted to make a Judas-hole. He looked out between the
knees, across the low bedrail, out through the tainted window. He heard snatches of a response from a dissertation
on the sixth precept of the Decalogue: *elevate his mind his
mind to God, invoke Him, signo crucis se munire . . . Deum
placidum placidumdumdum invocare. B. Virginem . . . an-
gelum custodem . . .* He lay on his back on the bed gawk-
ing out like a fool at the end of the day. First, the bare tree,
dripping; then, behind, smoke from the janitor's chimney-
pot, rising stiff like a pine of ashes; then, beyond, beyond
the world, pouring a little light up the long gully of the
street that westers to the Luxembourg, half blinded by the
sodden boughs, sending a little light into the room where
he lay spreadeagled on the hot bed, blessed and ineffably
remote, the tattered flowers of the evening, sweet colour of
sapphire, an uncharted reef of flowers. There the harlot
lives for ever, the throttled harlot, breaking with her hands

the yellow gold and dividing the enamel. There she squats, Yang, for ever and for ever, crying on a spray of blossom, Yang, the geisha Rahab, garotted by the eunuchs, the princess of the eunuchs . . .

His Mother had bought turf from two little boys who had stolen it off the bog, whose parents incited them to steal turf off the bog. On two counts, subsequently, by the Civic Guards, those plush bosthoons, they were indicted: breach of turbary and cruelty to the ass. They hawked it round from door to door in an ass and cart, and his Mother wrote to say she had bought half a load. Now therefore the room where they sat was more sanctum than ever when the lamps were lit and the curtains drawn. His Mother went to sleep over the paper, but when she went to bed she would lie awake. "The perils and dangers of this night . . ." What were they? John came slouching down from his forge for a cup of scald. His father assembled his arsenal of cold pipes, turned on the book, connected up, and it did the rest. That was the way to read—find out the literary voltage that suits you and switch on the current of the book. That was the mode that every one had known, the corduroy trousers and bunch of blue ribbon mode. Then it goes. The wretched reader takes off his coat and squares up to the book, squares up to his poetry like a cocky little hop-me-thumb, hisses up his mind and pecks and picks wherever he smells a chink. And the old corduroy mode, when you switched on and put in the plug and dropped everything, let yourself go to the book, and it do the work and dephlogisticate you like a current of just the right frequency, once gone is gone for ever. Except with luck on certain occasions that may bring it back, and then you know where you were. To the convalescent, well again and weak, the old mode may come back; or in winter, in the country, at night, in bad weather, far from the cliques and juntas. But his Father had never lost it. He sat motionless in the armchair under the singing lamp, absorbed and null. The pipes went out, one after another. For long spells he heard nothing that was said in the room, whether to him or not. If you asked him next day what the book was like he could not tell you.

Chas, the dark seraphim in his heart, turned off all the lights in his big room, and with a little heavy hammer that he had, pounded up his gramophone records. "Je les ai *concassés*" he wrote "tous jusqu'à l'avant-dernier." The trams, the Blackrock, the Dun Laoghaire, the Dalkey, one Donnybrook and a little single-decker bound for Sandymount Tower, cried up to him from the causeway of Nassau Street, and passed.

The Alba in pain sat in the kitchen, nec cincta nec nuda, in a royal peignoir of cloth of gold, sipping her Hennessy. The trams cried to her passing up and down, the Radio played Avalon, a sad rag and old, she sat on, derelict daughter of kings, undaunted daughter, in the sunken kitchen, she sucked great packets of smoke down her ruined larynx, she thought bitterly of the old days, she finished her Hennessy, she called angrily for more. "Shall I be mewed up like a hawk" she cried "shall I, all the days of my life? Shall I?"

And Belacqua on the hot bed, the work of prayer over, the blessed island spent, the streets full of darkness, said her name, once, twice, incantation, abracadabra, abracadabra, and saying it felt the tip of his tongue between his incisors. Dactyl-trochee dactyl-trochee, he said it wetly, biting at one and four on the viscid tip.

There the wind was big and he was wise who stirred not at all, came not abroad. The man, Nemo to be precise, was on his bridge, curved over the western parapet. High over the black water he leaned out, he let fall a foaming spit, it fell plumb to the top of the arch, then was scattered, by the Wild West Wind. He moved off left to the end of the bridge, he lapsed down blankly on to the quay where the bus rank is, he set off sullenly, his head sullenly, clot of anger, skewered aloft, strangled in the cang of the wind, biting like a dog against its chastisement.

Bel Bel my own beloved, *allways* and for *ever* mine!!
    Your letter is soked with tears death is the onely thing. I had been crying bitterly, tears! tears! tears! and nothing els, then your letter cam with more tears, after I had read it ofer and ofer again I found I had ink spots on my face. The tears are rolling down my face. It is very early in the morning, the sun is riseing behind the black trees and soon that will change, the sky will be blue and the trees a golden brown, but there is one thing that dosent change, this pain and thos tears. Oh! Bel I love you terrible, I want you terrible, I want your body your soft white body naked! naked! My body needs you so terrible, my hands and lips

and breasts and everything els on me, sometimes I feel it very hard to keep my promise but I have kept it up till now and will keep on doing so untill we meet again and I can at last have you, at last be "Deine Geliebte". Whitch is the greater: the pain of being away from eachother, or the pain of being with eachother, crying at eachother beauty? I sopose the last is the greater, otherwise we would of given up all hope of ever being anything els but miserable.

I was at a grand Film last night, first of all there wasent *any* of the usual hugging and kissing, I think I have never enjoyed or felt so sad at a Film as at that one: *Sturm über Asien*, if it comes to Paris you must go and see it, the same Regie as *Der Lebende Leichnam*, it was realey something quite diffrent from all other Films, nothing to do with "Love" (as everybody understands the word) no silly girls makeing sweet faces, nearly all old people from Asien with marvellous faces, black lakes and grand Landschaften. Comeing home there was a new moon, it looked so grand ofer the black trees that it maid me cry. I opened my arms wide and tryed to imagine that you were lieing against my breasts and looking up at me, like you did thos moonlight nights when we walked together under the big chestnut trees with the stars shining through the branches.

I met a new girl, very beautiful, pitch black hairs and very pale, she onely talks Egyptian. She told me about the man she loves, at present he is in Amerika far away in some lonely place and wont be back for the next 3 years and cant writ to her because there is no post office where he is staying and she onely gets a letter every 4 months, imagine if we only got a letter from eachother every 4 months what sort of state we would be in by now, the poor girl I am very sorry for her. We went to a 5 o'clock tea dance, it was rather boreing but quite amusing to see the people thinking of nothing but what they have on and what they look like and if there lips are painted well and the men settling there tyes every 5 minutes. On the way home I sudenly got in to a terrible state of sadness and woulden say a word, of course they were rageing with me, at the moment I dident care a dam, when I got in to the bus I got out a little Book and pencil and wrot down 100 times: Beloved Beloved Beloved Bel Bel Bel, I felt as if I never longed so much in my life for the man I love, to be with him, with him. I want you so much in every sence of the word, you and onely you. After I got out of the bus and was walking down the street I yelled out wahnsinnig! wahnsinnig! wahnsinnig! Frau Schlank brought down your sock and that made me cry more than ever. I dont think I will send it to you, I will put it in to the drawer with your sweet letters. I had allso a letter from a man who asked me to go out with him to dance on Saturday evening, I sopose I will go, I know my beloved dosent mind and it makes the time go round quicker, the man is a bit of a fool but dances quite well and is the right hight for me. A flirt is very amusing but shouldent go further than that.

Then I met the old man with the pipe and he told me I had a blue letter, and then the fat man with the keys in the passage and he said Grüß Gott but I dident hear him.

Soon I will be counting the hours untill I can go to the station and find you amongst the crowded platform but I dont think I will be able to wear my grey costume if it is too cold and then I will have to wear Mammy furcoat. You will be by me on the 23th wont you Bel, my Bel with the beautiful lips and hands and eyes and face and everything that is on you, and now with your poor sore face it would make no diffrence. Two more weeks of agony pain and sadness! 14 more days oh! God and thos sleepless nights!!! How long? how long?

57

I had a very queer dream last night about you and me in a dark forest, we were lieing together on a path, when sudenly you changed in to a baby and dident know what love was and I was trying to tell you that I loved you more than anything on earth but you dident understand and wouldent have anything to do with me but it was all a dream so it dosent count. There is no object in me trying to tell you how much I love you because I will never succeed, I know that for sirten. Is he the man I have allways been looking for? Yes! but then why cant he give that what I have been longing for for the last 6 months? I ofen wonder what is on you that makes me love you so greatly. I love you über alles in dieser Welt, mehr als alles auf Himmel, Erde und Hölle. One thing I thank God for that our love is so vast. I ofen wonder who I am to thank that you are born and that we met, I sopose I better not start trying to find out whose fault it is that you are born. It comes back to the same thing, and that is, that I onely know *ONE THING* and that is that *I LOVE YOU AND I AM ALLWAYS YOUR SMERRY* and that is the thing that matters most in our life *YOU LOVE ME AND ARE ALLWAYS MY BEL.*

Analiese is hacking round on the piano and there is no peace so I will stop. Now I am going to go on reading my Book called *Die Große Liebe* and then perhaps I will try and struggel through the Beethoven sonate, it is the onely thing that can take me away from my misery, I love playing quietly to myself in the evenings it gives me such a rest

Bel! Bel! Bel! your letter has just come! Even if you cease to be all and allways mine!!! Oh! God how could you ever say such a thing, for lord sake dont!!! for god sake dont ever suggest such a thing again! I just berry my head in my hands and soke your letter with tears . . . Bel! Bel! how could you ever doupt me? Mein Ruh ist hin mein Herz ist schwer ich finde Sie nimmer und nimmer mehr. (Herr Geheimrat Johann Wolfgang Goethes Faust.) Lord Lord Lord for god sake tell me strate away what agsactly I have done. Is everything indiffrent to you? Evedintly you cant be bothered with a goat like me. If I dont stop writing you wont be able to read this letter because it will be all ofer tears. Bel! Bel! my love is so vast that when I am introduced to some young man and he starts doing the polite I get a quivver all ofer. I *know* what I am lifeing for, your last letter is allways on my breast when I wake up in the morning and see the sun rise. Ich seh' Dich nicht mehr Tränen hindern mich! My God! my true dog! my baby!

I must get a new nib, this old pen is gone to the dogs, I cant writ with it any more, it is the one that I got from Wollworth so you can imagine how good it must be.

Mammy wanted me to go out for a walk this afternoon, but I hate walking, I get so tired putting one foot delibertely in front of the other. Do you remember last summer (of course he dose!) and how lovely it was lieing hearing the bees summing and the birds singing, and the big butterfly that cam past, it looked grand, it was dark brown with yellow spots and looked so beautiful in the sun, and my body was quite brown *all* ofer and I dident feel the cold any more. Now the snow is all melted and the wood is as black as ever and the sky is allways grey except in the early morning and even then one can onely see spots of red between the black clouds.

My hairs are freshily washed and I have a bit more energie than usual, but I still feel very passiv. For god sake dont overdo yourself and try and not get drunk again, I meen in that way that makes you sick.

We cam home in the bus this evening but we dident go that way through the fields with all the little paths because the big road was mended. Mammy allways asks after you. She says the time is *flying*, it will be *no* time untill Xmas and she says she hopes Frau Holle makes her bed ofen. I heard her saying to Daddy: I wonder how it is that Ivy and Jacky get on my nerves when they go on together and Smerry and Bel never did. She ment when we are sitting on eachother knee and so on, I think it is because the love between Ivy and Jacky is not real, there allways seems to be some sort of affection about it.

I curse the old body all day asswell because I have some dam thing on my leg so that I can bearly walk, I dont know what it is or how it got there but it is there and full of matter to hell with it.

To-day is one of the days when I see everything more clearer than ever and I am sure everything *will* go *right* in the end.

Der Tag wird kommen und die stille
NACHT!!!

I dont know genau when, but if I dident think so I would cullaps with this agony, thes terrible long dark nights and onely your image to console me. I like the little white statue so much and am longing for the day when you and I will be standing like that and not haveing to think that there is somebody outside that can come in any minute.

You ask me to give you a taske. I think I have gived you a big enough a taske, I am longing to see the "thing" you wrot about my "beauty" (as *you* call it) I must say (without wanting any complements) I cant see anything very much to writ about except the usual rot men writ about women.

Arschlochweh is married and gone to the Schweiz with his wife.

Darling Bel I must close. My bed is lonely without me and your photograph is waiting to be kissed so I better give them both peace. Soon it will all take an end, you will be by me and will feel that marvellous pain again that we did in the dark mountains and the black lake blow and we will walk in the fields covered with cowslips and hedges of Flieder and you will hold once more in your arms

your own sad beloved

Smerry

P.S. One day nearer to the silent night!!!

A severe bout of hepatic colics confined him to his room. They were very severe. They pulled him down, they reduced him to a shadow of his robust self. He groaned in spirit. How intempestively, he groaned, am I pulled down. Just when I wanted so much to be at the top of my form, à point, to wrestle with the Madonna. God, he made moan, forgive me, but I'll arrive like Socrates, as cold as January, as little and unable as a child, a mere bedful of bones. Now he was as sad as a hare on this account. A procella raged in his sweetbread. Non est vivere, he was absolutely of that famous opinion, sed valere, vita. He declined the darkest passages of Schopenhauer, Vigny, Leopardi, Espronceda, Inge, Hatiz, Saadi, Espronerda, Becquer and the other Epimethei. All day he told the beads of his spleen. *Or posa per sempre*, for example he was liable to murmur, lifting

61

and shifting the seat of the disturbance, *stanco mio cor.
Assai palpitasti . . .* and as much more of that gloomy composition as he could remember. To his chafing Braut he
scribbled a line whose burden was: that feeling a little
inclined to be seedy he might be detained, that he might
not feel up to undertaking so long a journey so soon, that
she must not allow herself to be disappointed, must not
worry, on no account get it into her head that there was the
least thing *seriously* amiss, that he simply wanted her to be
prepared for the possibility of his being obliged to arrive a
day or two later than he had hoped and led her to expect,
immer Dein, tuissimus, and gave it to post to the cyanosed
valet de chambre. Well, would you believe it, promptly by
return a letter from Mammy that made him sit up in the
bed and no error:

"Smerry nearly had a fit on receipt of yours. She went off
in a hysteria (sic) and the family daren't approach her. She
seems to have got it into her head, whatever you said in
your letter, that either you are dying or have ceased to care
for her. For God's sake pull yourself together, throw a
bottle and a toothbrush into a bag, and come on. Expect
you without fail for --- by the midday train."

Hah! So he was to pull himself together. It did not
matter about his feeling as sick as a dog, he was to pull
himself together and dash off into the unknown with no
more luggage than a bottle and a toothbrush.

He fell back very cross indeed on the bed. He
stretched out his legs and put on his considering cap. To do
this he had to liquidate Limbo, he had to eject the grey
angels, and disperse with light the shoal of spirits. This
moment will do to mark the term of his beatitude, the
relâche of the tunnel, the centroid of the massive ictus that
began to descend with the arrival of the Smeraldina's let-

ter, the colics and concomitant anxiety. This was the moment if ever, now that he was alone in his chamber and pricked into anger, to slay his old man, to give, there and then, this love the slip. But the moment passed with the dull and drowsy formula. Anon, he said, anon, take your hurry, and he opened wide the lids of the mind and let in the glare. The beaver bites his off, he said, I know, that he may live. That was a very persuasive chapter of Natural History. But he lost no time in reminding himself that, far from being a beaver or the least likely to sympathise with its aspirations, he was no less a person than the lover of the Belacqua Jesus and a very inward man. Hold your horses, was again his coarse thought, there's no sense in trying to bawl down an echo.

Out from the tunnel therefore he came, it clanged behind him, the libido sentiendi flared up, and he purled along in a foxy meditation. To begin with he considered offensive the tigress tone of the old multipara's letter. "Pull yourself together and come on"! It was easy to talk. He composed a letter in his mind:

". . . had you gone to the trouble of taking cognisance of the terms of my letter to your delicate and third or fourth daughter (and no doubt, in the excitement of the moment you might have *arranged* to do that) you would scarcely, I believe, have conveyed so unreflected a tone to your recommendations. My letter was affectionately to the effect that I, unwell and confined to my room, might be obliged to postpone my departure for a day or two. I occupy one of the many positions that separate death from indifference to your daughter the Smeraldina-Rima. I am suffering from DIARRHŒIA. There is no reason why this affliction should turn out to be fatal, nor yet jeopardise my feeling for the Smeraldina-Rima . . ." and so on. Then he thought better, he thought, no, I can't send a thing like that, and anyway I don't know how to write a stinger in English, I always overdo it. In French I can write a fine stinger, but in English I overdo it. And it is possible that Mammy is acting for what she conceives to be the best for all parties. It's that great heifer of a pucelle bawling out of her beauty-sickness—that's the one I want to get. I'll get up, I'll take a train this very day, I'll arrive beginning to look like St Francis skull-gazing, and then when the thing fiascoes I can I told you so.

He lay there working it all out on the bed and already the Reisefieber burned him. He left the bed in a spasm, he wired "Gewiß" and went.

Down you get now and step around. Two hours menopause at least. Drag your coffin my lord. Half a day and I'll be with. HIER! The bright beer goes like water through the shortsighted fliegende Frankfurter porter. In Perpignan exiled dream-Dantes screaming in the plane-trees and freezing the sun with peacock feathers and at last at least a rudimentary black swan with the blood-beak and HIC! for the bladderjerk of the little Catalan postman. Oh who can hold a fire in his hand by thinking on the frosty Caucasus! Here oh here oh art thou pale with weariness. I hope yes after a continental third-class insomnia among the reluctantly military philologists asleep and armed as to na-sals and dentals. Laughter. Ten Pfenige in such a dainty slot gives the la I am bound to concede and releases the appropriate tonic for the waning love. Moderate strength rings the bell. Like hell it does. Così fan tutte with the magic flute. Even in the Xmas holidays. Half a day and I'll be in.

Up to time then after this little railway-station rectification here she comes advancing up the railway-platform like a Gozzi-Epstein, careful not to lose the platform ticket that yet ten Pfenige cost had, insisting on the Garden of Eden in Mammy's furcoat, scarcely suggestive within the mild aphrodisiac of cheap loose black cardboard Russian buskins legs and limbs that even flexed nervously in black hose stretched to breaking point and viewed from a carefully selected Blickpunkt against a very special quality of hard light during œstrum were not alas even reasonably exciting. The truly tremendous bowel of the hips (frequent and easy) breaking out and away from the waistroot (Lupercus a liability) like a burdocked bulb of Ruffino and the two hoops of the buttocks received an almost Rhineline from the dark peltsheath. Sheath within sheath and the missing sword. Not forgetting for a moment this was the suit he had bought for next to nothing from a lefthanded indivisible individual, with a charitable desire to justify his fatigue, he forced his right hand down past the craggy coxa (almost a woman's basin in these trousers) into the glairy gallant depths and fished up a fifty. A cigarette quick for maxillas and malas and the ticket handy there in the breast of my reefer and the heavy valise to snatch him down skilfully detached and meagre into the loveglue and a smoke after that was nearly as good as in the Maison du Café.

"At last!"

"Beloved!"

"Taxi!"

Vie de taxi. Je t'adore à l'égal.

Carry your coffin my lord. Männer. Moving east to the segregation of the sexes. Ausgang on the right. Rule of the road. Lady on right arm. Nonsens unique. Astuce. But sleep on the right side. Gentle reader don't overlook will you the fact that he celebrated the signing of the Armistice with a pubic lanugo and

BELACQUA

we had to call him and no indolent virgin is his sister (indolent virgin!) and he does not much care whether he plays the tinkle-tinkle of a fourhander or not but he won't facing the keyboard observe the rule of the road (a megalomaniac you see with his head in his thighs as a general rule) so we ask you to humour now what naturally looks merely like so much intestinal incohesion, remember he belongs to the costermonger times of a pale and ardent generation, pray that he will let a few good sighs out of him ere it be too late and speedy promotion from the Godbirds.

And the lady that even in this very short and public space of time and notwithstanding that fur has no conductive properties of the appropriate kind worth speaking of has succeeded in transmitting certain unexpectedly stimulating sensations to her young visitor, were we not obliged to dub her the

SMERALDINA-RIMA

though most anything else would have done as well and notably Hesper we fancy would have been better and anything that comes in handy for short. He handed her into the cab of the Wagen with its charming deep Bluepoint zoster and spoke the address confidently to the chauffeur who but a moment previously had thought to light a cigarette and now naturally was in no kind of humour to start his engine and set off but was not slow to yield to the promising accent of the callow tourist whose heavy fibre case he hoisted vigorously on board on his left beside him and clipping the yet intact Ova between a rubbery helix and hypertrophied mastoid process gratified in his dialogue doubtless his nearest colleagues with what no doubt was a passionate Hessian epigram, set his machine angrily in motion, suffering with a kind of hopeless interest the refracted deportment of his clients.

Down the cobbled alley then of bitter Xmas trees, trembling in many and many an umbral stasis twixt tram and trottoir, the superb Wagen flew towards the spire that eliminates in impeccable imperial alignment the now dim height of Hercules and the mean cascade sullen and abandoned dropping, the little there was of it and because it bloody well had to, down the choked channel of Hohenzollern rocaille, snowclad, upon the castle.

"Where did you get the hat?" Another glaucous helmet.

"Do you like it?"

"Very nice do you?"

"Oh I don't know do you?"

Snotgasp of reliefhilarity in honour of private joke.

"It goes with the ring."

He turned over the hand and looked at the warts. Two dwindling warts in the shadow of the Mount Venerean. Warts in the valley of the shadow of.

"Your warts are better."

Ostentatiously he clapped his mouth upon the place. She squeezed the Giudecca of her palm against the centre of distribution, nailing his malas with thumb and index. That was lovely. In the rue Delambre with a silk handkerchief did he not stem and staunch the vomitdribble of littérateur deaddrunk and cornuted what's more into the bargain on Pernod Fils and Pick-me-up? How often had he not denied all knowledge of Hernani? Poor Hamlet rolling his belly waxes and tapers the spike of his navelthread for the red waistcoat. The beadlust. By no thinking shall he consume that enterprise, by no new thoughts shall he altogether be released from the postulate of his undertaking. Fast in the black sand.

Let us off the tutti chords now and tell us frankly shutting your eyes like Rouletabille what you think of our erotic sostenutino. Crémieux hold your saliva and you Curtius, we have a little note somewhere on Anteros we do believe, in fact we seem to remember we once wrote a poem (Nth. Gt. George's St. triphthong Corporal Banquo, *if* you please) on him or to him cogged from the liquorish laypriest's Magic Ode and if we don't forget we'll have the good taste to shove in the little ducky-diver as a kind of contrapuntal compensation do you comprehend us and in deference to your Pisan penchants for literary stress and strain.

Well really you know and in spite of the haricot skull and a tendency to use up any odds and ends of pigment that happened to be left over she was the living spit he thought of Madonna Lucrezia del Fede. Ne suis-je point pâle? Suis-je belle? But certainly pale and belle my pale belle Braut with a winter skin like any old sail in the wind. The root and the source betwixt and between the little athletic or æsthetic bit of a birdneb was indeed we assure you a constant source of delight and astonishment, when his solitude was not peopled and justified and beautified and even his sociabilities by a constipated coryza, to his forefinger pad and nail, rubbing and plumbing and palping and boring it just as for many years he polished (ecstasy of attrition!) his glasses or suffered the shakes and gracenote strangulations and enthrottlements of the Winkelmusik of Szopen or

Pichon or Chopinek or Chopinetto or whosoever it was embraced her heartily as sure as his name was Fred, dying all his life (thanks Mr Auber) on a sickroom talent (thanks Mr Field) and a Kleinmeister's Leidenschaftsucherei (thanks Mr Beckett), or crossed the Seine or the Pegnitz or the Tolka or the Fulda as the case might be and it never by any possible chance on one single solitary occasion occurring to him that he was on all such and similar occasions (which we regret to say lack of space obliges us regretfully to exclude from this chronicle) not merely indulging in but pandering to the vilest and basest excesses of sublimation of a certain kind. The wretched little wet plug of an upperlip, pugnozzling up and back in a kind of a duck or a cobra sneer to the nostrils was happily to some small extent mollified and compensated by the fine full firm undershot priapism of underlip and chin, a signal recovery to say the least and a reaffirmation of the promise of sentimentic vehemence already so gothly declamatory in the wedgehead of the strapping fizgig. From time to time she positively only had to snatch off her amice to be a birdface and to have put Pope John Kissmine and Orchids in mind of his Puerpetually Succourbusting Lady as she positively must have appeared on at least two probabionary occasions: *primo*, skewered, there's no other word for it, to her loggia by the shining gynaecologist; *secundo*, confined, by Thermidor, in the interests of her armpits, to her bathroom, shamed in mind, yes, and yet—grieving for the doomed olives. Well we must say and no offence meant, that class of egoterminal immaculate quackery and dupery gives us the sick if anything does. Whatever she was she was not that kind. We suppose we can say she looked like an ulula in pietra serena, a parrot in a Pietà. On occasions that is. Not we need scarcely point out in the helmet of salvation.

69

By Jove when we look back and think how chaste was the passion of mutual attraction that juxtaposed those two young people in the first instance! It is out of the questions, it is beyond our poor powers, to give you any idea of the reverence with which they—how shall we say?—clave the one to the other in an ecstasy and an agony of mystical adhesion. Yessir! An ecstasy and an agony! A sentimentical coagulum, sir, that biggers descruption. Don't we know for a positive fact that th'unhappy Belacqua, separated from his douce Vega by two channels and 29 hours third if he went over Ostend, tossing and turning and tightening the tender white worms of his nervi nervorum with the frogs' and the corncrakes' Chinese chromatisms, inscribed to his darling blue flower some of the finest Night of May hiccupsobs that ever left a fox's paw sneering and rotting in a snaptrap. E.g.

At last I find in my confusèd soul,
Dark with the dark flame of the cypresses,
The certitude that I cannot be whole,
Consummate, finally achieved, unless

I be consumed and fused in the white heat
Of her sad finite essence, so that none
Shall sever us who are at last complete
Eternally, irrevocably one,

One with the birdless, cloudless, colourless skies,
One with the bright purity of the fire
Of which we are and for which we must die
A rapturous strange death and be entire,

Like syzygetic stars, supernly bright,
Conjoined in the One and in the Infinite!

Lilly Neary has a lovely gee and her pore Paddy got his B.A. and by the holy fly I wouldn't recommend you to ask me what class of a tree they were under when he put his hand on her and enjoyed that. The thighjoy through the fingers and what do you suppose she wants for her thigh-beauty? A bitch-melba and a long long come and go before breakfast, toast and. Keycold Lucrece the chaste and the castaway in the cruel tights and Christ the useful culmination, fouterpounds through the fingers. No, more— more?—other, than that to my bright agenesia. No no don't admire that. No but I thought I thought perhaps honey-suckle round the cradle, custard and nutmeg on my grave, and the Eingang? Then he reddied his nose with the hand that came off her. Christ that was fine too. I wouldn't be seen looking at your Haus Albrecht Dürer, Adam Kraft my iron buck virgin. No smoking in the torture chamber. Not really you don't mean to tell me well well! Now the thin little sandy bony with the fine little stout son in Hanover, furchtbar all of a sudden with tears, now I must go and dien in the, the others do the streets but I go and dien in the, furcht*bar*, find a hotel, take a Wagen, no?, write, to hell with you, strive for your stout little hoffentlich ballbearing bastardpimp, I'll spend the night in the station, without the Benedictina, my old bald darling, your garret stinks of, I won't kiss your playful hand, daß heißt spielen, my do-lorific nymphæ and a tic doulheureux in th'imperforate hymen, what's the Dutch for randy, my dirty little hungry little bony vulture of a whorchen away up first-floor Burg-ward over the stream, I'll send you a Schein when I have a Schwips. No effing smoking do you hear me in the effing Folterzimmer. I had to ask her little sister and she closed me the vowel. I wonder did I do well to leave my notes at home, in 39 under the east wind, weind please. Well then to get back to what we were saying when he'd picked his nose for a little bit and the thighs there Gott sei dank he rose did he not and left her playing there against the oak before the ash, oh don't infuriate me don't bother me, let me pay let me buy you etwas, eat my little Augen Celery-ice Celeryice, did he not, and wandered up hill and down dale like the cat and the mouse in business together or the Marientotenkind. No no I *won't* say everything, I *won't* tell you everything. No but surely you see now what he am? See! Heiliger Brahmaputra! A hedgecreeper! A peeping Tom in bicycle-clips, the ones that go round! Well then up he rose and apprehended without passion round and about the Sabbath brushwood foothill couples. Yes to be sure of course you are right, it would be hard for you to understand my meaning, you see he led a fairly small fleshy lipped maiden I might have said Jungfrau into the wood I might have said Wald and creeped and peeped instead of. Oh did I do well to leave my notes at home. So then after another little bit he came back and stood looking with his tongue in his cheek instead of.

J'aime et je veux pââââlir. Livid rapture of the Zurbaran Saint-Onan. Schwindsucht and pollution in the umbra in the tunnel in the Thebaid. Rapturous strange death! Plus précieuse que la vie, the dirty dog. But right enough all the same what more miserable than the miserable man that commiserates not himself, cæsura, with new grief grieves not for his grief, is not worn by a double sorrow, drowns not in ken of shore? Who said all that? Turned he hath the audacious soul, turned he hath and turned again, on back, sides and belly, like little Miss Florence on the tick while Virgil and Sordello—yet all was very sore. As an herpetic taratantaratarantula (have you spotted the style?) hath he consumèd away. He dared to go off the deep end

with his shadowy love and he daily watered by daily littles
the ground under his face and beerbibbing did not lay
siege to his spirit and he was continent though not in the
least sustenant and many of his months have since run out
with him the pestilent person to take him from behind his
crooked back and set him before his ulcerous gob in the
boiling over of his neckings and in chambering and wan-
tonness and in bitter and blind bawling against the honey
what honey bloody well you know the honey and in can-
vassing and getting and weltering in filth and scratching off
the scabs of lust. All on a mild scale, of course, don't be
misled, Paterson's Camp Coffee is the Best with Sanka.
Perhaps the pen ran away, don't for a moment imagine
Belacqua is down the drain, of course he has got a bit
wasted that was bound to happen and his bitch of a heart
knocks hell out of his bosom three or four nights in the
week and to make a long story short Lucy and Jude are
kept going pretty well from dawn to dark with his shingles
and graphospasmus and weeping eczema and general condition, but for all that we will all agree that it's a long call
from feeling a bit slack and run down to lying senseless in
a deathsweat.

Here we are. Out we get. Step around. Thank you
dear. You put on the light. Up we go. Out of step. Randy-
gasp of ruthilarity in honour of private joke. Here we are.
There they are. Hello hello. Great to be here. Grand to be
here. Same old Wohnung. Wunnerful to be here. Prosit.
God bless. Lav on the left. Won't be a sec. Mind the bike.
Mind the skis. Beschissenes Dasein beschissenes Dasein
Augenblick bitte beschissenes Dasein Augenblickchen
bitte beschissenes

*   *   *

73

All that sublimen of blatherskite just to give some idea of the state the poor fellow was in on arrival. We would not wish our young hero to be misjudged, or hastily judged, by the reader, for the want of a few facts. We strive to give the capital facts of his case. Facts, we cannot repeat it too often, let us have facts, plenty of facts.

Now there is a lull, now the Madonna's Mammy, the eternal grandmother if all worked out according to plan, dared be the very bowels of compassion. She put him lying down on the settee.

"Poor Bel" she said "look Smerry, he is ill."

Smerry, biding her time in a corner, casting up the pubic content of this lover haggard before the fact, had a great look of the B.V. before the tidings.

"Drink this" said the Mandarin.

"Domine" responded Belacqua, sitting up and dipping the glass of fiery liquor at parents and child "non sum dignus."

"Don't you think" said Mammy "that Smerry looks rather a pet in that frock?"

Belacqua, the brandy drunk, was well able to do the false and the suave and the bland demon.

"Your third or fourth daughter" he said "looks to me more beautiful if possible than ever before. Would" he sucked in his cheeks and launched a heavy sigh "that the same could be said of me."

"Poor Bel" said Mammy. "But we'll look after you, won't we, Smerry?"

"A chaser" insinuated the Mandarin "a cognate chaser."

The Smeraldina-Rima had worked it out and felt very cross.

"What's wrong with him anyhow?" she demanded.

Belacqua unleashed the chaser and exchanged a leer of intelligence with Mammy.

"Collywobbles" he said slyly.

The Smeraldina, very touchy as we know already on the subject of her small vocabulary, had no patience with this kind of thing.

"What's that?" she moaned "something to eat?"

The Mandarin took a fleet pace to the rere, clapped a long yellow finger to the wing of his nose, and, poised with flexed knee on one tiptoe like a ballerina, dangling the bottle, announced in a general way:

"Der Mench ist ein Gewohnheitstier!"

"Something you've et, dear" said Mammy facetiously.

The Smeraldina-Rima held aloof from the salvo of merriment that greeted this little effort of Mammy's.

"Don't be so horrid" she cried "making jokes that I can't understand. How am I to know what are cobble-wobbles . . ."

"*Colly*" corrected Mammy "wobbles."

"Egal!" exploded the Smeraldina "how am I to know anything when you never sent me to school?"

"My dear young lady" said the Mandarin gravely "your education has cost us thousands. Nothing short" he said "of thousands of pounds."

"Cheer up Smerry" exhorted the multipara "if I was young and beautiful and had a nice young man" holding up the apodasis to ogle the hope of her grandmaternity "to take me out, I wouldn't care whether I knew what colly-wobbles were or not. You'll know soon enough. Wait till you're my age" she exclaimed, as though that were hardly to be expected, "and you'll know."

The Smeraldina-Rima surveyed the nice young man

who was going to take her out. He was stretched on the settee.

"Out!" she loosed a piercing cackle "so siehst Du aus!"

Indeed what with his slugging-a-bed in the morning and soaks with the Mandarin in the evening and in the afternoon his absorption in a Vasari he had found in his host's library and the latest pictures hanging on his host's wall and the inneffectual darts he was liable to make at the piano at any hour of the day or night and his objection to going out to be frozen to death when there was nothing to prevent him from hatching a great thought over the stove, he was only able, in the week that elapsed between his arrival and Silvester, three times to promenade her, and two of these times Mammy, whose Spreegeist infuriated the Madonna beyond measure, came with. The Madonna was displeased, this was not the treatment she was used to. So the only evening they spent alone together was marred by a copious tiff with tears to follow.

All this pitted of course with the usual fiascos and semi-fiascos, he doing his poor best to oblige her and she hers to be obliged, in an absence of all douceness; Mammy getting more and more fed up as herself as happy beldam waned in her mind, the Mandarin very bottle-nosed and courtly and gestural and somehow Venetian, waiving his patria potestas on all available occasions.

Silvester, when high tea had passed from them, found him seated to himself on the settee in the candlelight of course with a bottle of course again. If they were not there they would be in a minute. He felt very bad. Would he last into the New Year, that was the question. He feared to fall to pieces. He thought he was going light, not so much in the head as in the centre, vaguely the midriff. The least heedlessness now on my part, he thought, and I fly at once to pieces.

He had read all the opening of Vasari and wondered why, so little did it matter. The even-fisted pettifogger. What mattered? He mattered.

He goggled like a fool at the shrieking paullo-post-Expression of the Last Supper hanging on the wall fornenst him, livid in the restless yellow light, its thirteen flattened flagrant egg-heads gathered round the tempter and his sop and the traitor and his burse. The tempter and the traitor and the Jugendbund of eleven. John the Divine was the green egg at the head of the board. What a charming undershot purity of expression to be sure! He would ask for a toad to eat in a minute.

Ask (we are sorry, we fear he is off again under the limen, it is not our fault) for your toad, John, to eat, swallow a viper or a scorpion or a morpion and let me tell all you boys what it feels like to be in Old Nick's bath. I am in the extreme centre of Old Nick's bath, I have gone light in the centre, I am at the frontiers of the boundless, I am the scourged cream of human adversity, yes, the quintessence and the upshot. A whore, boys, is a deep ditch of diabolic water, there am I, shall I then be hot in a cold cause, is it fair to expect that, would it not be much nicer to know a few good digs of compunction and clip Jesus straight away and stand fast for ever? Oh sometimes as now I almost think: nothing is less like me than me. It must be either that I am not adequately alkaline or that there is a cavity needing filling under my navel spiral where the big weight ought to be. Fire and stone and torment by skewering. Four skewers and a good dig with a blade and there you have a Pro-Cathedral. And the pros and cons.

Oh very well so then in that case since you insist my

77

fiery petrifactors, first of all then algebraically, take the firstfather in the eburnine sacristy. No appetite for the Passover, boys, but have it your own way. A dream of lines palped the dust the dust of the ground. Yah! My time is at hand. Now come off it out of that on to` the gravel. The difficult art of shortening, boys, temper and fresco, in oil and miniature on wood and stones and canvas, tarsia and tinted wood for stories, etching with iron and printing with copper, follow the man with the pitcher, niello, the enamel of the goldsmith and gold and damask having a high time together, go upstairs with the goodman, figures on glass and flowers and figurines on cloth of gold and stories and waterpassions on earthern jars, is it I, the most beautiful invention of the woven arras, the carving the vexing of steels and jewels, is it I. Yah! Now what would be very nice to know is what all this lapidary catlap that we hear about a heavyweight majority putting the shot to the glory of got to do with one little putto, ah the dear little putto, for the colours and the hair-pencils and the most modest predella. I go as it is written of me. A fico and a fouter for your stags of amber and your pines of bronze and your marble love-potions and your frozen fugues, as it is written so help me but woe to that man, and your mard of gold sculpppt and foil of silver painted and the swivelling snivelling miracle of your belly-cum-bum totalities and realities, dee 'and is wid me, and the fatal slip of a hairy hand. Who are your patrons? Greeks? Kings? Lovers? Gladly for Apelle a warrior's lust, the ravishing Campaspe. Yah! Wid me on dee table. You can keep your George Bernard Pygmalion. *And* your prostated elephantiatics. The man of my peace. Did you never hear tell how Big George cubed a nude in a corslet and a mirror and a sleeping cistern? Hath lifted up his heel against me. Wet doom of lime. That thou doest do quickly. A ewe can grow gold. And it was night. Oh the moon shines bright on Aceldama, his boots are crackling, for want of . . .

Pardon now just consider the treasurer's bowels clotting the lush blood. Always trust the medical vestry-man for the stercoraceous detail.

Quick now with an eight cylinder accelerando there I am the twilight mummyfœtus, the old heart becalmed in snowbroth, paralysed before this diademitonic Cæsarian of a livid spectrum, ripped from Dan unto Beersheba, tight-lipped, rapt in the upper torture-chamber. The Rabbi, the lemon-egg, the non-playing captain, wearing the blazer wove, would you believe it, from the throat, where it must have been clasped, throughout, facing, not seeing, down the operating-table's length, on his right hand naturally, his green of course toady. What a desolation of Bullscrit hesitation and the Y of the crossroads to run between this head and that boosom. My darling from the power of the dog, whose darling, bloody well you, was it wine and myrrh that like the last breakfast or the white handkerchief of any polyglot musical pallid brigand of a pessimist he received not? Pink of course for the insidious chairman, the perfid-ious very much more than papal key, with the little phallic pouch trapped in his plump pink palpers, his lips parted for the garden, or was it vinegar and gall maybe, a boil on his neck that I cannot see, his Gilles de Rais orbs, quite too Rio-Santo, *focussed* on the patibulary melancholy of the lemon of lemons, was it vinegar then or hyssop on the sponge or the reed of hyssop, and of course before gliding on to more pleasant topics allusion must be made to blood-faced Tom with his bow-tie moustache disbelieving in the Sherry Cobbler that is my. A masterly study, boys, there's no getting away from it, of what I once saw described as the

79

bulliest feed in 'istory if the boyscouts 'adn't booked a trough for th'eleventh's eleventh eleven years after, and there not as much as the weeniest gutta of Sehnsucht between the eloquent boards of this book. Did they slit your palate Thérèse Philosophe? Only the labia minora? Well I am glad to know that.

"Of all the Bitchlein" he said "speaking as a cad, that schweigen niemals im Wald, or ever unclasped a starchèd snood before my incompetence and of all the respectably abgeknutscht (pump it out, pump it out like a very snot-cork: abbb-gekkk-kkknnn-nutscht) heifers that ever wasted collop-tight bloomers on my bloodless nonchalance, you are the champion, you are the Queen of Spain, and I do not care for cocoanuts, I never did care for cocoanuts."

Oh Florence Florence concerning the branny desquamation of my papular pustular variola inform the medical man. Dust me Florence with violet or starch powder. Rub me with spirits of wine or brandy. See how the litmus is depressed by my incontinence. Place me in an airbed. Raise me slightly. Lower the drawsheet. Hoist the restraining-sheet. See I am seized with a vomiting. My tongue is foul and my bowels are confined. I am irritable in manner. I resent being disturbed. I am intolerant of light. I am observed to pick at the bedclothes. It is the end. My breathing stops for half an hour. I pass everything nolens volens under me. My face becomes not merely pale but dusky. I perspire profusely. I sink gradually. I die in a convulsion. Swathe me oh swathe me in oakum or charpie. Knot my cord twice. Place me in my flannel receiver, gently does it. The brightest bottle and the best is the one with the caoutchouc teat. At eighteen months, not before, give me pounded meat and light puddings. I have a rather third or fourth generation snuffle, very trying, and my buttocks ache in the absence of emerald stools. Give me koumiss and manna and a torrestial clyster of Revalenta Arabica. Wrap me in my isolation sheet. Mammy I am sorry to say has pigmentation of the mammæ, a clavus hystericus, a phantom tumour, a spurious pain, two vats of colostrum, the whites and a white leg. She is a domestic servant of pale aspect. Enquire carefully into her lochia. Pharoah her nipples with Kölnischeswasserbrand. Shin up her udder-rope with glycerine of belladonna. I am found after a pleasant little supper of cheese wine and spirits sleeping soundly in the knee-and-elbow position, my head enlarged, my abdomen distended and my cute little fontanelle wide open. There is only one thing to do: stupe me in turpentine. The bed shakes and I go blue. I attempt to drink boiling water from the spout of the tea-kettle. Remove the fire-dogs, fleams, knives, razors, round pans, batteries, slipper pans, catheters, rods, écraseurs, probes, bougies, pumps, bistouries, charcoal, Allingham's clamp, don't forget Allingham's clamp, and Higginson's syringe. Bind me oh bind me in huckaback. Telephone for Surgeon Battey, Ballsbridge two and a bit. See how my sweat is yellow, see how it stains my pilch. My pus is laudable yellow sweet and faint. Sponge me down quickly the night sweats of phthisis. Sterilise the harelip needles for my Cockburn nævus, I have five. Wipe him with a soft cloth, put him into his glass, tempt him with a little milk, salt him a little and he'll disgorge, rinse him a little and he'll do again. Pass over the flexile collodion of the British Bulldog's Pharmacopœia. Rub me in neatsfoot. Pinch my feet firmly but not too firmly all the same, twist my toes in all directions, knead my small muscles, knead my large muscles, grasp my legs, one by one, run the hand up me firmly, strike the muscles *very* firmly, effleurage you know and pétrissage and a tantinet of tapotement, pinch my abdomen all over, in both hands firmly grasp my abdomen, firmly draw the flesh downwards to the colon, be firm in all things, pinch the whole of my back, make a sweep—whoosh!—several times downwards quickly the length of my spina bifida, skate-roll my bottom, bruise my flexors, batter my extensors, leave me in the blanket. Inunction for my exanthem and—handy-dandy!—I expire in my Gorgonzola varnish. His pinky-spongies floated.

Calm, her lovely white face averted, bosom and belly well forward, shoulders back, holding with both hands the long stiff scroll, she sustained his girds with a kind of anti-aircraft vigilance that brought a fleer to his mobile lips as he trundled through the Tuileries on the platform of the A1 bis now the AA clenching his bladder beneath his chic shower-proof. The wattmen tittered as I tottered on purpose for radiant Venice to solve my life. Mes pieds. Mes larges pieds. Aux cors sempiternels. Very neat. Very smart and astute to be sure. Calvary through the shock-absorbers. Con . . . stan-ti-no.pel. S.M.E.R.A.L.D.I.N.A.R.I.M.A. How long oh Lord has this been going on. Nicht küssen bevor der Zug hält.

"That is bad dialogue" she said bitterly "God has tormented me all my life" she said, with an extraordinary movement of expansion, "that is no way to speak to Ophelia. Why do you complicate the Sauladen with trying to be yourself? Such a babby" she sneered "I haff to laff."

Without turning her head or loosening her pose she let out sideways at him smartly with the scroll.

Oh and I dreamed he would come and come come come and cull me bonny bony double-bed cony swiftly my springal and my thin Wicklow twingle-twangler comfort my days of roses days of beauty week of redness with mad shame to my lips of shame to my shamehill for the newest of news the shemost of shenews is I'm lust-belepered and unwell oh I'd rather be a sparrow for my puckfisted coxcomb bird to bird and branch or a coalcave with golden veins for my wicked doty's potystick trimly to besom gone the hartshorn and the cowslip wine gone and the lettuce nibbled up nibbled up and gone nor the last day of beauty of the red time opened its rose struck with its thorn oh I'm all of a gallimaufry and a salady salmagundi singly and single to bed she said I'll have no toad-spit about this house and whose quab was I I'd like to know that from my cheerfully cuckooed Dublin landloper and whose foal hackney mare toeing the line like a Viennese Taübchen take my tip and clap a padlock on your Greek galligaskins ere I'm quick and living in hope and glad to go snacks with my twingle-twangler and grow grow into the earth mother of whom clapdish and foreshop.

"Hure!" backing away to face her against the casement "Hure! Hure!" with a sudden yearning for the life and passion of Dmitri Karamazov. But being Belacqua he settled his bottom on the sill, evacuate, his heart more moved than with a trumpet, his want upon him as a man of shield, "Hure! Hure!" in his waistcoat-pocket prose-poem diapason now, seeking an arsehold. Then the proud hell-blond beauty receded or perhaps seemed only so to do as gravely with the indifferent movement of my succubus my Infanta defunct oh Schopenhauer stepped across her the hard breastless Greek slave or huntress the hard nautchgal through the appointed evening down the shingle that sweats already for the algor of Bilitis to the act of darkness on the hard rucks of shingle that knuckle into our hot pelts our dry pelts and bruise the bones of our loins of our shoulders, all night, if she comes the lil pute, shaming wasting the flesh, forcing down my shoulders my buttocks on the hard icy berries of shingle that lapse and wedge and drive up like knuckles into the kidneys the withers, Lesbia, rather stiff and small and oh so compact, she tailed off very da capella into a kind of stela you might nearly say and back into the picture loomed the Smeraldina-Rima looking momently I thought sodden flav mammose poppata immensely slobbery-blubbery.

"How comes it" he expostulated "even making allowances I know after all these years in a foreign land you speak your native tongue so badly?"

Breasting the air ridiculously it seemed she kept a sharp look-out over his shoulder. Like a big white-and-liver bitch sitting in a window wanting to bark. He wanted to say come off it in the name of God and was going to when she dropped everything.

"Egal" she said, loud and rude, "egal."

"So *badly*" he insisted "so *badly*."

Thirteen not twelve times impure. Got you there merde snarled the prognathous Commendatore grinding his bicuspids in a rictus. Quip. Name. Age. Birth. Premature or Fulltime. Nursed or Handfed. By a polar bear Sam oh the fulva vulva merde in one or other of the Hebrides peeping and creeping at the hontes sangsuelles of the gutter Nicolettes squatting bereft of diaper and pilch merde merde merde in the dews of the stews, just look at my cephalic index the browstone crushing the eyes, and looking I recall with some pleasure as being almost a touching won't you thing or moving like a far bugle in glades at sunset though maybe inclined to be a bit too Yellow Love and An Ankou for the liking of such as you and me an anecdote not relating this time for once for a wonder to the sphincter of poor Lelian prostated probably in some horrid nasty station hotel with the Muttering Delirium and the Summer Diarrhœa and confluent noli me tangere rodent ulcers lancinating his venter, incubating the nits what nits bloody well you in the scarf of his cuticle, the black spots encrimsoned on his sacrum, his mouth a clot of sordes, his clubbed digits plucking at the counterpane, his rhonchi not to mention his inspirating (there's no call to labour this particular aspect of his malaise) crepitous mucous sonorous sibilant crackling whistling wheezing crowing and would you believe it stridulous, strangled with the waterbrash and a plumjuice sputum, the big slob of a catamite, dear oh dear how did he ever get himself into such a state, and a complete Racine drowning in the bidet . . . Douceurs . . . ! Ugh that word gives me the chinks doesn't it you? There are souls that must be saved and. When I peter out in a nightsweat as we all high and lowly must sooner or later one of these fine days Florence shall be instructed shall she not or reminded to foist deep down oh douceurs the antiseptic tampons. Father to-day woman mygodmygod I thirst basta father into thy hands. With his mind a blank (now that is a point that cannot be too stringently stressed) he suddenly was pleased to want all the candles quenched but one and it set carelessly on the good grand and draw not the curtains you stupid girl, Mammy a taste of the moody, a wagon for me who am weary on the way, something too soft without the notes, break the chords for the love of God, soft and low and slow and pleasant as a signet of rubies and ad my libidinem, though I declare I'm in such great form to-night that I wouldn't put it past me to weasel a whimper out of Bacharachnidean Eggs without Words.

The way the Madonna threw up her shoulders and

collapsed all damp disappointment one would think she had been looking for milk in a little bird or a male tiger. That is clear enough anyhow. Mammy slammed the piano and the Mandarin looked up fiercely from his pyrotechnics.

"Silvester" said Mammy, in a dead voice.

By heaven but the paramour turned very nasty at this. And then, he would like to know, what might that have to do with the tide coming in, he would be intrigued to know that, flinging himself about in a regular pet.

"If you don't bring her out" (he might well tremble at such an ominous recitative) telescoping her neck till the vast mottled jowl came to rest on what putting such an opportunity steadfastly behind us we'll call the sternum, bowed forward over the dangling bloodballast of her swollen paws, "you're a b--- ".

The pyrotechnist responded to the trigger with a superb shoulder-elbow-palm-and-eyebrow ikey.

"Between the yeeeears" he groaned, convulsed, "look at the night." Anguish of supplication. "The old town" he wheezed "Gewohnheitstier don't be a goat."

The spasm was very severe. Death may occur on third or fifth day. Don't break my incisors, merely pass a suppository of pancreatised caviar and bankerout my wits. If there is any difficulty in removing my trousers cut down the off seam, don't be afraid, a warm bland drink of warm wan wine and tickle my fauces, for the redness swelling heat and pain opium guttatim.

Now then oh my Helper. The Greek bath drives sadness from the mind. Free among the dead. Oh in peace oh for the Selfsame. Optumo optume optumam operam. The demon of irony the life of irony the diamond. Lean on the orange-peel wonderfully made by the Lemon-sole that your . . . er . . . soul may arise from its weariness. So. Viel Vergnügen.

"Now" she bickered, toiling up the steps, "of course we can't get in."

He felt weak after his visions. But his little mind was clear, clear as a bell, the poet's mind, par excellence and parenthèse:

> Clear and bright it should be ever,
> Flowing like a crystal river,
> Bright as light and clear as wind . . .

With his mind then in this condition for the moment, brilliantly lit, canalised and purling, he said:

"Yes of course we can, it's not twelve yet."

They pushed at the heavy door together and passed through the crowded vestibule to the stair-head.

"Didn't I tell you" he said "that we could get in?"

The Ratskeller was a revel-rout. They stood at the stair-head looking for a table.

"Now" she said "of course we won't get a table. Why wouldn't you come on when I wanted you to?"

It did look indeed as though they would not get a table.

"There is no good staying here" he said "there is nothing to be done here. We can't get a drink. Come on."

"Come on where?"

"We'll go to the Barberina and get a drink."

"It'll be gleich at the Barberina."

"Not at all" he said. "Come on."

"Anyhow we'll miss midnight." There was certainly evil and madness in her heart at that moment. "Why wouldn't you . . ."

"We won't" he recited "if you'll come on now quick."

He coaxed her back through the vestibule and pulled at the big door. It was locked.

"We can't get out" he said.

The Madonna scrabbled at the door. She panted with anger. He, evacuate, leaned up against the wall. He stood in great need of a drink.

"It's no good" he said "you can't get out."

She turned on him like a leopardess, but he had not the smallest inclination to have her ruin him or anything of that kind.

"Quick" she frothed "try the other."

These things take time. In due time he was back.

"Locked" he said "we're locked till the year's out."

The Smeraldina-Rima began to giggle:

"We're locked in between the years!" She fell back against the wall and began to make limp passes at him with her hands, tittering from head to foot. He looked at his watch.

"It will all be over in a minute" he said "and then we'll get out and go to the Barberina and have a nice quiet drink. It's just twelve."

The Madonna did not want a nice quiet drink. She catapulted herself off the wall and swaggered past him, the bold allumeuse, to the stair-head. She curved herself over the rail and her thin black dress clung to her posteriors. He followed up beside her.

"Back in a sec" he said, and walked gingerly down the little stairs.

"Fow-fow!" she called gaily down after him. That was a

private joke and he fluttered a hand to it without turning round however. She watched him thread a passage through the press with his usual exaggerated aloofness. A man or two noticed and hailed. The women, after a glance, dismissed him from their minds. This circumstance did not escape her. She watched him waddle remote and nonchalant into the W. C. Abandoned on the crowded stair-head, watching him limp into the W. C., she suddenly understood that there was nothing to be done, that poor Bel was lost and that perhaps his life was over. She felt sorry for him and tears collected in her eyes.

A hand descended with familiarity on her shoulder. She pushed herself off the rail without resentment and turned to face the plump chess champion and petty financier who, as well she knew, coveted vaguely her favours. He exulted.

"The beautiful girl" he said "will come to our table? She will join us at our table?"

He was fat and fascinating like a satrap. He had the women he wanted, and he wondered did he want this one. So he had not had her yet.

"Who's with you?" she asked, warding him off. He named three bucks or toffs, notorious gigerls, and pointed them out.

"Sorry" she said "I'm with Bel."

Now he had beaten Belacqua at chess, he had brought him home incapable from the old town, so he knew him. He found him naïf and a dull vain dog and a patent babylan. He was a shrewd man.

"That's not a reason" he mocked "when there is place for two."

"Sorry" she repeated.

He pushed his head forward at her.

89

"But why not?" he insisted, softly, more night of Egypt than ever.

"He wouldn't sit with you" she said, after a moment's hesitation.

"So!" he smiled without the least resentment "So!" he was genuinely touched. "See you later" dared he hope, and withdrew.

The clock of the Rathaus now struck the hour, the revellers joined hands and sang their chorus. The remarkable divisibility of twelve entered the head of Belacqua who, having underestimated his need, was now pressing his forehead against the cool porcelain. "Prosit Neujahr!" he said in a very weak and scranny voice indeed and pulled the joystick. On the way back he was stopped by the Belshazzar who had spied him approaching from afar and broken away from the three gigerls, leaving them swaying in a restricted garland, to intercept him.

"So" he opened "and how are you?"

"A little unwell" said Belacqua "and how are you?"

"Come and join our little party" moved the Belshazzar.

"Sorry" said Belacqua "I am with the Smeraldina."

"Come" whispered the Balshazzar, to an indescribable spasm of his gross attractive face, "come with the Smeraldina, both of you come."

That seemed to Belacqua fair enough. When he reached the stair-head he found his partner conversing with a most charming young fellow.

"Dare I?" said Belacqua, hovering on the outskirts.

The young man receded for the Madonna to step smartly up to her escort. She eyed him attentively.

"What is it?" she said "you're as white as a sheet."

"I'm unwell" he said "but you'll be glad to hear I have found a table."

"Where?"

"That fat bastard" he said "of an indoor playboy asks us to sit at his table, and I am tired and I want a drink and you want to stay here, so . . ."

He started off down the stairs.

"Who?" cried the Madonna. "What are you talking about. Who asks us . . .?"

"How do I know?" he groaned. "Will you come on. That fat dentist of a chess-player . . ."

"Stop!" said the Madonna. "Come back. I'm going to the Barberina."

He came back a step.

"We can't get out" he objected most violently to the idea of going to the Barberina. She turned her long back on him and disappeared into the vestibule. At the door he came up with her.

"What's the good" he said "where's the sense in talking about going to the Barberina when we can't get OUT?" But she opened the door with her own frail hand and he had no choice but to follow her out.

Sitting in the bar of the Barberina she exposed the combination.

"He'll be here in a minute" she said "so we better go. Drink out and come on."

"Didn't himself say he'd come out after the fireworks" he said, knowing that in an hour or so he would want to talk "and bring Mammy?"

"Give me a cigarette" she said.

He suggested that he might light it for her. She looked at him in astonishment. He held up the cigarette before her. He felt like playing with her a little.

"Will I?" he said.

"Give me the one you're smoking" she said at last "and light a new one for yourself."

He leaned forward across the table and she pulled the half-smoked cigarette away from his lips. Such a pop it made coming away!

"Now" she said "light your own."

But he fell back into his corner without doing anything of the kind. He proposed to sulk now because she would not make a game of it.

"What about your boy-friend?" he said. "It isn't the beer that gives you the head next morning, but all the smoking you do with it."

"What?"

"I say it isn't the beer . . ."

"No, before that."

"Oh, your boy-friend . . ."

"What boy-friend?"

How the hell did he know what boy-friend!

"Maybe I was thinking" he said vaguely "of the one be-yond in the Keller."

"How do you mean, maybe you were thinking?"

"I don't know."

"Do you know anything?" she groaned. "That's not a boy-friend, that's the glider-champion."

"How, the glider-champion?"

"He did the longest fly in a Flieger."

"Not a boy-friend?"

"No."

"What is a boy-friend?"

"I don't know. Do you?"

"No. Do you?"

"No."

"Am I a boy-friend?"

"Are you my boy-friend?"

"Yes."

She thought over this.

"No" she said "you are not."

"Who am I?" he said.

She thought again over this.

"You are my man" she said.

"But not with two enns" he said.

"What?"

"I say I'm not your man with two enns."

She frowned terribly.

"What?" she cried.

"I mean not your M-A-N-N."

"Don't annoy me" she moaned "don't bother me. Drink out and come on."

"Come on where?"

"Anywhere. That brute will be here if you don't."

"But I thought you wanted to dance."

"No" she said sharply "what's the good of wanting to dance when there's nobody to dance with."

"Can't you dance with me?"

She stood up in that case and pulled down her dress behind. Poor girl, it was always rutsching up on her, the poop of her behind was so kolossal.

He rose up painfully.

"I can't dance" he grumbled.

She stood looking at him across the table.

"Du lieber Gott!" she whispered.

Now he was frightened and furious.

"I'm sorry Smerry" he whined, with all kinds of angry

waftures, "I can't dance. I'd like to be able to dance, but I can't. I don't know how to dance. I get tired. I don't know how to do it."

She sat down.

"Take a seat" she said.

To hell with you anyhow, he thought.

"What" she enquired in a low voice "did you come from Paris for?"

"To look at your face" he said, very short and sure of himself.

"But you don't look at it."

"I do look at it."

"But you *don't*, Bel, you know you don't."

"You don't see me" he said.

"You used to say you only wanted to look at my eyes, to look *into* my eyes."

He let that pass.

"Bel!" she implored.

He hardened his little heart.

"He doesn't want" she whinged "to look into my eyes any more!"

"Because I want to look at your face?" he sneered, furious. "I'm a classicist" he said "didn't you know?"

"You couldn't love me or you wouldn't go on like that!"

"Go on like what?" he cried, striking the table.

"The way you always go on" raising the note to a pule "indifferent to everything, saying you don't know and you don't care, lying about all day in that verdammte old Wohnung, reading your old book and fooling around with Daddy. And he's supposed" she concluded hopelessly "to be in love with me!"

To hell with you anyhow, he thought.

"He wants to look at my face" she mimicked, forcing a

94

little cackle, "he came all the way from Paris" she cackled "third class to look at his darling Smerry's face!" She leaned across the table, closed her eyes and reared up the little angry face gone Judas-colour for inspection. "Now" she jeered "have a good look at it."

"You don't understand me" he said earnestly "it must be surreptitious."

"What's that?" she said, opening her eyes, "something to eat?"

"When I say" he explained "that I want to look at your face, what I mean is that I want to steal a look at it. *Steal a look at it.*"

"Are you drunk?" she said, restored to good humour by his seriousness.

"Leider!" he said.

"So he came all the way from Paris, third class, to steal a look at my face."

"Put it that way" he said "if you like."

"I'm not putting anything. That's what you said."

He thought it might be a good idea if they dropped it.

"You started it" she said.

The tiff had been so public that a hard case becalmed in a distant corner of the bar waved a big promiscuous hand at the Madonna, and the Ungeküßte Eva gratified the discomfited Belacqua with a slow hitch on her upper-lip. The Ungeküßte Eva was the barmaid. She had lost her looks, the virtuous girl, supposititiously, in Dickens's striking adverb, through her passion for Steinhägers and late hours. Steinhägers in abundance she cadged from the soft unhappy class of client, and she knew our young hero for an easy mark. Thus it was that now she bared her teeth in token of her desire. Belacqua snuggled up to his corner and helped himself to one of the series at the Madonna, who had reorganised her pallor and was exhibiting herself. Belacqua let a great sigh hoping to come back into the tableau. Far up the bar the vigilant Eva elevated her private bottle.

"Darf' ich" she piped.

Belacqua blushed.

"You've got off" mentioned the Madonna, over her shoulder, "with the barmaid."

Eva raised towards them the fruit of her derring-do.

The Pyrotechnist swaggered in. Belacqua was delighted.

"Have a drink" he gushed "do have a drink. On me" he added, this kind invitation not having been accepted with the speed he would have wished.

"Where's Mammy?" said the Madonna, in a very vicious tone of voice.

The Pyrotechnist stood at the threshold of the alcove, appraising the situation.

"Where's Mammy?" repeated the Madonna.

He caressed an unshaven Gioconda smile.

"This is the town of miracles" he said at last. "The Grauler drove me down in his superb machine."

"May I offer you a drink?" said Belacqua.

"It's what I have always said" groaned the Mandarin, very worried and resentful all of a sudden. "Can you imagine this" turning round to be dumbfounded "in Drogheda?" turning back with a flame in his pale blue eye.

"A feast of Cana" said Belacqua.

"But this" sobbed the Mandarin, following up his vision, "is the Drogheda of Germany. Not even the Drogheda, the Ballyboghill of Germany!"

"Daddy!" The Madonna was choking. Daddy pulled down his waistcoat.

"I am still wearing your excellent braces" he confided to Belacqua. "Is there a ruby left in the bottle?"

Just about as much as a "by your leave" interrupted Thibaud in the Sala Bianca. The glider-champion paused for permission, he was insolently erect at the Madonna's side.

"Please" said Belacqua, blushing again.

The Mandarin took the seat. Watching them dance out of the bar was the first ague of the new year. She danced all wrong, throwing herself about. She pranced, she waggled her seat of honour. A fessade, a chiappata, a verberation on the breech. He squeezed his palms together under the table. Oh a most superlative bastinado à la mode . . .!

"What does Horace say?" he said. "A defective . . ."

"Carpe diem" said the Mandarin.

"No. He says: *a defective bottom, a flat nose and a long foot* . . . The human bottom" he proceeded "is extremely deserving of esteem, conferring as it does the faculty of assiduity. The great Lawgiver urged his pupils to cultivate an iron head and a leaden posterior. The Greeks, I need hardly tell you, entertained a high notion of its beauty; and the celebrated poet Rousseau worships in the temple of Venus Callipyge. The Romans bestowed upon the part the epithet of 'fair', and many have thought it susceptible, not only of being beautiful, but even of being endowed with dignity and splendour. Thus Monsieur Pavillon, academician, bel esprit and nephew of a bishop, in his noble *Métamorphose du Cul d'Iris en Astre*. Oh Caterina" he cried in a transport "oh little Caterina of Cordona, how couldst thou unmask those charms to a lower discipline" he closed his eyes "and of chains and hooks!"

"Who is the lady?" enquired the Mandarin.

"I have no idea" said Belacqua "a rival of Saint-Bridget the Rose."

"I have never heard her called that before."

"She was never called that before" exclaimed Belacqua "she was never called that before! Saint-Bridget the Rose without the white goat! Blissful Saint-Bridget the Rose without the white goat and the bunch of keys and the besom!"

"Write a poem to her" said the Mandarin, sourly.

"Oh I will" cried Belacqua "a long poem to the tormented bottom of Caterina. I would have been an Adamite" he vociferated, ignoring the return of his mourning bride, "I would have died for Juniperus the Gymnosophist! Juniperus the Gymnosophist! I will write a long long poem on Caterina and Juniperus the Gymnosophist, how he dreamed her a naughty vestal in the dark gauze or Medusa in a Carmelite Ecce Homo or a barren queen bleeding, bleeding like a banner, bleeding in a Lupercal, and he filled his hands with rods . . ."

"Move up in the bed" said the Madonna.

"This is a kip" growled the Mandarin "come where the booze is cheaper."

"Or at the altar, a Spartan queenboy . . ."

"Go on" said the Madonna "who's keeping you?"

"Oh there's nobody *keeping* me" said the Mandarin, very suave, "as far as I know. I do not think there is anybody *keeping* me. Not what you could really call *keeping*. But I thought perhaps our friend here might care to join me possibly in the darker draught."

"A bottle" sighed the Juniperite "a bottle of the dark Export."

"Pree-cisely" said the Mandarin "the darker draught, the dark Export, call it what you will."

"Leave him alone" snarled the Madonna "go and drink your own dirty old beer."

The Mandarin beamed and struck a nervous posture.

"My dear" he chuckled, out of the midst of his contortion, "that is just the very thing, you have put your finger on just the very thing, that I was proposing to do. That is" he added "unless somebody would prefer I did not."

"But wouldn't you like to stay here" said Belacqua "just a little bit longer and have another dance with the glider and then follow us on?"

"No" wailed the Madonna. They were all against her.

"Go on Smerry" urged the Mandarin "don't be such a goat. We're only going round the corner to Meisters."

The recordman saved what was developing into a nasty situation. Heavenly God, but he was indeed the right height, when you saw them glued together like that for the take-off. Belacqua closed his eyes.

Her face appeared over his shoulder.

"Schwein" she said.

They had a fleeting consommation on their way out. Belacqua invited Eva to have a Steinhäger.

"If you don't mind" said Eva "I think I'll have a little Goldwasser."

"It's all the same to me" said Belacqua, with a blush, "what you have."

The Mandarin devoured his braised celery.

"This is not eating" he said "this is an æsthetic experience."

Belacqua was very red in the face.

"It confuses the issue" he said.

"Hast Du eine Aaaaaahnung!" cried the Mandarin.

Belacqua dropped his cigarette on the table-cloth. He was getting very close to where he wanted to be. Soon he would start to talk.

"Weib" he said, and stopped unexpectedly.

The Mandarin looked up with his fork in the air.

"God bless 'em" he said piously "we can't get on without 'em."

"Weib" said Belacqua "is a fat, flabby, pasty, kind of a word, all breasts and buttocks, bubbubbubbub, bbbacio, bbbocca, a hell of a fine word" he sneered "look at them."

"No ideeeea" panted the Mandarin.

"And as soon" proceeded Belacqua "as you are aware of her as a Weib, you can throw your hat at it. I hate the liars" he said violently "that accept the confusion, faute de mieux, God help us, and I hate the stallions for whom there is no confusion."

"Stallions?" echoed the Mandarin. He was shocked. "Liars? Confusion?"

"Between love and the thalamus" cried Juniperus "how can you ask what confusion?"

The Mandarin drew the heel of his hand sadly across his mouth.

"I'm only an incompetent married man" he said "with a family, but it never occurred to me that I was either a liar or a stallion."

"Nor ever a lover."

"In a most high and noble way of my own" said the Mandarin "not your way. Neither better nor worse. Just not your way. I know you" he said "a penny maneen of a low-down low-church Protestant high-brow, cocking up your old testament snout at what you can't have."

"Worse!" cried Belacqua, "baser! meaner! dirtier!"

The Mandarin was delighted.

"Hating the flesh" he guffawed "by definition."

"I hate nothing" said Belacqua. "It does not amuse me. It smells. I never suffered from pica."

100

"Weibery and corruption" sneered the Mandarin "and what about our old friend the Incarnate Logos?"

"Don't sneer at me" cried Belacqua "and don't try and sidetrack me. What's the good of talking to a Jesuit!"

"You are a sentimental purist, I suppose," said the Mandarin "and I, praise be to God and his holy name, am not."

"Meaning" said Belacqua "that you can love a woman and use her as a private convenience."

"If such" smiled the Mandarin "be her desire."

"She can work both ways."

"Since such is her desire." He suddenly threw out his great arms and sunk his head in a crucified invocation. "Lex stallionis" he said.

"Get thee to a stud" said Belacqua.

"Your vocabulary of abuse" said the Mandarin "is arbitrary and literary and at times comes close to entertaining me. But it doesn't touch me. You cannot touch me. You simplify and dramatise the whole thing with your literary mathematics. I don't waste any words with the argument of experience, the inward decrystallisation of experience, because your type never accepts experience, nor the notion of experience. So I speak merely from a need that is as valid as yours, because it is valid. The need to live, to be authentically and seriously and totally involved in the life of my heart and . . ."

"Have you forgotten the English for it?" said Belacqua.

"My heart and my blood. The reality of the individual, you had the cheek to inform me once, is an incoherent reality and must be expressed incoherently. And now you demand a stable architecture of sentiment."

The Mandarin shrugged his shoulders. There was no shrug in the world, and not many shoulders, like the Mandarin's.

"You misunderstand me" said Belacqua. "What you heard me say does not concern my contempt for your dirty erotic manœuvres. I was speaking of something of which you have and can have no knowledge, the incoherent continuum as expressed by, say, Rimbaud and Beethoven. Their names occur to me. The terms of whose statements serve merely to delimit the reality of insane areas of silence, whose audibilities are no more than punctuation in a statement of silences. How do they get from point to point. That is what I meant by the incoherent reality and its authentic extrinsecation."

"How" said the Mandarin patiently "do I misunderstand you?"

"There is no such thing" said Belacqua wildly "as a simultaneity of incoherence, there is no such thing as love in a thalamus. There is no word for such a thing, there is no such abominable thing. The notion of an unqualified present—the mere 'I am'—is an ideal notion. That of an incoherent present—'I am this and that'—altogether abominable. I admit Beatrice" he said kindly "and the brothel, Beatrice after the brothel or the brothel after Beatrice, but not Beatrice in the brothel, or rather, not Beatrice and me in bed in the brothel. Do you get that" cried Belacqua "you old dirt, do you? not Beatrice and me in bed in the brothel!"

"I may be stupid" said the Mandarin "and then again I may not . . ."

"A thousand times better" said Belacqua "Heep than the evenhanded dirt."

"I do loathe" said the Mandarin, with conviction, "the things you write about."

"Like hell you do!" said Belacqua.

"And your cock-eyed continuum!" The Mandarin paused

to find words for it. "What's wrong" he said suddenly "may I ask, with you and Beatrice happy in the Mystic Rose at say five o'clock and happy again in No. 69 at say one minute past."

"No."

"Why not?"

"Don't talk to me" implored Belacqua. He looked across at the coral face. "Forgive me" he groaned "can't you see you humiliate me? I can't tell you why not . . . not now. Forgive me" and he stretched out his hand.

The Mandarin beamed all over.

"My dear fellow!" he protested. "Dare I give you a little word of advice?"

"Do" said Belacqua "do."

"Never try and be able to tell me."

"But I don't have to" said Belacqua, taken slightly back. "Why do you say that?"

"We might have to mourn you."

Belacqua laughed.

Then said the Jew:

"Behold how he loved her" and joined in the laughter of Belacqua.

They were still cackling heartily when the Madonna came on, with the Belshazzar, no less a person than the Belshazzar, at heel.

"Just to tell you" she notified "that you are invited to Sauerwein's studio."

"Then" said the Belshazzar "I'll drive you all up to the Height in my new car." Everything was working out beautifully for the Belshazzar. Belacqua made a cast at a venture:

"J'ai le dégoût très sûr" he said.

"What do you say?" exploded the Smeraldina.

"Tell Mr. Sauerwein" said the Mandarin loftily "that we

103

cannot see our way to honouring his studio, but that we are more than happy to know that he is at home." He bestowed a leer on all whom it might concern.

"Speak for yourself" said the Smeraldina "haven't you done enough damage?"

"My beautiful new car" cooed the Belshazzar. It occurred suddenly to the Smeraldina that here at least was a man.

"Bel" called the Mandarin.

"Sir" said Belacqua.

"Another dirty lowdown German mechanic."

"Altro che" said Belacqua.

"What do you say?" fumed the Smeraldina "what does he say?"

"That is the Portuguese" said the Mandarin "for and how. Tell Mr. Sauerwein or Sauerschwein, will you my dear, from me . . ."

"Bel!"

"Hello" said Belacqua.

"Are you coming?"

"And the glider?" said Belacqua.

"Bel, you said you wanted to see that portrait."

"Portrait?" said Belacqua.

"Bloody well you know the portrait" guffawed the Mandarin.

"The one he did of me in my bathing-dress."

"His hand must have been trembling" said the Mandarin "when he was doing it."

"Tell Mr. Sauerwein . . ."

The Smeraldina whistled up the Belshazzar and plunged towards the door.

"Smerry!" cried Belacqua, staggering to his feet.

"Before Mr Sauerwein was" said the Mandarin "we are."

"What's biting her?" demanded Belacqua, despairingly.

"She'll be all right" said the Mandarin. "Why it is I don't know, she . . ."

So shall their voices pass away, begin and end, the syllables sound, sound and pass away, the second after the first, the third after the second, and so forth and so on in order, until the last after the rest, and silence, with a bit of luck, after the last . . .

"Now" said Belacqua "at last I can say what's on my mind."

A convulsion of attention pealed down the Mandarin.

"In the old town" said Belacqua "correct me if I am wrong, a certain Fräulein Anita Furtwängler sits by her window."

"Wisdom gleams through me" cried the Mandarin "I shudder and kindle."

"The perfection of her limbs" pursued Belacqua "has been weighing me up to the peace of Jerusalem. I have the address of Abraham's bosom."

"Zahlen!" cried the Mandarin. "Telephone for the Grauler!"

"The true Shekinah" said Belacqua "is Woman."

"Nastasia Filippovna!"

"In her latter days" said Belacqua, putting by his change, "wouldn't you be inclined to say?"

"That may be" said the Mandarin "you may be right."

Dawn. Belacqua rang at the studio of Herr Sauerwein. The blue-black seraphim in his heart, so that it bled.

"The Smeraldina?"

"Waiting for you" said Herr Sauerwein, contemptuously.

"From the rosa mundi" explained Belacqua "to the rosa munda."

"That can be" said Herr Sauerwein.

She recommended strongly a Wirtschaft on the Height and the Grauler drove them up to it in his superb machine, up and up from the dregs of the town to the snows. There they kissed again with any God's quantity of tears. She ordered a dish of soup to comfort him, she ordered it piping hot, and a Schokolade and cookies to comfort herself. When he realised what she had done, he said:

"My wonderful one, I don't want soup, I don't like soup."

"What then?" she said.

"Nothing" he said. "I want to look at you." He burst into more tears. "What I want" he whinged "is to look into your eyes, your beautiful eyes, and then out of the window at the morning, and then back at you. I don't want soup, I don't want anything."

"Just a little hot soup" she coaxed "to do you good? Nik?"

Now what he could not stand was being wheedled and made a fool of about his food. He really did abhor soup.

"I tell you" he said fretfully "I don't want the bloody stuff, I don't drink it." Then, perceiving that the dear girl was wounded: "Darling" he said in a calmer tone "call him back, there's a good girl, and countermand it."

She countermanded the soup. Now she was lashing into the cookies, she was bowed over her plate like a cat over milk, she was doing her best, the dear girl, not to be greedy. Every now and then she would peep up at him out of her feast of cream, just to make sure he was still there to kiss and be kissed when her hunger would be appeased by the Schokolade and cookies. She ate them genteelly with a fork, doing herself great violence in her determination not to seem greedy to him; often she paused to wipe her lips discreetly with the paper napkin, and she kept the best of each cooky for the last mouthful. She was like a cat or a bird feeding, making happy little pecks and darts and licks at the food and every now and again peeping up to see was everything in order.

When she had finished she moved over beside him and began to paw him. He did not want to be pawed, he had got all the pawing he could stand elsewhere; also he had counted on Herr Sauerwein and the Belshazzar, one or the other or both together, to assuage the Smeraldina. Was it possible they had not? Anyhow, he blocked her leads for a little while and then moved away to the window and looked out. The worst might come to the worst, but for the moment he could not bear to be pawed and slabbered on, and least of all by the reigning fetish. All he wanted was to know a few good prods of compunction and consider how best his quiet breath, or, better still, his and hers mingled, might be taken into the air.

He felt her exasperation behind him and heard her drumming on the table with her nails. She had polished off her little feast of cream and chocolate. Very well then: why wouldn't he come to her? He continued to look out of the window with his back turned to her, he ignored the drumming. He felt queasy from all the rubbing and pawing and petting and nuzzling, all the rutty gobble-gobble and manipulation. Suck is not suck that alters . . . All of a sudden he felt clammy, he felt a great desire to hurry out and lie down in the snow. He pressed his face against the rimy pane. That was lovely, like a glass of water to drink in prison.

In a paroxysm of pruritus she stamped, she set up a nasty caterwauling.

"Bel" she miauled "come." She tambourined a tatoo on the table. "Muß Dich haben, muß Dich haben . . ." The squalling fell to a thin snuffle of libido, ". . . haben, ihn haben . . ." What she meant by that and what pleasure she hoped to get out of that cannot be made clear.

Feeling very clammy and groggy he moved his face to a fresh cold patch of the pane. The snuffling and muttering went on behind him. It was like a drip of sanies into an empty bucket. A beastly noise. In another moment he would be catting all over the floor.

Suddenly he turned round, it was not possible to endure more, and he made a definite statement:

"I feel sick, I must get out into the air."

She was still now and hunched, her face in her lap, her hefty cambered spine presenting anything but an elegant appearance. At least she had stopped dripping.

"Go on" she said, without moving.

Oh, she need not fret, he was going. The question was, was she coming with, or was she staying there.

"No" she said.

Oh, very well, she could please herself, aufwiedersehen then in that case. You can stay there, he thought, stamping down through the snow alone, whining and dripping till the cows come home. There's as much pity, he thought, due to a woman caterwauling as to a goose going barefoot. He scooped a big pad of snow off the bank and crushed it against his face. That did him all the good in the world. Explicit, he said aloud, and gratias tibi Christe. And so it was. For once in his life he was correct in what he said.

108

Except of course, that certain aspects of her abode in his heart, like wind in a dyspeptic's stomach, and made themselves felt from time to time in the form of a sentimental eructation that was far from being agreeable. She continued to bother him as an infrequent jolt of sentimental heartburn, nothing to write home about. Better, he thought, the odd belch than the permanent gripe.

Thus that was that, and small credit to either of them. She knew and he knew, and God knows it was high time.

To be sure the next few days, ere he took himself off to Hamburg, were more tears and more recriminations and more tears and more huddling and cuddling and catch-as-catch-can hugger-mugger and more tears and sweats and fiascos, a most painful time. But he knew and so did she. It was all over bar the explanations and the jostling when he stepped off in the Wirtschaft on the Height that Silvester's morrow, leaving her to her own devices to begin the new year in whatever way she saw fit. She had an extensive repertory of devises and an accommodating sense of fitness. He saw the last of her through a veil of nausea, and she was metamorphosed into a hiccup.

She salted her chambering with remembrance of him.

Extraordinary how everything ends like a fairy-tale, or can be made to; even the most unsanitary episodes.

UND

The Empress Wu of China took the chair at Cabinet council wearing a false beard. The lily was nearly as fair and the rose as lovely as God Almighty the Empress Wu.

"Bloom!" she cried to the peonies "bloom, blast you!"

No. Not a stir out of them. So they were all extirpated, they were rooted up throughout her dominions, burnt and their culture prohibited.

Now, having got so far, our opinion is we might do worse than slip, in the elegant phrase, our sad spaniels and let them quest. We durst not, our taste, the literary cui bono, precludes it, make a sudden leap, princumprancum!, from the pleasant land of Hesse, the German garden, to marshy Dublin, its paludal heavens, its big winds and rains and sorrows and puddles of sky-flowers; from the merely snout-fair Smeraldina, that petulant, exuberant, clitoridian puella, who has not the first glimmering of an idea of how to set her cold bath on fire, whom now it is high time to turn round and dislike intensely, like collops of pork gone greasy, to Alba, Alba, royal diminutive, Du, dust of a dove's heart, the eyes the eyes black till the plagal east shall resolve the long night-phrase. Can't hop about like that, really can't, must make lull somehow

or other, let a little breath of the fresh into the thing somehow, little breather all round. Nik?

How would it be then if we took to that end our
bearing together and got an idea of just where we are?
Supposing precisely as the true mountaineer, loving
women, his pipe and wine, stalks, proud pioneer, into the
oyster bar of the hallway hut, deposits his ice-axe, ruck-
sack, ropes and other equipment, turns himself this way,
reviewing the path he has trod, and that, estimating with a
fairly expert eye the labours, not to mention the dangers,
yet to be undergone and overcome ere he spurn the peak
yet hidden from view in the cloudy, misty, snowy imbro-
glio, we, extenuate concensus of me, were to pause in our
treacherous theme, take a quick look up and down, ponder
what has taken place and what threatens to and renew,
with the help of Apollo, the reduced circumstances of our
naïveté? How would that be? Chi va piano, they say, va
sano, and we lontano. Haply.

Pride of place to our boys and girls. Ah these liŭs
and liŭs! How have they stayed the course? Have they
been doing their dope? The family, the Alba, the Polar
Bear, Chas, that dear friend, and of course Nemo, ranging
always from his bridge, seem almost as good as new, so
little have they been plucked and blown and bowed, so
little struck with the little hammer. But they will let us
down, they will insist on being themselves, as soon as they
are called on for a little strenuous collaboration. Ping! they
will no doubt cry with a sneer, pure, permanent lius, we?
We take leave to doubt that. And far be it from us to
condemn them on that account. But observe what happens
in that event, we mean of our being unable to keep those
boys and girls up to their notes. The peak pierces the
clouds like a sudden flower. We call the whole perfor-

mance off, we call the book off, it tails off in a horrid manner. The whole fabric comes unstitched, it goes unge-bunden, the wistful fabric. The music comes to pieces. The notes fly about all over the place, a cyclone of elec-trons. And then all we can do, if we are not too old and tired by that time to be interested in making the best of a bad job, is to deploy a curtain of silence as rapidly as pos-sible.

At the same time we are bound to admit, placing ourselves for the moment in the thick of the popular belief that there are two sides to every question, that the terri-torials may behave, at least to the extent of giving us some kind of a meagre codetta. May they. There is many a slip, we all know that, between pontem and fontem and gladium and jugulum. But what that consideration has to do with our counting on the members of the Dublin contingent to perform like decent indivisibilities is not clear. The fact of the matter is, we do not trust them. And why not? Be-cause, firstly, of what has gone before; and, secondly, and here is the real hic, the taproot of the whole tangle, of our principal boy's precarious ipsissimosity.

Consequently, we are rather anxious to dilate briefly of these two things: one, the lius that have let us down; two, Belacqua, who can scarcely fail to keep on doing so.

Shall we consider then in the first instance that pow-erful vedette that we have been hearing so much about, the Smeraldina-Rima? Shall we? To begin with, then, there was the Dublin edition that bewitched Belacqua, the un-opened edition, all visage and climate: the intact little cameo of a bird-face, so moving, and the gay zephyrs of Purgatory, slithering in across the blue tremolo of the ocean with a pinnace of souls, as good as saved, to the

113

landing-stage, the reedy beach, bright and blue, merging into grass, not without laughter and old K'în music, rising demitonically, we almost said: diademitonically, to the butt of the emerald sugarloaf. When she went away, as go she did, across the wide waters Hesse to seek, again Hesse, unashamed in mind, and left him alone and inconsolable, then her face in the clouds and in the fire and wherever he looked or looked away and on the lining of his lids, such a callow wet he was then, and the thought or dream, sleeping and waking, in the morning dozing and the evening ditto, with the penny rapture, of the shining shore where underneath them the keel of their skiff would ground and grind and rasp and stay stuck for them, just the pair of them, to skip out on to the sand and gather reeds and bathe hands, faces and breasts and broach the foothills without any discussion, in the bright light with the keen music behind them—then that face and site preyed to such purpose on the poor fellow that he took steps to reintegrate the facts of the former and the skin of the zephyr, and so expelled her, for better or worse, from his eye and mind.

Next the stuprum and illicit defloration, the raptus, frankly, violentiæ, and the ignoble scuffling that we want the stomach to go back on; he, still scullion to hope, putting his best . . . er . . . foot forward, because he loved her, or thought so, and thought too that in that case the right thing to do and his bounden duty as a penny boyo and expedient and experienced and so on was to step through the ropes of the alcove with the powerful diva and there acquit himself to the best of his ability.

Paullo post, when he decided it would be wise to throw up the sponge, he had her, the third edition, her pages cut and clumsily cut and bespattered with the most imbecile marginalia, according to his God, i.e. the current Belacqua Jesus.

So to the last scene, though of course she abides in his little heart, to allocate a convenient term to the repository for perilous garbage, the whole four of her and many another that have not been presented because they make us tired; the last scene, when they spring—zeep!—apart, as on collision bodies dowered with high coefficients of elasticity. Zeep!

Now what kind of a liū is that? What is one to think of that for a liū? We assert that we think most poorly of it. Is there as much as the licked shadow of a note there that can be relied on for two minutes? Is there? There may be. No doubt great skill could wring her into some kind of a mean squawk that would do as well as anything else to represent her. We can't be bothered. A respectable overtone is one thing, but this irresponsible squawking bursting up our tune all along the line is quite another. From now on she can hold her bake altogether or damn well get off the platform, for good and all. She can please herself. We won't have her.

Voice of Grock: *Nicht möööögliccchhh . . . !*

Similarly for the others—Liebert, Lucien, the Syra-Cusa, Mammy and the Mandarin. Mammy, whom, by the way, we may need for our tableau mourant, was the best of them. Her letter, for example, and her little explosion on the night of Silvester, they hang together, they produce the desired monotony. The reason for that is, we never let ourselves loose on her, we never called on her to any large extent. So that in a sense she is in the position of the Alba and Co., she has had practically no occasion to be herselves. Which does not prevent us from being of the opinion, having up our sleeve certain aspects of that amiable multipara that surprise even us, hardened and all as we are to this kind of work, that when and if we jerk her on for the terminal scena she will collaborate energetically in the general multiplication of tissue. We are of that opinion. Peace be with her, at all events, for a space.

The case of Liebert (such a name!) is self-evident, and does not merit to be treated separately. Did not we marry him away to a professor's daughter? Requiescat.

(Query: why do professors lack the gust to get sons? Elucidate.)

We thought we had got rid of the Syra-Cusa. No such thing, here below, as riddance, good, bad or indifferent. Not having the stomach formally to disprove her let us merely, quickly, cite a circumstance of no importance to tickle our fauces. For days, whole days, she came not abroad, she stayed mewed up in her bedroom. What was she up to? Hold everything now. She was doing *abstract drawing!* Heavenly Father! Abstract drawing! Can you beat that one?

It was crass ever to suppose that Lucien might play his part like a liŭ. Never yet have we come upon anybody, man, woman or child, so little concerned with abiding in being as our brave Lucien. He was a crucible of volatilisation (bravo!), an efflorescence at every moment, his contours in perpetual erosion. Formidable. Looking at his face you saw the features bloom, as in Rembrandt's portrait of his brother. (Mem.: develop.) His face surged forward at you, coming unstuck, coming to pieces, invading the airs, a red dehiscence of flesh in action. You warded it off. Jesus, you thought, it wants to dissolve. Then the gestures, the horrid gestures, of the little fat hands and the splendid words and the seaweed smile, all coiling and uncoiling and unfolding and flowering into nothingness, his whole person a stew of disruption and flux. And that from the fresh miracle of coherence that he presented every time he turned up. How he kept himself together is one of those mysteries. By right he should have broken up into bits, he should have become a mist of dust in the airs. He was disintegrating bric-à-brac.

Such a paraphrased abrégé would seem to indicate, unless there be some very serious flaw in our delirium, that the book is degenerating into a kind of Commedia dell'Arte, a form of literary statement to which we object particularly. The lius do just what they please, they just please themselves. They flower out and around into every kind of illicit ultra and infra and supra. Which is bad, because as long as they do that they can never meet. We are afraid to call for the simplest chord. Belacqua drifts about, it is true, doing his best to thicken the tune, but harmonic composition properly speaking, music in depth on the considerable scale is, and this is a terrible thing to have to say, ausgeschlossen.

E.g: we were strongly tempted, some way back, to make the Syra-Cusa make Lucien a father. That was a very unsavoury plan. If new life in this case, with the Syra-Cusa and Lucien, could be the fruit of a collision, well and good. One can always organise a collision. It is to be hoped that we have not sunk quite so low as to be incapable of organising a collision. But how could it? How could it be anything but the fruit of a congruence of enormous improbability? We are too easily tired, we are neither Deus enough nor ex machina enough to go in for that class of hyperbolical exornation, as devoid of valour as it would be of value.

Similarly for all other attractive combinations. We

117

dare not beckon for a duo much less spread our wings amply for a tutti. We can only wander about vaguely, or send Belacqua wandering about vaguely, thickening the ruined melody here and there.

Bearing now in mind the untractable behaviour of our material up to date, is it surprising that we should be unable to envisage without hurting of conscience (how seldom we approach home without that!) the imminent entrée en scène of its, so to speak, colleague? All that is necessary, it seems for the time being at least to us, in order that to the novel a whipped verisimilitude may be imparted, is a well-stocked gallery of Chesnels and Birotteaux and Octaves and sposi manzoneschi whose names we forget and such like types, doing their dope from cover to cover without a waver, returning, you know, with commendable symmetry to the dust from which they sprung, or, perhaps better, were forcibly extracted. And we with not a single Chesnel in our whole bag of tricks! (You know Chesnel, one of Balzac's Old Curiosities.)

Even our spaniels are on the gay side.

Next, in the interests of this virgin chronicle, we find ourselves obliged to hack through a most pitiless belt, a regular thicket as dense and stubborn and intolerant of penetration as that which confronted us some way back at the neck, if you remember, of the black blizzard corridor, and which we are shocked and pained to find cropping up like this at the very fringe of the clearing. It must now be our endeavour, no less, to pierce the shadows and tangles of Belacqua's behaviour. And we call the Book Society to witness that we do not propose, on the occasion of this enterprise, to concede ourselves conquered. The mind commands the mind, and it obeys. Oh miracle d'amour.

Much of what has been written concerning the reluctance of our refractory constituents to bind together and give us a synthesis is true equally of Belacqua. Their movement is based on a principle of repulsion, their property not to combine but, like heavenly bodies, to scatter and stampede, astral straws on a time-strom, grit in the mistral. And not only to shrink from all that is not they, from all that is without and in its turn shrinks from them, but also to strain away from themselves. They are no good from the builder's point of view, firstly because they will not suffer their systems to be absorbed in the cluster of a greater system, and then, and chiefly, because they themselves tend to disappear as systems. Their centres are wasting, the strain away from the centre is not to be gainsaid, a little more and they explode. Then, to complicate things further, they have odd periods of recueillement, a kind of centripetal backwash that checks the rot. The procédé that seems all falsity, that of Balzac, for example, and the divine Jane and many others, consists in dealing with the vicissitudes, or absence of vicissitudes, of character in this backwash, as though that were the whole story. Whereas, in reality, this is so little the story, this nervous recoil into composure, this has so little to do with the story, that one must be excessively concerned with a total precision to allude to it at all. To the item thus artificially immobilised in a backwash of composure precise value can be assigned. So all the novelist has to do is to bind his material in a spell, item after item, and juggle politely with irrefragable values, values that can assimilate other values like in kind and be assimilated by them, that can increase and decrease in virtue of an unreal permanence of quality. To read Balzac is to receive the impression of a chloroformed world. He is absolute master of his material, he can do what he likes with it, he can foresee and calculate its least vicissitude, he

119

can write the end of his book before he has finished the first paragraph, because he has turned all his creatures into clockwork cabbages and can rely on their staying put wherever needed or staying going at whatever speed in whatever direction he chooses. The whole thing, from beginning to end, takes place in a spellbound backwash. We all love and lick up Balzac, we lap it up and say it is wonderful, but why call a distillation of Euclid and Perrault *Scenes from Life?* Why *human* comedy?

Why anything? Why bother about it? It covers our good paper.

A great deal of the above marginalia covers Belacqua, or, better: Belacqua is in part covered by the above marginalia.

At his simplest he was trine. Just think of that. A trine man! Centripetal, centrifugal and . . . not. Phœbus chasing Daphne, Narcissus flying from Echo and . . . neither. Is that neat or is it not? The chase to Vienna, the flight to Paris, the slouch to Fulda, the relapse into Dublin and . . . immunity like hell from journeys and cities. The hand to Lucien and Liebert and the Syra-Cusa tendered and withdrawn and again tendered and again withdrawn and . . . hands forgotten. The dots are nice don't you think? Trine. Yessir. In cases of emergency, as when the Syra-Cusa became a saint or the Smeraldina-Daphne, that he might have her according to his God, a Smeraldina-Echo, the two first persons might sink their differences, the two main interests merge, the wings of flight to the centre be harnessed to flight thence. The same dirty confusion and neutralisation of needs when he wands her into a blue bird, wands whom, how the hell do we know, anybody, into a blue bird and lets fly a poem at her, immerging the better to emerge. Almost a case of *reculer pour mieux enculer*.

That was a dirty confusion. It stinks in his memory like the snuff of a cierge.

The third being was the dark gulf, when the glare of the will and the hammer-strokes of the brain doomed outside to take flight from its quarry were expunged, the Limbo and the wombtomb alive with the unanxious spirits of quiet cerebration, where there was no conflict of flight and flow and Eros was as null as Anteros and Night had no daughters. He was bogged in indolence, without identity, impervious alike to its pull and goading. The cities and forests and beings were also without identity, they were shadows, they exerted neither pull nor goad. His third being was without axis or contour, its centre everywhere and periphery nowhere, an unsurveyed marsh of sloth.

There is no authority for supposing that this third Belacqua is the real Belacqua any more than that the Syra-Cusa of the abstract drawing was the real Syra-Cusa. There is no real Belacqua, it is to be hoped not indeed, there is no such person. All that can be said for certain is, that as far as he can judge for himself, the emancipation, in a slough of indifference and negligence and disinterest, from identity, his own and his neighbour's, suits his accursed complexion much better than the dreary fiasco of oscillation that presents itself as the only alternative. He is sorry it does not happen more often, that he does not go under more often. He finds it more pleasant to be altogether swathed in the black arras of his sloth than condemned to deploy same and inscribe it with the frivolous spirals, ascending like the little angels and descending, never coming to head or tail, never abutting. Whether squatting in the heart of his store, sculpting with great care and chiselling the heads and necks of lutes and zithers, or sustaining in the doorway the girds of eminent poets, or coming out into the street for a bit of song and dance (aliquando etiam pulsabat), he was cheating and denying his native indolence, denying himself to the ground-swell of his indolence, holding himself clear, refusing to be sucked down and abolished. But when, as rarely happened, he was drawn down to the blessedly sunless depths, down and down to the slush of angels, clear of the pettifogging ebb and flow, then he knew, but retrospectively, after the furious divers had hauled him out like a crab to fry in the sun, because at the time he was not concerned with such niceties of perception, that if he were free he would take up his dwelling in that place. Nothing less exorbitant than that! If he were free he would take up his dwelling in that curious place, he would settle down there, you see, he would retire and settle down there, like La Fontaine's catawampus.

Excuse our mentioning it here, but it suddenly occurs to us that the real problem of waking hours is how soonest to become sleepy. Excuse our mentioning it here.

In this Kimmerea not of sleep Narcissus was obliterated and Phœbus (here names only, anything else would do as well, for the extremes of the pendulum) and all their ultra-violets. Sometimes he speaks of himself thus drowned and darkened as "restored to his heart"; and at other times as "sedendo *et* quiescendo" with the stress on the et and no extension of the thought into the spirit made wise. Squatting in the heart of the store he was not quiet. Cellineggiava finickety scrolls and bosses, exposed to the fleers of uneasy poets. *If to be seated is to be wise, then no man is wiser than thee.* That class of cheap stinger.

But the wretched Belacqua was not free and there-

122

fore could not at will go back into his heart, could not will and gain his enlargement from the gin-palace of willing. Convinced like a fool that it must be possible to induce at pleasure a state so desirable and necessary to himself he exhausted his ingenuity experimenting. He left no stone unturned. He trained his little brain to hold its breath, he made covenants of all kinds with his senses, he forced the lids of the little brain down against the flaring bric-à-brac, in every imaginable way he flogged on his cœnæsthesis to enwomb him, to exclude the bric-à-brac and expunge his consciousness. He learned how with his knuckles to press torrents of violet from his eyeballs, he lay in his skin on his belly on the bed, his face crushed grossly into the pillow, pressing down towards the bearings of the earth with all the pitiful little weight of his inertia, for hours and hours, until he would begin and all things to descend, ponderously and softly to lapse downwards through darkness, he and the bed and the room and the world. All for nothing. He was grotesque, wanting to "troglodyse" himself, worse than grotesque. It was impossible to switch off the inward glare, wilfully to suppress the bureaucratic mind. It was stupid to imagine that he could be organised as Limbo and wombtomb, worse than stupid. When he tried to mechanise what was a dispensation he was guilty of a no less abominable confusion than when he tried to plunge through himself to a cloud, when, for his sorrow, he tried to do that. How could the will be abolished in its own tension? or the mind appeased in paroxysms of disgust? Shameful spewing shall be his portion. He remains, for all his grand fidgeting and shuffling, bird or fish, or, worse still, a horrible border-creature, a submarine bird, flapping its wings under a press of water. The will and nill cannot suicide, they are not free to suicide. That is where the wretched Belacqua jumps the rails. And that is his wretch-edness, that he seeks a means whereby the will and nill may be enabled to suicide and refuses to understand that they cannot do it, that they are not free to do it. Which does as well as anything else, though no better, to explain, since it is always a question here below of explaining, why the temper of Belacqua is bad as a rule and his complexion saturnine. He remembers the pleasant gracious bountiful tunnel, and cannot get back. Not for the life of him. He keeps on chafing and scuffling and fidgeting about, scrib-bling bad spirals with an awful scowl on the "belle face carrée", instead of simply waiting until the thing happens. And we cannot do anything for him. How can you help people, unless it be on with their corsets or to a second or third helping?

It makes us anxious, we are quite frank about it, with such material and such a demiurge. Belacqua cannot be petrified in the moment of recoil, of backwash into com-posure, any more than the rest of them. *He has turned out to be simply not that kind of person.* Only for the sake of convenience is he presented as a cubic unknown. *At his simplest trine,* we were at pains to say so, to save our bacon, save our face. He is no more satisfied by the three values, Apollo, Narcissus and the anonymous third person, than he would be by fifty values, or any number of values. And to know that he was would be precious cold comfort. For what are they themselves—Apollo, Narcissus and the inaccessible Limbese? Are they simple themselves? Like hell they are! Can we measure them once and for all and do sums with them like those impostors that they call math-ematicians? We can not. We can state them as a succession of terms, but we can't sum them and we can't define them. They tail off vaguely at both ends and the intervals of their series are demented. We give you one term of Apollo: chasing a bitch, the usual bitch. And one term of Narcissus: running away from one. But we took very good care not to mention the shepherd or the charioteer or the healer or the mourner or the arcitenens or the lyrist or the butcher or the crow; and very good care not to mention the hunter or the mocker or the boy howling for his pals or in tears or in love or testing the Stygian speculum. Because it did not suit us and would not have amused us and because the passage did not call for it. But if at any time it happen that a passage does call for a different term, for another Apollo or another Narcissus or another spirit from the wombtomb, and if it suit and amuse us (because if not the passage can call until it be blue in the face) to use it, then in it goes. Thus little by little Belacqua may be described, but not circumscribed; his terms stated, but not summed. And of course God's will be done should one description happen to cancel the next, or the terms appear crazily spaced. His will, never ours.

Belacqua, of all people, to be in such a hotch-potch! Something might yet be saved from the wreck if only he would have the goodness to fix his vibrations and be a liŭ on the grand scale. But he will not. It is all we can do, when we think of this incommensurate demiurge, not to get into a panic. What is needed of course is a tuning-fork, faithful unto death, that is to say the gasping codetta, to mix with the treacherous liŭs and liūs and get a line on them. That is what we call being a liu on the grand scale. Someone like Watson or Figaro or Jane the Pale or Miss Flite or the Pio Goffredo, someone who could be always relied on for just the one little squawk, ping!, just right, the right squawk in the right place, just one pure permanent liŭ or liū, sex no bar, and all might yet be well. Just one, only one, tuning-fork charlatan to move among the notes and size 'em up and steady 'em down and chain 'em together in some kind of a nice little cantilena and then come along and consolidate the entire article with the ground-swell of its canto fermo. We picked Belacqua for the job, and now we find that he is not able for it. He is in marmalade. Like his feet.

It would scarcely be an exaggeration to maintain that the four-and-twenty letters make no more variety of words in divers languages than the days and nights of this hopeless man produce variety. Yet, various though he was, he epitomised nothing. Sallust would have made a dreadful hash of his portrait.

By them that knew him, by them that loved him and by them that hated him, he was not forgotten. By them also who when called upon could place him without any doubt subsisting in their own minds as to the correctness of their ascriptions but to whom he was not ordinarily very present, an unremarkable person at the best of times, he was not neglected. He was fatally recognisable and wilfully cut, so little capable even as a behaviourist of versatility did he appear. The hats of friends flew off spontaneously to him as he passed, their arms flared up on his passage, and very often, more often than not, because he waddled forward bowed to the ground or screwed inward to the stores, their kindly sheets of glass, he would not respond, and always he hastened to pass, that was a great need with him, to pass, not to halt in the street, even when the man was nice, or else they crossed over grossly like the Pharisee or if they saw the disaster coming too late put on a spurt and dashed past with faces most incompetently blank or broached a long complicated observation eagerly to their companion if they had the good fortune to be accompanied. What was curious was that never, never by any chance at any time, did he mean anything at all to his inferiors. No, there we are wrong, there were exceptions to that, and one most charming. Yet it is not so very wide of the mark to say that day after day, year in and out, he could enter at the same hour the same store to make some trifling indispensable purchase, he could receive his coffee at the same hour in the same café from the hands of the same waiter, remain faithful to one particular kiosque for his newspaper and to one particular tobacconist for his tobacco, he could persist in eating at the same house and in taking his drink before and after in the same bar, and never know his assiduity to be recognised by as much as a smile or a kind word or the smallest additional attention, say a little more butter on his sandwich than would naturally fall to the share of the odd chance client, or a more generous part of curaçoa in his apéritif. Almost it seemed as though he were doomed to leave no trace, but none of any kind, on the popular sensibility. Is it not curious that he should be thus excluded from the ring of habitués and their legitimate benefits? He had no success with the people, and he suffered profoundly in consequence. The purchase of a stamp or a book of tram-tickets or a book on the quay or in a shop entailed without fail, notwithstanding the humility, the timorousness, almost the tenderness, of his approach, a disagreeable passage of arms with the vendor. Then he became furious, red in the face. To register and post a packet was out of the question. In the bank it was torture to present a cheque even amply provided for.

He never grew accustomed to this boycott.

Children he abominated and feared.

Dogs, for their obviousness, he despised and rejected, and cats he disliked, but cats less than dogs and children.

The appearance of domestic animals of all kinds he disliked, save the extraordinary countenance of the donkey seen full-face. Sometimes also however, when walking through a series of fields, he would feel a great desire to see a foal, the foal of an old racemare, under the hull of its dam, bounding.

The fact of the matter is, we suppose, that he desired rather vehemently to find himself alone in a room, where he could look at himself in the glass and pick his nose thoroughly, and scratch his person thoroughly what is more wherever and for as long as it chose to itch, without shame. And troglodyse himself also, even though it were without success, if and for whatever length of time he was pleased to do so, banging and locking the door, extinguishing, and being at home to nobody.

To two sources he was prone to ascribe the demolition of his feet.

One: it was upon their outer rim that as a child, ashamed of his limbs that were ill-shaped, the knees that knocked, he walked. Boldly then he stepped off the little toe and the offside malleolus, hoping against hope to let a little light between the thighs, split the crural web and perhaps even, who could tell, induce a touch of valgus elegance. Thereby alas he did but thicken the ankle, hoist the instep and detract in a degree that he does not care to consider from the male charm, and, who knows, the cogency, of the basin.

Two: as a youth, impatient of their bigness, contemptuous of the agonistic brogue, he shod them à la gigolo (a position he never occupied) in exiguous patents.

In the little village of aged peasant men and women and their frail grandchildren, the hale having fled to a richer land, situated half-way down the vale, a sweet vale now we look back on it, that lies so unevenly between Como and a point that most likely shall be nameless on the Lake of Lugano, the sweet Val d'Intelvi, oershadowed north and south, or would it be north-west and south-east, by the notable peaks of Generoso and Galbiga, he interviewed as quite a callow signorino mighty nailed boots for climbing. The cobbler sat in his dark store, he twisted the uppers this way and that.

"Oh!" he cried "la bella morbidezza! Babbo è morto. Si, è morto."

Imagine what cunning was required to associate these affirmations, the second of which was so obviously true that no filial client of Piedmont could ever have had the heart to question the former.

Belacqua bought the boots, he bought them for 100 lire or thereabouts, on sound and strong feet the money had been well spent. In the morning he clattered off in them in high fettle, his comrade having first in vain exhorted him:

"Do now as I do, put on two pairs of socks, bandage the feet well with rags, soap well the insides."

Macchè! But lætus exitus etc., we all know that, the joyful going forth and sorrowful coming home, and sure enough in the afternoon declining Belacqua was to be seen, and in effect by a group of aged compassionate contadine was seen, crouched in the parched grass to the side of the cobbled way that screws down so steeply from the highest village of that region to the valley where he lived. He whimpered, he was utterly fatigued, the new boots sprawled in the ditch where he had cast them from him, the bloated feet trembled amongst the little flowers, with his socks he had staunched them, the bells of the cattle high above under the crags aspersed him, he cried for his Mother. A fat June butterfly, dark brown to be sure with the yellow spots, the same that years later on a more auspicious occasion, it was inscribed above on the eternal toilet-roll, was to pern in a gyre about a mixed pipi champêtre, settled now alongside his degradation. His comrade had left him, he had gone forward, he had gone up to the cloudy cairns, he would make a victorious circuit and sweep down home to his zabbaglione. Belacqua slept. Again he woke, the moon had raised her lamp on high, Cain was toiling up his firmament, he had taken over. Above the lakes that he could not see the Virgin was swinging her legs, Cain was shaking light from his brand, light on the just and the unjust. That was what he was there for, that was what he was spared for. Belacqua culled the boots, he plucked them forth from the ditch, thenceforward he would refer to them grimly as the morbid Jungfräulein, he knotted their cruel laces the better to carry them, and discalced but for his bloody socks, under the laggard moon, eternal pearl of Constance and Piccarda, of Constance whose heart we are told was never loosed of its veil, of Piccarda alone but for her secret and God, he picked his steps home as a barefoot hen in a daze would down the steep Calvary of cobbles to the village in the valley where he lived.

Of the morbid Jungfräulein some months later he made a present to a servant for whom he thought he cared. The servant, a neat little suave little ex-service creature, was fitted to them according to his own account à la Cinderella (more correctly, but there is no time to go into that, Arsecinder). But he pawned them and drank the proceeds.

Yet again, in the full swing of the premature Spring sales in the pleasant land of Hesse, he bought, though discouraged by his knacky beloved who was with him as it happened, what looked like, and no doubt was, a stout pair of elastic-sides. Five Reichmarks he payed for them.

"There is always, I know," he complained to the tickled salesgirl "one foot larger than the other. But it is the left foot, is it not, that is ordinarily the larger?"

The salesgirl gave way before a greater than she: the shopwalker. Falling at once, like all his frockcoated, lecherous, pommaded and impotent colleagues, for the mighty Smeraldina-Rima, he abounded in informations.

"But it is well known" he gasped, preening his morning-coat, "that the left foot exceeds the right."

"Sir" Belacqua corrected him "it is the right that pinches."

"No no" he said "the left, that is our experience."

"But I am telling you" said Belacqua, pausing in his lunges on the polished parquet, "that it is my *right* that is made to suffer by this pair of boots that I have not yet bought from you."

"Ah" the shopwalker was very urbane and sure of his ground "my dear sir, that is because you are *left-handed.*"

"That is not so" said Belacqua.

"What!" he was astonished, raking the bored Smeraldina with an X-Ray up-and-downer, "what! he is not left-handed?"

"In my family" conceded Belacqua "there is left-handling. Never was I left-handed, sir, never." That was a lie.

"Never!" echoed the shopwalker with filthy irony "never! are you quite sure, sir, of that?"

The salesgirl, an hypertrophied Dorrit, hovered on the outskirts, fearful to be amused and ready, in a manner of speaking, to be tapped whenever that might be required of her by her employers.

"Gnnnädiges Fräulein" said Belacqua, turning on his nose for the accent, "can you perhaps explain how it is . . .?"

"Well sir" began the Dorrit "I think . . ."

"Hah!" smiled the shopwalker, very narquois, "yes deary . . ."

"I think" the Dorrit spoke up bravely "that this is how it is . . ."

"Are you listening, Smerry" asked Belacqua anxiously "because I may not understand . . ."

"Since" pursued the Dorrit "it is the experience, as you have heard, of the trade, that the left foot exceeds the right, it has become the tradition, in the case of all wear not made to measure, to build the left boot rather more spacious than the right . . ."

"That is to say" cried Belacqua, in a sudden illumination, having understood all after all, "the right boot rather less spacious than the left!"

"So that" the Dorrit developed her thought in a superb cadence "the rare client whose feet are *equal* in size, you sir" she curtsied slightly to the rare client "is obliged to pay for the asymmetry of an article that is primarily addressed to the average client."

"Smerry!" cried Belacqua, in a transport, "did you hear that?"

"Brothers and sisters" said the Smeraldina heavily "have I none, but . . ."

The boots were bought for all that, but, strong and shapely as they were, they failed to give satisfaction, and some months later poor Belacqua, whose exclusion from the benefits of the group extended even unto a pair of feet that were, in the gross if not in detail, monstrously symmetrical, passed them on quietly, without any fuss, to an inferior.

The only unity in this story is, please God, an involuntary unity.

Now it occurs to us that for the moment at least we have had more than enough of Belacqua the trinal maneen with his wombtomb and likes and dislikes and penny triumphs and failures and exclusions and general incompetence and pedincurabilities, if such a word may be said to exist. And though we had fully intended to present in some detail his more notorious physical particularities and before switching over to Dublin cause him to revolve for a rapid inspection before you, just as many and many a time he himself had caused to girate on its swivelling pedestal, the better to delight in its ins and outs and ups and downs, the dear little Buonarotti David in the Bargello, we let ourselves be so carried away by his feet, the state they are in, that we have no choice now, you will all be delighted to hear, but to renounce that intention. In particular we had planned to speak of his belly, because it threatens to play so important a part in what follows, his loins, his breast and his demeanour, and spell out his face feature by feature and make a long rapturous statement of his hands. But now we are tired of him. We feel, we simply

133

cannot help feeling, that the rest must wait until we can all turn to it for relief.

Then we feel also that this hyphenating is getting out of hand. Cacoethes scribendi, the doom of the best of penmen.

From Cuxhaven, after a very dark night in Altona, he took ship back to the land. The second night out, Cherbourg that noon having been delivered of the Yanks, he drew himself forth and down from the hot upper couchette where he lay and climbed the steep little ladder out from the well of steerage-class, if steerage can be said to have any class at all. It was quiet at this hour, that was only to be expected, the spit of deck so it was, by day a reeking perturbation of Poles and Hamburgers, happy to get away or grieved to go, getting on to something good against the long Atlantic hours or staunching their national tunes. There was one enormous bosthoon of a Pole, like a civic guard, a fresh and young Pole, a button-burster, in brilliant check trousers that stuck, inter alia, to his opulent thighs, and cinched in a short ultramarine double-dugger. He was the cock, he owned the deck. It was quiet now, it had been scoured sweet and clean by the night, the night that was fine by the grace of God and his Abbé Gabriel. A fair September night on the bosom of the deep.

Now the day is over, Belacqua is on the deep blue sea, he is alone on the deck of steerage-class. What shall we make him do now, what would be the correct thing for him to think for us? To begin with, of course, he moves forward, like the Cartesian earthball, with the moving ship, and then on his own account to the windy prow. He can go no further with security. He leans out to starboard, if that

134

means landward when land is to the right of the ship's motion, and scans the waste of waters, the distant beacons. Was it Beachy Head or the Isle of Wight, was it Land's End or tragic lightboats standing afar out about the shallows of the sea, or lightbuoys moored over the shoals? They were red and green and white and they lancinated his heart, they brought down his lips and head over the froth of water. If I were in, he thought richly, and it up to me to swim to one of those lights that I can see from here—how would I know that land was there, I would see no light from the level of the sea, I would certainly drown in a panic.

Does he remain bowed over the rail, his hair in the wind, his spectacles in the breast of his reefer, peering at the seethe of flowers, the silver fizz of flowers, scored by the prow? Suppose, for the sake of argument, that he does. Then in his brain also the molecules must ferment in sympathy, panic-stricken they must seethe, saddened and stilled when he raises his eyes to the beacons, then off again on the boil when he brings his head down once more over the swell, the black swell where he might well be and it up to him to do something about it and trying to float and making a dreadful hash of that and spending rather than fostering his strength the while he cast round for an issue and a direction in which to paddle deliberately away, using the breast-stroke their Father had taught them, when they were tiny, first John, then him.

That was in the blue-eyed days when they rode down to the sea on bicycles, Father in the van, his handsome head standing up out of the great ruff of the family towel, John in the centre, lean and gracefully seated, Bel behind, his feet speeding round in the smallest gear ever constructed. They were the Great Bear, the Big Bear and the Little Bear; aliter sic, the Big, Little and Small Bears.

135

That will never be known for certain now. As in single file they sped along the breakwater each one of the vast iron lids of the shafts that had been sunk for some reason or other in the concrete coughed under the wheels; six wheels, six coughs; two great râles, two big and two little. Then silence till the next lot. Many was the priest coming back safe from his bathe that they passed, his towel folded suavely, like a waiter's serviette, across his arm. The superlative Bear would then discharge the celebrated broadside: B-P! B-P! B-P! and twist round with his handsome face wreathed in smiles in the saddle to make sure that the sally had not been in vain. It had never been known to be in vain. It would have been furnished by John or Bel had the occasion been let pass by Father. The occasion had never been known to be let pass by Father. The priest always pressed his trigger. He shared that distinction with, among other stimuli, a dish of curry. A dish of curry always pressed Father's trigger.

"Oh!" he was dumbfounded "oh! curry from the curry-comb!"

Then John and Bel would titter and their Mother fail to be amused only in the rare event of what she considered a housewifely negligence, a siphon, for example, forgotten, oppressing her conscience.

Belacqua, tired of the game of beacons and drowning, threw back his head for a mouthful of the starry, pressed himself in a more intimate manner against the bulwark, and, what do you think, set to think about the girls he had left behind him!

The opening passages were quite pleasant. It was because he was a poor performer that he was pleased to despise the performance. He was blind to the charms of the mighty steaks and jug-dugs of the Smeraldina-Rima and angered by the Priapean whirlijiggery-pokery of the Syra-Cusa because in both cases he was disarmed, he was really unable to rise to such superlative carnal occasions. It is time I learnt, he thought. I will study in the Nassau Street School, I will frequent the Railway Street Academies. But he was inclined to agree with Grock, when that faithful philosopher blew from his French horn the first throaty cui bono of the meditation, that it might be just as well after all to leave well alone. If he could not he could not. It was a bloody business and what did it matter? When he meets the angel of his dreams, hee! hee!, the issue will only arise in so far as it is compatible with his indolence. My indolence, the debility of my complexion, the honing of my soul after the penumbra, these, he reassured himself, are of more moment than a pimp's technique, these shall be my first care, my first and last care.

He launched, in token of this decision, overboard a foaming spit. Back adown the great hull, astern, by the way on the ocean greyhound it was swept. So shall their voices pass away . . .

Just a tincture of the sublime now, he thought, cocking up his eye at the starfield, before back to the bunk. But again she balked him, swinging her bright legs at the earthball, forcing back upon the boiling ocean his eyes that would not submit for any consideration to ransack those blessed skirts.

Vieil Océan! Well, it was to be supposed so, bad and all as it sounded, and notwithstanding the contributions of post-war sputum. Isodore, Hughetto plumed with a café liègeois, less than Byron of Lara. And Rimbaud, the Infernal One, the Ailing Seer. In his latter days, when he mastered the art of the tag, then he could hold up his curly head with the best of them. Shall he roll his eyes, blush and quote him in translation? You know of course, don't you, that he did him pat into English?

I shall write a book, he mused, tired of the harlots of earth and air—I am hemmed in, he submused, on all sides by putes, in thought or in deed, hemmed in and about; a great big man must be hired to lift the hem—a book where the phrase is self-consciously smart and slick, but of a smartness and slickness other than that of its neighbours on the page. The blown roses of a phrase shall catapult the reader into the tulips of the phrase that follows. The experience of my reader shall be between the phrases, in the silence, communicated by the intervals, not the terms, of the statement, between the flowers that cannot coexist, the antithetical (nothing so simple as antithetical) seasons of words, his experience shall be the menace, the miracle, the memory, of an unspeakable trajectory. (Thoroughly worked up now by this programme, he pushed himself off the bulwark and strode the spit of the deck with long strides and rapidly.) I shall state silences more competently than ever a better man spangled the butterflies of vertigo. I think now (he waddled up and down under the moon, il arpenta le pont, there is a phrase for a New England Lanson, convinced that he was a positive crucible of cerebration) of the dehiscing, the dynamic décousu, of a Rembrandt, the implication lurking behind the pictorial pretext threatening to invade pigment and oscuro; I think of the Selbstbildnis, in the toque and the golden chain, of his portrait of his brother, of the cute little Saint Matthew angel that I swear van Ryn never saw the day he painted, in all of which canvases during lunch on many a Sunday I have discerned a disfaction, a désuni, an Ungebund, a flottement, a tremblement, a tremor, a tremolo, a disaggre-

138

gating, a disintegrating, an efflorescence, a breaking down and multiplication of tissue, the corrosive ground-swell of Art. It is the Pauline (God forgive him for he knew not what he said) *cupio ·dissolvi*. It is Horace's *solvitur acris hiems*. It might even be at a pinch poor Hölderlin's *alles hineingeht Schlangen gleich*. Schlangen gleich! (By this time the unhappy Belacqua was well on his way up the rigging.) I think of Beethofen, his eyes are closed, the poor man he was very shortsighted they say, his eyes are closed, he smokes a long pipe, he listens to the Ferne, the unsterb-liche Geliebte, he unbuttons himself to Teresa ante rem, I think of his earlier compositions where into the body of the musical statement he incorporates a punctuation of dehis-cence, flottements, the coherence gone to pieces, the con-tinuity bitched to hell because the units of continuity have abdicated their unity, they have gone multiple, they fall apart, the notes fly about, a blizzard of electrons; and then vespertine compositions eaten away with terrible silences, a music one and indivisible only at the cost of as bloody a labour (bravo!) as any known to man (and woman? from the French horn) and pitted with dire stroms of silence, in which has been engulfed the hysteria that he used to let speak up, pipe up, for itself. And I think of the ultimately unprevisible atom threatening to come asunder, the left wing of the atom plotting without ceasing to spit in the eye of the physical statistician and commit a most copious of-fence of nuisance on his cenotaphs of indivisibility.

All that, conceded Belacqua, postponing the mare's-nest and the stars to another occasion, is a bit up in the rigging. If ever I do drop a book, which God forbid, trade being what it is, it will be a ramshackle, tumbledown, a bone-shaker, held together with bits of twine, and at the same time as innocent of the slightest velleity of coming unstuck as Mr Wright's original flying-machine that could never be persuaded to leave the ground.

But there he was probably wrong.

On that unwarrantable impression he clawed his way back through the raw flaws of wind and down the steep little ladder into the hot bowels of steerage-class. Now he lies on his right side, all but on his chest, in the upper couchette, in the hot bowels of the vessel. He thanks God, ere sleep dusk his eyes and his breath be faded, that his pleura had been pleased to weep where they did, that they had not washed into slush the pulsing snowball of his little heart that went pit-a-pat, à tombeau ouvert (was he not after all in the heart of the movement and was it not a fact that man trägt wieder Herzlein?), when darkness fell. He gives heartfelt thanks to whatever Gods there be for the merciful posture that could put such a various pair of birds to sleep, still the tempestuous poles of his thorax, pour painkiller on its zones.

Next dusk shall gather round him seated in the tug. It rocks itself upon the evening water livid under the bright decks. The whistler has come out with the emigrants and their friends, they have climbed aboard, with a slow frail music he feeds their lament, they cry down from the rail and their silence weaves an awning over the tug, the tug is grappled to the high bulwark by their cries and their silence and the tendrils of the whistling. Beyond Cobh across the harbour fireflies are moving in Hy-Brasil's low hills, the priests are abroad there with bludgeons. The captain of the tug stands by his wheel on his little bridge, his head is thrown back, he is abusing the young German mate in charge of the unlading, he is not afraid. The saloon band vomits Dear Little Shamrocks, it pukes the crassamenta of

140

its brasses down on top of the tug, we are all boys together, we belch therefore the chorus, the liana of silence and whistling is sundered, we are set adrift. Next to Belacqua the slut bawn is now weeping, she is weeping and waving a fairly clean portion of Bourbon bloomer. That is very meet, proper and, given her present condition, her bounden duty. Before Xmas she shall be in Green St, she shall be in Railway St under the new government. She was born well, she lived well and she died well, Colleen Cresswell in Clerkenwell and Bridewell. Now they are free, they are flying across the harbour to the landing-stage, a pinnace of souls. Belacqua lights a cigarette quick for malas and maxillas, he hoists his heavy fibre case up on the gunwhale beside him. Now he is all set, he is ready to skip ashore. Jean will be there to meet him, Jean with the grace of God will be there, his dear friend, Jean du Chas.

Thus dusk shall ere long gather about him—unless to be sure we take it into our head to scuttle at dead of night the brave ship where now he lies a-dreaming (creeks and springboards), the noble Hapak and all its freights, crew and cargo, and Belacqua along with his palpitations and adhesions and effusions and agenesia and wombtomb and æesthetic of inaudibilities.

L'andar su che porta? . . .

Oh but the bay, Mr Beckett, didn't you know, about your brow.

THREE

They took the dull coast road home, three days and three nights they dawdled up homeward along it, by Youghal, Tramore, Wicklow Town, living on the fat of the land. Chas payed, Belacqua having spent his last shillings in Cork on scent for a lady, a neat involucrate flasket of Cologne water, very fine, for his Mother, she stands listening on the perron, for all the stout in bottle they drank on the way, he shelled out for all the stout that helped to bloat the sadness of the sad evenings, and they went down to all the shores, they paced up and down, up and down, side by side, on the firm sand near the waves, and there Chas, in the chill evening and rain of course threatening, did develop his unheard of musical relations with one Ginette Mac Something, the hem of the hem of the hem of the hem of whose virginity (vidual) toga he would never, jamais au grand jamais, presume and was not worthy to lift the littlest notch let alone hoist aloft thigh-high.

"Je la trouve adorable, quoique peu belle. Elle a surtout beaucoup de GOUT, elle est intelligente et douce, mais douce, mon cher, tu n'peux pas t'imaginer, et des gestes, mon cher, tu sais, très désarmants."

Belacqua saw at once how lovely she must be, he was

quite sure she was very remarkable, and dare he hope that on some not too distant occasion he might be privileged to catch a glimpse of her sailing through the dusk when the dusk was she?

"Elle a une petite gueule" moaned Chas "qui tremble comme un petit nuage."

Belacqua found that a striking rapprochement, and in the long gloomy silence that ensued he was at some pains to fix it for ever in his mind:

> le ténébreux visage
> bouge comme un nuage . . .

> j'adore de Ginette le ténébreux visage
> qui tremblote et qui bouge comme un petit nuage

"I have a strong weakness" he assured his dear friend "for the epic cæsura, don't you know. I like to compare it, don't you know, to the heart of the metre missing a beat."

Chas thought this was a remarkable comparison, and a long gloomy silence ensued.

"There is much to be done, don't you think" said Belacqua "with a more nervous treatment of the cæsura", meaning there was nothing at all to be done don't you think, with the tenebrous Ginette, "just as the preterites and past subjunctives have never since Racine, it seems to me, been exploited poetically to the extent they merit to be. You know:
        'Vous mourûtes aux bords . . .' "

"Où vous fûtes laissée" whistled Chas.

"And the celebrated 'quel devint . . .' of the unfortunate Antiochus."

Chas shivered.

"Shall we go in?" he said.

Thus every night for three nights they left a dark shore, the dark sand, on which a soft rain would ere long be softly falling, falling, because it would bloody well have to.

Belacqua was heartily glad to get back to his parents' comfortable private residence, ineffably detached and situated and so on, and his first act, once spent the passion of greeting after so long and bitter a separation, was to plunge his prodigal head into the bush of verbena that clustered about the old porch (wonderful bush it was to be sure, even making every due allowance for the kind southern aspect it enjoyed, it never had been known to miss a summer since first it was reared from a tiny seedling) and longly to swim and swoon on the rich bosom of its fragrance, a fragrance in which the least of his childish joys and sorrows were and would for ever be embalmed.

His mother he found looking worn. She had not been in the best of health lately, she said, not at the top of her form, but she was much better now, now she felt fine.

It was really wonderful to get back to the home comforts. Belacqua tried all the armchairs in the house, he poltrooned in all the poltrone. Then he went and tried both privies. The seats were in rosewood. Douceurs . . .!

The postman flew up with letters, he skidded up the drive on his bicycle, scattering the loose gravel. He was more pleased than he could say, but compounded with his aphasia to the extent anyhow of "Welcome home" in the attractive accent and the old familiar smile there under the noble moustache "master Bel." Yes, yes, évidemment. But where was the slender one, where was he, that was the question, as thin and fine as the greyhound he tended, the musical one, a most respectable and industrious young fellow he was, by cheer industry, my dear, plus personal charm, those were the two sides of the ladder on which this

145

man had mounted, had he not raised himself above his station, out of the horrible slum of the cottages, did he not play on the violin, own an evening suit of his own and dance fleetly with the gentry, and: as he lay as a child wide awake long after he should have been fast asleep at the top of the house on a midsummer's night Belacqua would hear him, the light nervous step on the road as he danced home after his rounds, the keen loud whistling: *The Roses are Blooming in Picardy* . . . No man had ever whistled like that, and of course women can't. That was the original, the only, the unforgettable banquet of music. There was no music after—only, if one were lucky, the signet of rubies and the pleasant wine. He whistled the Roses are Blooming and danced home down the road under the moon, in the light of the moon, with perhaps a greyhound or two to set him off, and the dew descending.

Now he was dead, we thought it more reverent to put that into a paragraph by itself, dead, grinning up at the lid. The dead fart, says the Preacher, vanity of vanities, and the quick whistle. Blessed be the name of Thanatos.

The Polar Bear:
cursing, blaspheming, purple in the face with a terrible apprehension, he stampeded miserably through the vortex. He lurched up safe and sound on the sidewalk.

"God b--- the bastards" he snarled "merde and remerde for the bastards."

He snatched off his huge old hat and his head shone high above the crowd. He was an enormous stout block of a man. "Merde" he snarled "merde, merde." Still it was a relief to be across at all. It was only the mercy of God that he was across at all with what little life was still in him.

Now, what the hell had he got to get now? Oleum ricini for his ailing sister. Merde for his sister. Then there was some other bloody nonsense he had said he would get. What was that? Straining every nerve he suddenly got it: a two shilling chicken for his ailing family. Merde for his family. Though they really were darlings, they were pets, with all their little faults and shortcomings, and so good to him. He ground his teeth together, he gnashed them in the extremity of his affection for his ailing family. Hawking oleum ricini and two shilling pullets (they do not exist) all over the fornicating city.

He set his course now for where he knew he could pick up the oil on the cheap, he stumped along now, gasping and humped and enormous, ponderously in the middle of the sidewalk. He was gone in the legs. Hearing himself named he drew up, and on perceiving Monsieur du Chas he raised the old hat courteously.

"If you like" he said in his distinguished voice, tinged with a lallation, "you can come along and help me buy a bottle of oleum ricini for my blasted sister."

They made ground together.

"Merde" said the Polar Bear agreeably "for my sister."

"Hoffentlich" said Chas.

That was a quip, so the P.B. loosed a great guffaw.

"You can carry my bag, you know" he said "if you like."

Chas took over the bag.

"It's full of bloody shockers" said the P.B. "for my ailing family."

"What ails it?" enquired Chas.

"That is why it is such a weight" said the P.B. "I am tired, truly I am tired out, hawking the bastard round. And you are young and I am old . . ."

He turned now and stormed venomously through the

flux of pedestrians and made irruption into the pharmacy where he was known.

"And so he fears" carried forward Chas "to be a . . ."

That was the worst of Chas, that was his weakness, the ham that his any foe at any time could slit and string, this abominable production of text, as well as a great number of original and spontaneous observations, to a mysterious terminus of fitness closing the line or the couplet or the quatrain or the phrase or the period, whatever the area to which he felt dimly closure should be applied, we don't presume to know how that point was established. Anal complex anyway. Many a time had Belacqua, responding to the obscure need to verbalise a wombtombing or such like, murmured a syllable or two of incantation: "La sua bocca . . .", "Qui vive la pietà . . .", "Before morning you shall be here . . .", "Ange plein . . .", "Mais elle, viendra . . ." "Du bist so . . ." "La belle, la . . .", only to have this filthy little hop-me-thumb Bartlett-in-the-box pop aloft with a hod of syllables, gash a glaring Cæsarean in the nightfall of the ambiente, stitch and hemistich right left and centre the dying meditation, and drum the brain back into the counting-house. Then Belacqua loathed his dear friend. Not but that Chas was not a modest man, not but that it ever occurred to him, we feel sure, to preen himself however little on this infallible instinct of his for context. Twas as has been said, the alto of an inhibition, like the Platonic prancing and gallivanting before the Ginette seen through the glass rose-darkly, through the tissue of tears.

Why, why this sudden dart at Chas of which no good can come? He fades soon away. That we hope we can vouch for. Then why the sudden dart? Stuffing or padding, flagrant concealment, élan acquis, catamenia currente calamo.

We know (are we likely ever to forget!) that early on

we said we would look to Chas to garrot this chronicle. Well now on second thoughts we find we can do very well without his help. It is even possible that we be pricked into anger to marry him away to a slick Shetland Shawly we have in mind, not Ginette Mac Somebody, another, she shall be made get him with a tale told at twilight of tears idle tears shed in the heather (extraordinary when we come to think of it the amount of tears and twilight in this book), it comes just up to her navel she is such a snug little maid, she is just one plump little snug little odorous spasm of Nietzsche, Freud, oppoponax and assafœtida, Dublin is full of them. Let him push us just a little too far and that is what is coming to him. We shall pack off the pair of them to a thalamus that by day folds up for psycho-analysis. On no account does he get a curtain or share in one. And that is the least that can befall him.

We also mentioned we might have to whistle up Mammy for a terminal scena. But now thinking it over again from the point we find we have reached of view, we think no, we think it would be better, less trouble, if we left her fairly respectably where she is, cuddling and coddling and chiding for her good her lovely daughter and building her up for a German match on Fleischsalat and Ungarischer Gulasch . . . A passing reference, a fleeting evocation of that competent multipara doing the handsome by the Madonna and even putting her own expert lips in the interests of her pecker in moderation to the Krug, that ought to dénouer that. Let her stay where she is.

About the final curtain: if there be one to be taken, instead of which you know it may flicker down like Pecksniff's palpebra in the full flowering of the antepenultimate turn, say, come suddenly asunder, if there be any final curtain to be taken we rather fancy Belacqua is the

149

boy that will take it, all on his own, bowing left and right, bowing slightly to the plaudits. Now the figure solicits to be carried forward. It proffers fire-curtains, emergency exits, the green room and the stage door. We harden our heart and will not let ourselves go. Are we a tram of burden, trolley-plumed? We say courteously to the figure that perhaps some other evening.

And so he fears to be a . . .

"Where" the P.B., inexpressibly relieved now that he had the oil safe and sound in his pocket, would be interested to know "is it possible to acquire a chicken for the sum of two shillings? At the great poulterer's of D'Olier Street, at Brady's of Dawson Street, or in the Market?"

"You would need to keep vigil all night" said Chas "and go to the Halles with the first streaks of morning."

"Haffner's pork sausingers" the Polar Bear narrowed down the field of research "are prime, but their birds are dear. And if my family thinks" cocking the jaws "that I am going to burst myself sweating up George's Street . . ."

"Well sir" said Chas, tendering the gravid bag, "now I must fly. I have an A.P."

"Well" said the Polar Bear "I hope she is very nice."

"With Belacqua" said Chas, refusing to play, " 'aven't you seen him?"

The P.B. admitted gloomily to having seen him but the day before. He had found him very much—how would he say—changed.

"Not altered?" Chas hoped.

That was not for the Polar Bear to say.

"Other" was as far as he cared to go. "A lot of people have been asking after him tenderly."

"That so" said Chas "well" advancing the bag "I must fly."

The Polar Bear raked his nose and swallowed it.

"Notably" he said "the Alba."

"Alba?"

"A girl" sighed the P.B. "wunnerful girl. Great friend or was of your friend and colleague Monsieur Liebert."

"Indeed . . ."

"Well" the Polar Bear was tired of Chas "now I must fly." Suddenly he became aware of the bag. "Here!" he growled "don't run away with the bag. If I went home without the bag" he said slyly, when he had it safe in his grasp, "do you know what would happen?"

Chas had no idea.

"I'd be beaten" said the Polar Bear.

They flew apart.

He found the pullet, hard and taut and small, tant pis, but for the budgeted amount. That was a great satisfaction. Beat the thieving bastards down. Half-a-crown for a sabre-breasted hen! Merde. The Baby he could buy on his way home. The oil and the bird entered the bag.

"Now" he said, scraping his throat and swallowing it, launching a high red cacklebelch of duty done, "now."

Silence now we beseech you, reverence, your closest attention. For whom have we here. Follow us closely. Behold it is she it is the

ALBA.

Behold her gliding ahead of schedule—for to keep him waiting is not her genre, no, that is too easy,—into the hotel lounge where she has granted him rends-toi. She was alive, there she was, living in pain, alive and in pain. She would have brandy, hijo de la puta blanca! but she would indeed and be damned to the whole galère. Carajo! but she

151

would have brandy and in a glass of degustation what was more into the bargain, Hennessy in a tulip in a bucket. Salt in my mouth, she thought, salt and sand for ever and ever. Forth from her balmy brassière she drew his last letter her latest's last. He applied for a gage of her affections.

He was a terrific lump of a chap, quite the reverse of her frail Princess-ship, our ladysloop, our Lope flower, positively at the opposite pole.

"Massive!" exclaimed the Venerilla "a massive man."

Massive was the Meath, the West Meath, for épatant, and the Venerilla was the Alba's abigail. Devoted! She would most gladly have laid down her life without the slightest velleity of salvation in corollary, for Miss Alba her little royal mistress. She is not to be wondered at, not for a moment.

His name it was Jem, a weight-lifter, a Rugby man, a pugilist, not even a shinty or camogie man, a feller of ladies with the pillared muscle-fluted thighs bulging behind the stuff. He applied for the gage of the horny-handed prelude, the gage was to take the form of the marginalia of the penetralia, it was to be handed over in the antichambers of the arcana.

"You little she-devil" he had been moved to write "you little witch you have bewitched me. I am not much of a hand at writing as you may know, I am not a literary cove in any sense of the word, but you have stolen my heart away and I am yours body and soul and I love you more than words can utter. From that first wonderful night we met never again to part if I had my way I felt that nothing else mattered if I could be yours some day and you could be mine, in the highest sense of course I mean. I need not tell you . . ."

The Alba broke off to guffaw with great heartiness and

openness on the divan. Carajo!, she giggled, achieving a superb aspiration for her own pleasure, body and soul and in the highest sense of course he means!

". . . need not tell you. I would give over all, work and play and career and all the little tarts that for some reason I can't think why make a great fuss of me as you may have heard . . ."

Ciel ! but he would give over the little tarts!

". . . if I could think that you loved me half as much as I love you that is more than all the world. 'I'll be loving you always!' I will always dream of you whenever I hear that air. May I bring you out for a run in the car next Sunday? You were divine that evening in that stunning evening frock, where on earth did you raise it? All the fellows I knew there think you are marvellous. I am so crazy about you I can hardly sleep thinking about you. You were like an angel come down from Heaven in the middle of all those little tarts. Do say I may. And do please send me a photo or snap if you have not anything better and please do not think me impertinent or pushing if I ask you for a photo so soon after so short an acquaintance. I would rather have a side face one if you have one, in evening dress if you have one, you look so divine in evening dress, or on the beach, I am sure you can rake up the very thing I want. I enclose a snap of myself taken by a pal at Douglas this summer for the T.T., not much good, just a little souvenir. We were just over for a few days and we had a pretty hot time I can tell you. But that is all over now, now that I know you I would not be bothered any more.

Do write and send me that and say I may call for you Sunday afternoon about three if you do not think that would be too early. It could not be early enough for me. You will make me the happiest man in the world if you say yes. I could go on in this strain for ever, but will only bore you probably if I go on. Saturday we are playing the Rangers. May I send you a touchline seat? I lead the forwards you know. It should be a good game. We could meet after for tea at Fuller's or if you prefer that Bon Bouche place in Dawson St.

Hoping to have reply by return.

Ever your passionate but respectful admirer
Jem (Higgins)

P.S. I know now that I never knew what love was until I met you. J."

Alba sighed. More money for jam. That she might thus sigh alone in pain with brandy she turned her eyes on him, she pulled off the petticoats and outwards of her gaze, she unleashed the claws and crotchets of her brain, they crept out and grappled the bosthoon. Or put it this way, that she showed herself at the high turret window so that the birds came flying through the evening; she appeared as Florina at the high window and sang her couplet so that the birds, settling furtively on the great cypress of swords and daggers, gashed suddenly their wings, flittered their talons. Then they cawed the bloody caw: Never knew, what Love could be, till I met you, 'n you met me. And not a blue feather in the entire colony.

Trincapollas! sighed Alba, raising her glass, but all men are homo-sexy, I wish to Christ I'd been born a Lesbian.

The sooner, since she had not, that she became Mie-Souillon and slept and wept in a Cabinet of Echos and ate astrologers and doctors and musicians in a pie, the better, par la vertuchou! Yes, but would her health stand

154

it? No, her health would not stand it. She must build herself up a little first, she must lead a simpler life, Benger's
and a dander daily in the gardens. Then she would take the
rags of her Venerilla, her scullion, her foil, and she would
set out.

She would set off through the forests and she would
take her time. No forced marches. The birds would scuttle
above bleeding in the tree-tops. A fizz of scampering birds,
it would lead her to the honey. What honey? They would
not fly, their wings were in tatters, she would not see
them, desperately they would sprawl and flounder high
overhead through the treacherous stools, it is a poor shoal
of wounded noddies threshing aloft. In the heat of their
endeavours they loose their siftings unashamed, they cannot help it, a dew of white dung it lapses down through the
green sunlight, it drenches the leaves, the fizz of their
endeavour leads her forward to the court of honey. What
honey? The green of Circe? Alas, a pint of that and a gallon
of gall, salt in my mouth for ever and ever.

She plunged her hand into the stuff of her hat as
though it were a tuft of grass growing, she extirpated the
smart bowler in a rage. With a scroll of the blackest hair
she swathed the eburnine distemper of her temple. She
tottered to her feet, she disengaged herself from the divan,
till she was a slight, vigilant figure, still, erect, the big head
lowered, the finger-tips earthing her through the low table, cabling her fast to the earth. She waited. She listened
for the lounge to be centralised. She thought she had fever.
Then ten to one the waiter would come.

"Madame" said the waiter.

"My coat" she said, breaking the circuit, "and I ordered
another glass of brandy" she said, reseated, "if you remember."

She had not, and the waiter remembered nothing of the kind.

"Hennessey!" she cried "3-star—double—degustation—hurry!" she cried "can't you see I am dying?"

She folded up her high-bred legs, she nested against the arm of the divan. The lounge had slipped back to its natural slipshod, tangle of private spirals and foci.

But the heated brain of the beautiful Alba was off: why am I thus abroad, why in the name of God do I come thus abroad, maltworm, girlfish, frog in a puddle? Am I then to be baptised? married? buried? Then why am I not in my chamber, giving ear to the big wind. And the eyes of a man are upon me, as those bloodshot of Orestes up and down his sister's rags. The old ruffian, why does he not come, and entertain me?

"Sugar" she said to the trembling waiter.

Now the day was over, it was quite the busiest hour of the day for the lounge-attendants, the better-to-do of the city were taking refuge from the dusk. It was the hour of the nimble lamplighters, flying through the suburbs on bicycles, tilting at the standards. The local poets, in this respect differing from the better-to-do, crept forth at this hour and came abroad, each from his public-house, for the daily snipe of inspiration. It was soon known in the snug that Seum or Liam or Harry or Sean had gone out but was expected back ere long. They would not have long to wait for him. He would return, his voice, his familiar step, advancing down the body of the public-house, would make it known that he had returned. He would pay his round, for was he not a very decent man and a great bard and a great man to talk later in the evening?

Belacqua cowered beneath the battalions of the sky. He had disembarrassed himself rapidly of his dear friend who had said:

"He mentioned some Alba who had been enquiring tenderly after you."

She had not. The Polar Bear used words loosely, he threw them about.

Now Belacqua is on the bridge with Nemo, they are curved over the parapet, their bottoms are outlined and not in vain in the dusk descending. He lifts his head in due course to the doomed flowers, the livid tulips. Very poignant, yes, they lancinate his little heart, they seldom fail to oblige. His lips are brought down and his head again, yes, the gulls were there. They never miss an evening. They are grey slush in the spewing meatus of the sewer. Now it is time to go, it is yet time. They lapse down together and away from the right quays, they have ceded, they are being harried from the city. It is the placenta of the departed, the red rigor of post-partum.

The Polar Bear came cataracting—too late; the tram had gathered way, now it is screaming past the Mansion House. He tore at the strap.

"Can't the bloody thing be stopped?" he cried.

"Next stop the Green" said the conductor.

"Damn the Green" cried the P.B. "damn you and your damn Green."

He drew his plump hand's glabrous crown across his raw mouth. Three nouns, three adjectives.

"The Dublin United Tramways Bloody Company" he vociferated "seems to exist for the sole purpose of dragging its clients forcibly out of their way to Greens. Isn't there enough green in this merdific island? I get on to your accursed bolide at the risk of my life at the College Green and get fired out at the next of your verminous plaguespots whether I like it or not. If it's not the Stephen's Green it's Green's bloody library. What we want" he screamed from the sidewalk "in this pestiferous country is red for a change and plenty of it."

Alas the conductor was slow, he was Irish, his name was Hudson, he had not the Cockney gift of repartee. He might have made a very nice use of Green St, and he did not, he missed his chance. Very much later in the day, brooding over this incident, the right answer came to him, or one of the answers that would have done, and from that moment forth he had at least a presentable anecdote for his colleagues at the depot. But too late. Once again the Polar Bear had been let go unscathed.

Fiercely now retracing his steps, weighed down by the bag, he had occasion most bitterly to upbraid a wall-eyed employee of the R.A.C., a little mousy ex-service creature known to the members as Dick Deadeye. With a courtly gesture Dick motioned back the pedestrians that the cars for whose comings and goings he was responsible might issue forth unimpeded from the garage. It was the rush hour for the little man. The Polar Bear was among the pedestrians, one of those pedestrians was he.

"Curse you" he snarled "oh, curse you. Shall I stand here all night?"

"Sorry sir" said Dick, motioning him back, "duty."

"B--- your duty" snarled the P.B.

"And you sir" said Dick.

The Polar Bear raised the bag.

"You damned little impertinent pimp of hell you" he frothed at the commissures.

158

Dick stood his ground, he would do his duty.

"If you lay a finger on me sir" he was moved to mention over his shoulder "I'll have the law of you."

In this black city of ours that comes out seventh in occidental statistics, or did, such painful scenes are of daily occurrence. Men of the high standing of the Polar Bear, men of culture and distinction, occupying positions of responsibility in the City, permit themselves, condescend, to bandy invective with the meanest of day-labourers. Gone is patrician hauteur, gone, it almost seems, with the Garrison. The scurvy dog has taught the snarl to his scurvy master, the snarl, the fawn, the howl and the cocked leg: the general coprotechnics. And we are all dogs together in the dogocracy of unanimous scurrility.

(Overstatement. Dickens.)

The point it seems almost worth our while trying to make is not that the passing of the Castle as it was in the days of the Garrison is to be deprecated. Not at all. We hope we know our place better than that. We uncover our ancient Irish wedgehead in deference to that happy ejection. Nor are we the least prone to suggest that the kennel is a less utopian community than the pen or coop or shoal or convent or any other form of natural or stylicised pullulation. If these or similar termini were capable of providing us with the point, any point, would we not have been guilty of *ad quem?* And we cannot but feel, after all our toil, that it is rather late in the day for *ad quem*. We mean, dem it all, do we tolerate buffers in our regiment?

Con moto, then, for we have not a moment to lose, and not to overdo the tedium, we come to our point which is one of departure, an *a quo* that we fancy Watteau himself would not have turned up his nose at, not for us, we stay where we are, but for the eager young sociologists that abound in our midst (Merrion Row, Portobello, Mary St and passim) and particularly the more serious few that have not forgotten the striking phrase of the Paris schoolman, the master and author of them that are anxious to have an opinion, the bearded bonhomme: *one commences to re-read Proudhon, or, perhaps better, one recommences to read Proudhon.* He only has to place himself at this centre of focus, he only has to gird up his lusty loins at this point, blick from this Punkt, the ardent young politico-social psycho-scientific sleuth that we have in mind, and he shall command an ample perspective: the French provincial towns, the Five towns, the Tweed, emigration in the west, the alas rapidly waning Italian commune, the plight of the small farmer in the Europe of our time, the impressive decadential trend in the great cities of the west (and the east, for all we know) from the sale and purchase of labour in the market-place to the saving of same in the tavern. Etc.

Thus here in what immediately precedes we have an example of how, if instead of pressing à la Titania asses to our boosoms, of being satisfied to strain in healthy hypnosis to our boosoms the Hudsons and Deadeyes of daily, yea and hourly, encounter, their duties and their fleers, we could only learn to school ourselves to see all things great and small about us and their emanations, all the articles of bric-à-brac through which we move, as so many tunics of so many onions, if we could only learn to school ourselves to nurture that divine and fragile Fünkelein of curiosity struck from the desire to bind for ever in imperishable relation the object to its representation, the stimulus to the molecular agitation that it sets up, percipi to percipere, of how then there is no knowing on what sublime platform, nonpolitical, Beobachtungspost at once and springboard, we

160

may find ourselves poised and watchful, potential beyond measure ere we take off, unafraid, swallow-wise, through reefless airs for a magic land.

From the Hudsons and the Deadeyes and the P.B.s to a magic land! It is only necessary to follow the directions. For magic here is not milk and honey (Gawd forbid) nor Heaven's High Halls where all at last is in the very best of health nor everlasting sweet pea, no, it is the absence of Polar Bears and Deadeyes and the coprotechnics in which they are co-ordinate. It is the abolition of that class of person and that class of thing. There is not a trace, not as much as a suspicion of the old stench, of the premises in the conclusion. How is that for a fine figure of a syllogism? That is how you get away from the ignoble scuffling and snarling of bosthoonery and tinned Kultur. Presticerebration. That is how you can get rid of gowned poets and uniformed peasants. You Roentgen them to start off with, you strip off the millions of leathery tunics. It takes time but it is pleasant work. Then you find when you come to the core and the kernel and the seat of the malady that behold it is a bel niente. Now there are few things more bel than a niente but considered as a premise, and be you Abbot himself, it presents certain difficulties in the manner of manipulation. So you draw your wand and strike from the air ad your own sweet lib whatever premises you fancy. You will have to live on them, you cannot get rid of them, so take much thought, tis a critical moment. Then proceed in the ordinary way. The public never spots the deception. The public is too busy admiring the seamless tights of the performer and listening to the patter of the parable. All that is necessary is to follow directions.

Now he is drawing nigh, in a spouting and ingurgitation of crassamenta he joins issue with the perron, straining and heaving against the great load of himself he stamps the steps behind him in a cruel flatfooted diagonal, one by one he spurns them out of his path.

Oh where now are the hard nervous soles, smelling of bracken and thyme, of Bilitis or a chaste huntress or even a sinuous nautch-gal, scaling prestly from the sea shallow tiers of pale red marble? They are elsewhere Doctor Scholl. Or the muddy chubby feet of little Stoebli, he was an idle young herd, he was a blue flower in the mountain, he is akimbo on his lil bottom in the mountain dew, by the outposts of the dark forest he whittles his staff, he is like a starved della Robbia, we are told there is peach-down on his cheeks but what does that matter, there are his feet, muck caking in the toepits, the arches laced with mire. All the belled cattle for leagues around, above and below, are his father's stock. They are in his keeping. Then James, the hero, the steel mountaineer, comes striding through hornbeams. Then in a minute it is morning.

The P.B. lowered himself, his great load, coat, bag, hat, mucus, fury and exhaustion, on to the divan as soon as it occurred to the Alba to unfold her noble legs and make room for him beside her. After a few moments of silence and withdrawal, she waiting, he panting, to lower the temperature of this man and still the clamours and alarums of the trying hours through which he had passed, and the customary feintes and passes obiter between her amused that he should present himself so frankly after his time and him so glad and grateful that she had not bounced off in a huff on the tick but permitted herself to grant him a few moments' grace, then the pretty smart slap-up dialogue, transcribed herewith without frills or falbalas (tired of them) as follows, took place.

162

P.B. Frankly I find Belacqua changed more than l could have believed possible after so short an absence. Physically sadly so and mentally a hardening, I trust not a sclerosis, and a sourness, if I am to judge by the few words he has bestowed on me since his return, that are new in him and particularly shocking for me in one whose curiosity and enthusiasm for cosa mentale were charming without ever being merely naive. Perhaps I exaggerate. I hope I do. I told Chas, you know Chas . . .

A. No.

P.B. A colleague and friend of Liebert, a bit of a bore and a morpion, but means well, friend of Belacqua—I told him to tell Belacqua that you had been asking after him. That will gratify him. You know, he has a great gradh for you.

A. But I was not asking after him. How would I be asking after him when I don't know him. Now I'll have him skipping round to the house and pestering me. You might have known I had had enough of that . . .

P.B. But, my dear Alba, it was only the other day that you spoke so well of him to me, you know you did. Is it possible that you have forgotten?

A. I may have referred atonily to the creature in the current of conversation, but I did *not* ask after him. How would I ask for him when I scarcely know him?

P.B. But . . .

A. You live on indiscretions. Now I'll have him cantering round to pay his respects.

P.B. And wouldn't you like to see him?

A. What's the good? What is the good of starting again? You know, or you ought to, how it is with me and

163

how it has always been. You of all people ought to know that I don't want to and that it's no good. I can only do him injury and open my own. It has always been so. It might amuse him for a bit, but it won't amuse me. I'm tired flogging the trivial excitement. What did you want to say anything to Chas for! Why couldn't you leave it alone? Now I'll have to choke him off. More work.

P.B. I don't think I know exactly what you mean, and I am sure you are making a song about nothing. I assure you he is neither vulnerable nor troublesome. On the contrary. It is simply that he would like to see you and talk to you.

A. But don't you see that he cannot *simply* see me and talk to me? I find myself unable to permit it. If he sees me at all it must be non-simply. And I shall be obliged to complicate our conversation. I cannot have a simple relation with the cerebral type, and you can see he is that from a mile off. I have to make it a mess and a knot and a tangle. I can't help it. So what's the good? It's too difficult to untie.

P.B. Well, if I had known . . .

A. God knows you might know by this time. But I don't want to talk about people and things—bulks. Not even about myself. Entertain me. Tell me about Louise Labbé or the Holy Ghost or the unreal coordinates. And more brandy if you have the price of it. Tell me about the Egyptian Book of the Dead.

The Polar Bear disposed of a large information on these subjects and the Alba listened and did not interrupt. Of the Holy Ghost, however, he did not care to speak.

164

"Even were it not an impertinence" he said "for me, a spoilt Roundhead, to speak to you, brought up on real unspottednesses, of the Holy Ghost, I prefer" with a leer and a lowered voice "not to deal with that subject in a public place. Nor are the epigrams with which I would be obliged, so pungent and to the point and in every way excellent do I consider them, to punctuate my relation, for the ears of a maid. You are broadminded, not squeamish, but I prefer not."

A ridiculus mus of mucus was born in an ear-splitting eruption to the orator. He savoured it and put it away.

"Now Louise Labbé" he said "was a great poet, a great poet, perhaps one of the greatest of all time, of physical passion, of passion purely and exclusively physical. She did not know the love from which the body has been refined, in which the body has been consumed. She did not care for the Chanson de Toile's extremities of tenderness and service, the nostalgia of Doon for his "belle Doette". But what she did know and care for and enshrine in imperishable verse . . ."

The Alba folded up her legs, more under her this time, and listened, he had a pleasant voice, and did not interrupt.

Then, after a time, she ceased to listen. He had nearly polished off the unreal co-ordinates, he was saying: "and so we invent them", and she ceased to be bothered listening. Then he, sensing that she had withdrawn her attention, ceased to speak. They sat on in silence, not at all embarrassed by this cleavage.

The Alba allowed herself, against her better judgement, to be absorbed in the review of how her days up to then had been spent, of how she had been spent, of how she had been spent and almost, it seemed to her and to many that knew her, extinguished by her days. The days were not hers to spend, they were waste land to earn. She had earned her days. It was she who had been spent, she and the richness of days that were not hers until she had earned and impoverished them. She had been spent in daywinning. Poor in days she was light and full of light. Rich in days she was heavy and full of darkness. Living was a growing heavy and dark and rich in days. Natural death was black wealth of days. The brightness of day-poverty was music unscored for the need of keeping alive and well so that she might die, the music of days that were not hers and of which each hour was too manifold for possession. She made a version of each hour and day, she made a grotesque song of their music, she carried the version and song away hers, a growing weight of darkness upon her, she called the days thus earned and impoverished hers. She reviled the need, the unsubduable tradition of living up to dying, that forced her to score and raid thus the music of days. The heavy gloom of carnal custom. To extirpate the need and remain light and full of light, to secede from the companies of the dutifully dying and go with them no more from heaviness to heaviness and from darkness to darkness according to their law, to abide, light and full of light, caught in the fulness of this total music of days . . . She was a rock, dayless, furled in a water that she was not doomed to harness. Alone, unlonely, unconcerned, moored in the seethe of an element in which she had no movement and from which therefore she was not doomed to filch the daily mite that would guarantee, in a freighting and darkening of her spirit, the declension of that movement. The days, unopened and unmapped, would not spend her. They would break over in their fulness, uncashed. She would abide unladen and undarkened.

The Polar Bear, having ceased to rest and speak and having eaten his cake, began to fidget. He was getting hot. The great heat that was within this man began to make itself felt. He said he was navré, he must go, he found, looking at his watch, that he really must go, otherwise he would miss his bus and then the family would worry. His blasting ailing sister, moreover, would be clamouring for her haply merdiferous lubricant. It had been a real pleasure to have had this little chat. When would they foregather again?

"Yes" said the Alba "time to go. This evening there is a visitor, I should be back. In the morning there is a priest to deal with and a dress to come into town about, I must get to bed in good time. And then no doubt your precious Belacqua will be round in the afternoon, bursting with simple profundities. Then in the evening I am going on the skite with the Venerilla."

At the end of the street they parted. The Alba boarded a tram and like a Cézanne monster it carried her off, it moaned down Nassau Street into the darkness, little thinking what a royal and fragile tuppenny fare it had in keeping. The poor old P.B. plunged sadly on foot towards the quays. He had not a moment to spare, he had yet to buy the Baby.

Seeing as how we are more or less all set now for Belacqua and the Alba to meet at least, make contact at least and carry along for a time side by side, failing to coalesce, or, better said, dropping for once the old sweet song of failure, just not doing so, either because each in his and her own way was made of sterner stuff than, say, any single bee in d'Alembert's dream of the coagulum of con-

tinuous bees or because they had no particular lust to min-
gle or because the duration of their mere contiguity was on
the short side for the answer to the love tot to be 1 or
because they abode a pair of articles of such a hard, het-
erogeneos and complex constitution that they were a great
deal more likely to break down and come unstuck in two
separate non-synchronised processes each on his and her
side of the fence than sink their differences and pool their
resources in the slush of platitudinous treacle that is wont
to grace these occasions, take your choice and pick your
fancy: seeing as how then, to repeat that beautiful conjunc-
tion, it is now or never the time to sidetrack and couple
those two lone birds and give them at least a chance to
make a hit and bring it off, would it not be idle on our part
to temporise further and hold up the happy event with the
gratuitous echolalia and claptrap rhapsodies that are
palmed off as passion and lyricism and the high spots of the
creative ecstasy, the crises, no less, in our demiurgent
tension after unity of consciousness (as if we bothered our
arse about our pestilential consciousness), and which, as a
matter of fact, are nothing more or less, if any dear reader
would care to come in on a good thing, than padding: the
fall-back and the stand-by, don't you know, of the gentleman scrivener who has no very near or dear or clear ideas
on any subject whatsoever and whose talent is not the
dense talent of the proselytiser and proxenete but the rarer
article in the interests of whose convulsions clouds of words
condense to no particular purpose.

Yet even to such a one, notwithstanding his horror
of the *ficum voco ficum* buckram and swashbuckle, comes
the one clear cry and earnest recommendation to spigot the
faucet and throttle the cock, the cockwash, and cut the
cackle. This tergiversator lends ear in accordance, and with

168

the terrible scowl, with the very worse will in the world, he drags himself across the threshold of the gehenna of narratio recta.

We had no idea ars longa was such a Malebolge.

He galloped round sure enough according to plan to pay his respects and in the most morose of humours. For his native city had got him again, her miasmata already had all but laid him low, the yellow marsh fever that she keeps up her sleeve for her more distinguished sons had clapped its clammy honeymoon hands upon him, his moral temperature had gone sky-rocketing aloft, soon he would shudder and kindle in hourly ague.

All went off more or less as she had predicted. Out of the kindness of her heart, the sympathy that had been lit for him within her, she unleashed her eyes on him, she gave them carte blanche and he bled.

"I read your poem" she said in her soft ruined voice "but you will do better than that. It is clever, too clever, it amused me, it pleased me, it is good, but you will get over all that."

The "too clever" was a cropper and she felt it, without having to refer to his expression, as soon as it was out of her mouth. They were rare with her, these deviations of her instinct, but she was subject to them. Well muffled, however, in the sure phrase, alleviated by the charm of her husky delivery, it damaged her position scarcely at all and would not have jarred on any sensibility less tremulous than that of her interlocutor, shrinking away as it always did, and more of course than ever at this moment, from the least roughness of contact, ready to cry out at the littlest scratch.

"Already" he said, calmly, "I have done better."

The hair-spring of her instinct kept her silent and that silence, together with a new quality in her presence, a silence of body, did work. This was the complicating of conversation of which she had spoken to the Polar Bear in the lounge that evening with the bitter shrug that took its seat so well upon her, that rode her with such grace, we mean that she brought off with an aisance and a naturel that enchanted all beholders apt to apprehend that most tenuous of all the tenuous emanations of real personality, charm. Cæsura.

"Better" he was obliged by her immobility to hedge "is perhaps not quite the word. What I mean, when I say that already I have done better, is, that I have achieved a statement more ample, in so far as it embraces and transcends the poem that you are good enough to remember, and with that more temperate, less mannered, more banal (oh, Alba, a most precious quality, that), nearer to the low-voiced Pushkinian litotes. Better? Other. Me now, not a production of me then. In that sense, and of course that is the sense in which you speak, better."

He turned it off, but she was not quite ready for him.

"There is a shortness of poetic sight" he proceeded wildishly "when the image of the emotion is focussed before the verbal retina; and a longness of same, when it is focussed behind. There is an authentic trend from that shortsightedness to this long-sightedness. Poetry is not concerned with normal vision, when word and image coincide. I have moved from the short-sighted poem of which you spoke to a long-sighted one of which I now speak. Here the word is prolonged by the emotion instead of the emotion being gathered into and closed by the word. There are the

170

two modes, say Marlowe and Chenier, keeping the order, and who shall choose between them? When you say 'he will do better' you may mean: 'he will write a poem of a more perfect short-sightedness', or again you may mean: 'he will express himself more totally in the long-sighted mode'. Already, I repeat, I have expressed myself more totally in the long-sighted mode. I dislike the word better."

There seemed no reason why he should stop, and doubtless he would not, had not her instinct (this time I suppose we might say, her taste) broken the silence and she moved.

"Yes" she said "but don't do yourself an injury trying to circumvent it." Suddenly, flickering out at him like a sting, putting it up to him, the hard word. "And *verbal retina*" she said "I don't get. Can a word have a retina?"

He stiffened his neck against her at once. Observe how their relation already is thickening, soon it will be a monstrous tangle, a slough of granny's-bends.

"I could justify my figure" he said, with a great show of fatigue and altitudino, "if I could be bothered. Words shall put forth for me the organs that I choose. Need I remind you how they relieved themselves under Apollinaire?"

Satisfied that she had goaded him into stiffening himself against her, she moved now on suave words away from the ravaged zone. She wanted to hear all about Liebert who made no sign of life though he owed a letter this long time. Had Belacqua set eyes on the new Madame?

"Platinum" she was bound "they always are."

It was Belacqua's turn to be at a loss. What could she mean?

"No matter" she said "is she or is she not?"

"Not" he was sorry to say "what you might call hell-blond, that lovely shade russet, if you think that would do to translate *rousse*. It's silly of me, I know" he lisped "but I hate to be a snob and use the mot juste."

"Mamon!" she said, letting herself out just at the right moment, "don't be so squeamish, my dear, say it the best way first, the best people will understand. The lady, russet, you say, and with that ravishing, she must be to have got him?"

Got was the second slip so far.

"He was supposed to love me, you know" she hastened, but not too precipitately, to say "so I have what you might call a vested interest in his vicissitudes."

Such long words for such a little girl!

"Good rather than beautiful, I would have said; a good, non-beautiful gal."

"You did know he loved me?"

"He gave me to understand."

"But I could not . . ."

"That also."

"Ah, so he knew?"

"Did you not arrange that he should?"

The Alba reared up her head sharply, she started to her feet, it was very sudden, and declared that since the tea appeared to be undrinkable she would see was there a drop of brandy left in the cupboard. Did he drink brandy in the afternoon, before his dinner?

"Preferably" he was happy to say "in the afternoon, before my dinner."

She brought big tumblers and a dying noggin. She zigzagged in and out through the furniture with little fleet steps, grousing an Irish air:

'Woe and pain, pain and woe,
Are my lot, night and noon . . .'

"She is not heavy enough" the thought came to him watching her flicker from point to point "upon my word she is not heavy enough to hang herself."

They drank.

"Permit me to appreciate" he said "that superb and regal peignoir. It is like a Rimbaud Illumination, barbarous and royal. Cloth of gold, if I have an eye left in my head. Most insidiously flagrant and flamboyant, yes. You could say 'sortez!' with Roxane."

"But since there are no mutes at my beck . . ." She spoke from a real sorrow. "Beyond the door, a loudspeaker, it only wounds; beyond that again a melancholy gardener, watering the dying flowers; then you are in the street and free."

"Free?"

"Of the seraglio." She folded up her legs and looked at him with her mouth. "Didn't you know?"

Belacqua began to feel ill at ease. He fidgeted on his seat.

"Don't tell me" exclaimed the Alba "the child has piles!"

Then, he remaining remote and blank, she thought she could safely let it come, she felt it would be all right, the fiery question that had been threatening this long time back, itching in her ears.

"What is love?"

Belacqua withdrew his little finger sadly from his nostril and shanghaied his catch on the chair-arm.

"A great Devil" he said.

"No. A little devil, an imp."

"A great Devil, a fiend."

"He is young" she sighed "but that will pass."

"I am" he admitted sadly "a juvenile man, scarcely pubic. But I will not agree that love is an imp when I am of

the opinion that love is a fiend. That would be fake blasé.
And fake blasé" here his voice rang, it was suddenly proud,
"is a vulgarity that I cannot tolerate and to which I decline
to bend."

He sat bolt upright, declining to bend, red in the face.

"Sans blahague !" she mocked grockly, she would be
sorry for this, "ce qu'il est sentimentique !"

The Homer dusk, mutatis mutandis, lapsed, as
through the deeps of ocean a drowned body lapses. They
kept their seats, they delved into the subject, they treated
it coldly and carefully. She got his measure, he was not
altogether unworthy. The aged gardener, brooding over
the fragility of all life, moved vaguely in the little garden,
assailing, he did not want to, he would have much preferred not, but he was forced to, his rose had been taken
and hidden, with hard jets of water the vanquished flowers. The trams moaned up and down across the maw of the
avenue, and passed. In the house not a mouse was stirring.
It was the magic hour, the magic tragic prépuscule, alluded
to and torn to tatters passim above, when the poets come
abroad on the lamplighters' spoors, when Nemo is in position, when Night has its nasty difficult birth all over the
sheets of dusk, and the dark eyes of the beautiful darken
also. This was the case now with the Alba, furled in her
coils upon the settee, the small broad pale face spotted in
a little light escaped from the throttled west. Her great
eyes went as black as sloes, they went as big and black as
El Greco painted, with a couple of good wet slaps from his
laden brush, in the Burial of the Count of Orgaz the de-
bauched eyes of his son or was it his mistress? It was a
remarkable thing to see. Pupil and white swamped in the
dark iris gone black as night. Then lo! she is at the window,
she is taking stock of her cage. Now under the threat of

174

night the evening is albescent, its hues have blanched, it is
dim white and palpable, it pillows and mutes her head. So
that as from transparent polished glass or, if you prefer,
from tranquil shining waters, the details of his face return
so feeble that a pearl on a white brow comes not less
promptly to his pupils, so now he sees her vigilant face and
in him is reversed the error that lit love between the man
(if you can call such a spineless creature a man) and the
pool. For she had closed the eyes.

"Spirit of the moon" he said.

She begged his pardon.

He said it again.

"There is one poem by the Ronsard" she said, moving
back gaily towards him into captivity, "entitled: *Magic, or,
Deliverance from Love*. If you are familiar with it we could
give earth to this conversation there."

"A great poem" he gushed "a great poem. But why do
you say *the* Ronsard?"

She had just felt like it, she had felt she would like to.

"He was a comic old lecher" she said. Her jaw dropped
in a way that made him a little anxious. "So we are of one
mind" she said "think of that!"

After that he had no excuse for prolonging his visit.
He had paid his respects. Perhaps even he had got copy for
his wombtomb.

In the vestibule, the safe side of the Radio, he hoped
that he had not fatigued her. No, that was not possible. At
the garden gate he told her a storiette.

"You know what the rose said to the rose?"

No, she did not seem to have heard that one.

" 'No gardener has died within the memory of roses.' "

"Very neat" she said "very graceful. Adios."

She stood watching him waddle through the gloaming.

175

There is a class of lady that stands at the gate (though more usually in her porch) witnessing the recession of her visitor. His posteriors, she thought, are on the big side for his boots . . . Otherwise . . . She turned to go in, she strutted in a slow swagger prisonwards down the garden path, she flaunted the glittering peignoir for the envy of Mrs ---, her neighbour, her enemy.

They do much time side by side, azure skies come and go, the waters go. And they go from intimacy to intimacy, that is to say, about them rises the marsh of granny's-bends that is their relation.

Bear in mind, we are particularly anxious that you should, how his want to go—no matter where, anywhere, anywhere bar Moscow and England, increases with the climbing frequency of the place-ague. She too has said she wants to go. She must be off, she says. That is true, but frivolous also. She does not seriously want to move, she is past that. Still, she clasps and unclasps her hands, she does and undoes them, her hands that are just right, on the large side for her body as his posteriors for his boots, and says that carajo! but she must go, must get away, that she will go out of her mind. But she works herself up to it, she drinks and starves and smokes and dopes herself into a regular how-dee-do, she plunges into town to buy a ticket and drags home in the tram with a fish or a bag of buttered eggs. She is not serious, she does not seriously want to stir, not in her most buried forum. Her inner spectator, the good and faithful witness, yawns the usual, turns over on her other haunch, and the Alba lets it go at that. Still, great mangling and laundrying of hands goes on between the pair of them, even suicide is dragged in by the cork of the bottle, its pros and cons piously sifted. He comes out in hard and full pulses all over his public parts and in spasms of subsultus bungles a petit mal ult. horis. But she, does not really care about moving (must we drum that drum for ever?), she puts not her trust in changes of scenery, she is too inward by a long chalk, she inclines towards an absolute moral geography, her soul is her only poste restante. Whereas he does care, he prays fervently to be set free in a general way, he is such a very juvenile man. But he will get over all that. Hence, she shall not go. She can talk and talk and take trams into Cook's, but she shall not go. She can talk and talk and suddenly crucify her hands, saying: Shall I be mewed up, shall I, like a falcon, all the days of my life, shall I, in this stenching city?, she shall not go. He shall go. Wait till you see. He would be gone long ago but for the morass of nerve-squitch and beauty and that most tenuous of all the tenuous etc., where bogged beside the royal Alba he wallows caught in the reeds of their relation.

He has not lain with her. Nor she with him. None of that kind of thing here, if you don't mind.

What we are doing now, of course, is setting up the world for a proper swell slap-up explosion. The bang is better than the whimper. It is easier to do. It is timed for about ten or fifteen thousand words hence. We shall blow him out of the muck that way.

And the family? And Chas? And the P.B., the poor old P.B? To say nothing of the boys and girls he left behind him, *and whom soon he runs the risk of rejoining.* Are they then to be let slide? Are they, squeezed dry, to be cast aside into the gutter, the tragic gutter of not being referred to any more in this book? You fondly ask. Because we (concensus of me) we have not the slightest idea where they come in or if they come in at all. Beyond a few neb-

177

ulous directions we have no plans, but none at all, for the late Fall and Winter. We hope to keep our hands off all families, because they tend to make us magdalen. And Chas? We find that the body of our feeling corresponds with that enunciated by the Polar Bear, to wit, that Chas is inclined to be rather a bore and a crab-louse. We can always fire him into the aching boosom of his Shetland Shawly if at any moment we find ourself short of copy or at all uncertain as to how to proceed. In what concerns the Polar Bear, we confess ourself totally at a loss. He may loom large yet, he may have to be called on to do the best he can as an out-at-elbow down-at-heel gone-in-the-legs Colossus. But it is not possible to make any statement. How much more pleasant it would be for all parties all round, he is such a nice fellow, were it but feasible to arrange for him to be left in peace. He merits peace. *Per viam pacis ad patriam perpetuæ claritatis*—that is the fond hope and the vow, may it gleam through the horrid latin and light him, that we make, both now and ever, for the poor old P.B. We cannot do fairer than that. We would not ask better for ourself. By paths of peace to the land of everlasting clearness . . ! Can you beat it?

Clearness standing here of course for us for the *obscure clarté* that already more than once has been flogged to within one candle-power of its life, way back in the wilds of this old maid.

Now once more and for the last time we are obliged to hark back to the liu business, a dreadful business, feeling heartily sorry that we ever fell into the temptation of putting up that owld Tale of a Tub concerning Christopher Lîng-Liûn and his bamboo Yankee doodle. Our excuse must be that we were once upon a time inclined to fancy ourself as the Cézanne, shall we say, of the printed page,

178

very strong on architectonics. We live and learn, we draw breath from our heels now, like a pure man, and we honour our Father, our Mother, and Goethe.

The observation we feel we simply must place now, this very moment, preparatory to saying no more at all about it, is: that just as we feared the Alba and Co. have turned out to be as miserable a lot of croakers as Belacqua at his best and hoarsest and the entire continental circus. Such a collection of Kakiamouni wops, scorching away from their centres, no syndicate of authors, it is our stiff conviction, ever had the misfortune to have to do with. What would Leibnitz say?

Still and all we love 'em one and all, we can't be cross with 'em long, they are such charming and engaging creatures after all when all is said and done, *when* it is. Their very artlessness puts wrath to flight quite. How could anyone be angry with 'em for any length of time? They have such winning little ways. It is utterly out of the question. Even the Syra-Cusa, though we think she might have sent him at least *one* of her eyes in a dish. Even Chas, that bit of a nit. Pets one and all.

Now a most terrible and unexpected thing happens. Into the quiet pages of our cadenza bursts a nightmare harpy, Miss Dublin, a hell-cat. In she lands singing Havelock Ellis in a deep voice, itching manifestly to work that which is not seemly. If only she could be bound and beaten and burnt, but not quick. Or, failing that, brayed gently in a mortar. Open upon her concave breast as on a lectern lies Portigliotti's *Penumbre Claustrali* bound in tawed caul. In her talons earnestly she clutches Sade's *Hundred Days* and the *Anterotica* of Aliosha G. Brignole-Sale, unopened, bound in shagreened caul. A septic pudding hoodwinks her, a stodgy turban of pain it laps her horse-face. The eye-hole is clogged with the bulbus and the round pale globe goggles exposed. Solitary meditation has furnished her with nostrils of generous bore. The mouth champs an invisible bit, foam gathers at the bitter commissures. The crateriform brisket, lipped with sills of paunch, cowers ironically behind a maternity tunic. Keyholes have wrung the unfriendly withers, the osseous rump screams beneath the hobble-skirt. Wastes of woad worsted are gartered to the pasterns. Aïe!

What shall we call it? Give it a name quick. Lilly, Jane or Caleken Frica? Or just plain Mary? Suppose we make it Caleken to please the theologasters and Frica to please ourself, and of course whatever comes in handy for short.

The Frica had a mother, and thereby was partially explained: a bald caterwauling bedlam of a ma with more toes than teeth. As a young mare she had curvetted smartly, lifting the knees chin-high, and had enjoyed a certain measure of success in certain quarters. And if the dam trot, as the saying runs and we all know to our cost, shall the foal then amble? She shall not. Nor did. For did she not caper caparisoned in those nightmare housings and in her absinthe whinny notify Belacqua that her darling ma bade him to a party with back-stairs, claret-cup and the intelligentsia. Belacqua uncovered cautiously his face.

"I couldn't" he said "I could not."

Now she was springing the garters. What did she want? That was what he could not understand.

"I do wish" said Belacqua "that you would take a tip from Madame your noble mother and wear a respectable perforated rubber suspender-belt in place of those houghbands. Please do not flick them at me like that."

"But I must" she snuffled, setting the eyes in motion, "don't you see, Bel, that I simply must?"

"No!" cried Belacqua "shall I be gehennate in my own chamber by a Blue-stocking?"

"Oh Bel" she whinnied "do you really and truly mean to say you think I am?"

Under the anger of the moon, Rubens embolus, Belacqua let fall his poor head.

"If now" he found it in his fading breath to implore "you would please to go and say to Madame your mother that Belacqua regrets he is unable . . ."

Belacqua regrets he is unable . . . That makes, he reflected, casting it up in great anguish of spirit, toads and vipers, three more of each, in their torture chamber. Without warning she loosed a high sexual neigh:

"Chas is coming! Chas and the Polar Bear are coming!"

Belacqua roared with laughter. Wot a sop!

"Chas!" he coughed "Chas! Chas! But that is what Chasses are there for!"

"The Alba" she bugled.

But he waxed stiff, he heard no more that day. Suddenly there was no clot of moon there, no moon of any kind or description. It was the miracle, our old friend that whale of a miracle, taking him down from his pangs, sheathing him in the cerements of clarity. It was the descent and the enwombing, assumption upside down, tête-bêche, into the greyness, the dim press of disaffected angels. It was at last the hush and indolence of Limbo in his mind proddied and chivvied into taking thought, lounging against the willpricks. It was the mercy of salve on the prurigo of living, dousing the cock-robin of living. In a word in fact he was suddenly up to the eyes in his dear slush.

Plane of white music, warpless music expunging the tempest of emblems, calm womb of dawn whelping no sun, no lichen of sun-rising on its candid parapets, still flat white music, alb of timeless light. It is a blade before me, it is a sail of bleached silk on a shore, impassive statement of itself drawn across the strata and symbols, lamina of peace for my eyes and my brain slave of my eyes, pressing and pouring itself whiteness and music through blindness into the limp mind. It is the dawn-foil and the gift of blindness and the mysteries of bulk banished and the mind swathed in the music and candour of the dawn-foil, facts of surface. The layers of Damask fused and drawn to the uttermost layer, silken blade. Blind and my mind blade of silk, blind and music and whiteness facts in the fact of my mind. Douceurs . . .

It was shortly after this terrifying experience that the Twilight Herald inserted in its horrid latin a succinct paragraph to the effect that:

"C.J. Nicholas Nemo saltabat sobrius and in amore sapebat and had in consequence in the prepuscular gloom of Good Friday's or was it Lady Day's autumnal octave been withdrawn more dead than alive from under the stairs of the Salmon Leap at Leixlip by Adam of St Victor that most notorious poacher who on being interrogated turned a little yellow as well he might and was understood to depose that Ireland was a Paradise for women and a Hell for hosses and that he had no doubt at all in his own mind that the Lord would have mercy on whom he would have mercy.

The Cast-iron Virgin of Nürnberg having most furiously

been administered personally by the pitiless News Editor, Adam of St Victor, of no fixed address or occupation, was coaxed into the following addendum: how that the poor young gentleman, before coughing up and commending in a vague general way his spirit in the well of the jaunting-car that was bearing them post-haste to the Stillorgan Sunshine Home or was it the Lucan Spa Hotel, had embraced him with a wild Spanish light in his duskèd eyes, how that he had called upon him (Adam of St Victor) weakly as the Bride of his Soul, how that he had harnessed his latest breath, positively its last audition, to one of those smart nut-shell turn-outs that it had not been his (Adam of St Victor's) good fortune to clap ears to since the dear partner of his porridge days (God rest her) had turned to Him with a pain in her chest and furled her skirts from the Sirens' Isle and cast all over and moored in the millpond of curds that was Abraham's boosom, viz: *te præsente nil impurum.*

A rod was plunged forthwith in pickle and with the first weals of dawn the miscreant's filthy trousers were plucked down and a positively superlative verberation inflicted by the Art Editor in the presence of his swooning staff of camera-mattoids, shots of which vicious mortification will shortly be copiously promulgated.

A finding of Felo-de-se from Natural Causes was found.

Et voici le temps qu'il fera demain . . ."

Belacqua took cognisance of this corpulent reportage on his way home from the Fox and Geese over cheese and porter in the tabernacle of a wayfarers' public near the Island Bridge that has since been destroyed and consumed utterly by brimstone the bishops all say.

Intolerably moved almost immediately he sinks

down there and then in the sand and plumjuice on his hands and knees and with a good prayer truncates copiously the purgatorial villeggiatura. (We flatter ourself that from spits to plumjuice via sputa is a nice little bit of formal purification.) For from what he knew of Nemo, having now for some little time past conferred almost daily with that soured citizen and even more frequently of late in the intermittences of ague consulted him, no doubt could subsist in his mind that the late man, far from having done away with himself, had but by misadventure fallen in. In the life of such a gauche and burly body, habitually stooped over, and absorbed in the contemplation of, water, such a mishap, the loss of balance and then the splash and despairing cry, was bound sooner or later to supervene. And, no doubt, the sooner the better. But that he had despaired of God's mercy to the point of consigning himself, irremissible fortes peccatorum, to the pretty reaches developed by the Liffey at the locus delicti was altogether on the sandy side for a working hypothesis. The most valued possession of this man, indeed a most precious margarita, possibly his unique possession, certainly the only one in which he had ever been surprised into evincing the least proprietary interest, was a superb aboulia of the very first water. And where is the felo-de-se thus wonderfully gelt of will? Bah! He fell in and could not get out. Or he fell in and could not be bothered getting out. But he *fell in*. Ergo it was death by drowning by misadventure. The official finding was very fine. But it was erroneous.

The meditation thus concluded was as rapid as a zebra's thought, as thoughts of love, as peninstantaneous as the snap of the shutter for a snapshot. (The multiplication of figure to detriment of style is forced upon us by our most earnest desire to give satisfaction to all customers. We trust

184

we give satisfaction.) And when Belacqua, on a ringing
Amen in the male soprano register, extracted himself painfully from the spit-pitted arena of sawdust or sand or whatever we said it was, he felt himself heavenly enflamed as
the Cherubim and Seraphim for all the world as though his
mouth had been tapping the bung of the heavenly pipe of
the fountain of sweetness instead of just coming from clipping the rim of a pint pot of half-and-half. For about two
minutes he floated about the snug as Gottesfreund and
disembodied as you please. This sudden strange sensation
was of a piece with the ancient volatilisation of his first
communion, long forgot and never brought to mind in all
the long years that had run out with him since and rolled
over that delicious event. Alas! it was a short knock and
went as it had come, like that, it vacated him like that,
leaving him bereft and in his breast a void place and a
spacious nothing.

Years later, when in the course of a stroll in the
Prater (yes, it was in the Prater, we were strolling in the
Prater, we were strolling to the horse-races) he furnished
us with the details of this visitation, he affirmed that never
on any previous or subsequent occasion did he suffer such
a hateful sensation of emptiness, of being integrally turned
out.

On this emotion recollected in the tranquillity of
those celebrated bowers he scaffolded a theory of the mystical experience as being geared, that was his participle, to
the vision of an hypostatical clysterpipe, the apex of ecstasy
being furnished by the peroration of administration and of
course the Dark Night of the Soul (and here we were scandalised by slight consonantal adjustments) and the Great
Dereliction coinciding with the period of post-evacuative
depression. When we protested that we did not think this

would hold water he replied angrily that it was not meant to hold water.

Strictly speaking this Belacqua of later days stands outside the enceinte of our romaunt. The blame of this sally we lay therefore, since it is always a question here below of laying blame somewhere, on a phrase that he let fall on the way back to the city after a disastrous day on the course, a phrase that we propose now to the reader as a red-letter term in the statement of Belacqua and a notable arc of his botched circumscription .

"Behold, Mr Beckett" he said, whitely, "a dud mystic."

He meant mystique raté, but shrank always from the mot juste.

Guardedly, reservedly, we beheld him. He was hatless, he whistled a scrap of an Irish air, his port and mien were jaunty resignation.

"John" he said "of the Crossroads, Mr Beckett. A borderman."

And to be sure he did at that moment suggest something of the ascetic about town. But from that, from the live-and-let-live anchorite on leave, to *dud mystic* was a longer call than we cared immediately to undertake.

"Give me chastity" he mentioned "and continence, only not yet."

Nevertheless in the twilight, in the evening, in the black and dark night, after music, with the wine of music, Rhine wine, it was given to us to cotton on, to behold him as he was, face to face, even as he sometimes contrived to behold himself.

Thus through Nemo came Belacqua to a little knowledge of himself and we (though too late for insertion) to a little knowledge of Belacqua, and by the end of Nemo were forewarned.

186

*   *   *

Now we are anew in the muck, two channels and 29 hours if we went over Ostend from the pleasant Prater. Nor merely in the muck, but in that particular annex of the muck reserved for our two young people, their muck, the Holy of Holies, so to speak, of the muck, the slough where in the reeds and rushes of their relation the Alba and Belacqua loll. Ark and mercy-seat have sunk, the Shekinah has fizzled out, the Cherubim are drowning.

Side by side, touching, they recline in the shadow of a great rock, chosen by him for the shadow it gave, on the Silver Strand. She has rummaged in her fathomless bag, she has taken out from it scissors and file, she is beautifying his fingers, hurting him slightly in her determination to leave not one lunula undiscovered, pleasantly aware that she is causing him a little pain, grousing *Avalon* this time, the refrain over and over again, swallowing from time to time little flaws of saliva, born of her absorption. They are entrenched behind a low palissade of bottles driven into the pale sand. Beyond the palissade two gulls skirmishing for a sandwich fascinate the wincing lover.

"Look at the birds" he cried "just look at them."

"Yes" said the Alba.

"Like man and wife."

They flew away together far out over the sea, leaving the sandwich mutilated on the shore. Then in the lofty slips they wheeled and hovered, like eyelids over grit they trembled, and starting fair, getting away to a good start, came flying down to the goal of bread. The next thing was that the bread was between them, it was at the centre of the line joining them. Stiffly then on their tender bare feet, polarised across the bread, they stepped the diameter round, they screwed themselves round the sandwich of contention. It was a game, a love-game. They were not hungry, they were man and wife.

Alas cang of emblem . . .

"Now" she said "the other."

The way people go on *saying* things . . ! Who shall silence them, at last?

Let it be said now without further ado, they were just pleasantly drunk. That is, we think, being more, becoming and unbecoming less, than usual. Not so far gone as to be rapt in that disgraceful apotheosis of immediacy from which yesterday and to-morrow are banished and the off dawn into the mire of coma taken; and yet at the same time less buttoned up in their cohesion, more Seventh Symphony and contrapanic-stuck, than usual. Not, needless to say, melting in that shameless ecstasy of disintegration justly quenched in the mire and pain of reassemblage; no, it was not the glory of coming asunder in an apotheosis of immediacy, it was merely an innocent and agreeable awareness of being and that less clocklaboriously than was their habit. Pleasantly drunk.

As near as no matter it was a year ago now that he had been inland in another land with another girl, a bigger, less bountiful one, in fact not in the same class at all, the Smeraldina (whom now of course, too late in the day, we wish we had called, say, Hesper) to be sure, that lady dog for ever proud. Inland with the withered leaves, and very handsome they were too in their own way, spurned by the agile sandals of the Evites or drowning slowly in the canals that watered to no other purpose that arch-dukes' disaffected plaisaunce, or simply pulped gently into mould by the punctual equinox.

This, not the Springtime, was the season for the labours of love. And that, we feel, is a proposition holding specially good for the very last days of Autumn, Limbo, to drag in that old veteran once again of Winter. And Venice, where the waters wither and rot and pomegranates bleed their sperm and Dickens is forgotten, is nonpareil for that class of thing. The very place. Made for it.

Not that the Silver Strand—looking back through our notes we are aghast to find that it was Jack's Hole; but we cannot use that, that would be quite out of place in what threatens to come down a love passage—not that it were (mood of Fall indispensable) by any manner of means definitely hostile as atmosphere and scape to the Olympian romance that may break over it now at any moment. For *oui, les premiers baisers, oui, les premiers serments* it was as nice a site as any in the country. The rock was there, crumbling beyond a shadow of doubt, into dust; the wind was on the job, exfoliating the wrack; the inconstance of the sky was incontestable. And, over and above all these conditions, the fickle sea and sand. Lying there to a casual eye so calm between its headlands this little beach, without being the Bride of the Adriatic or anything of that kind and in spite of its leaving a few trees to be desired, furnished as neat a natural comment on the ephemeral sophism as any to be had in the Free State. Which is saying the hell of a lot.

With a calmness that excluded interpretations she gave him back his hand, she put it definitely away from her, she had done with it. She wiped her instruments on her sleeve and put them away.

"Your hands" she said, not having seen his feet in the nude, "are a disgrace."

"Ah" said Belacqua. Belacqua opened his mouth and

said "ah" when he felt nothing, or when words could not convey what he felt.

"Your hands" she said "are not bad. A little attention would improve them."

A little attention. He looked at them and saw that they were all bumps.

"They are all lumps and bumbs" he gave voice to this simple sentiment, "there is nothing to be done."

"No" said the Alba "they have their quality. But the nails . . ."

"Ah" he said "the nails."

"My child" she said "you have the nails of a body-snatcher."

He gave his preoccupation with his nose as a possible explanation.

"Yes. And you bite them and polish your glasses."

"Please" he threw himself on her mercy "please do not apply anyone to me, do not apply any system at me."

"Without systematised interpretations" she replied "I can suppose you nervous I suppose when I see you clawing your face without ceasing."

He was only too willing to admit that he was nervous, just nervous, technically so. He extended his hand in corroboration.

"It trembles" he said "like an aspen. Look. I have a genuine tremor. Look."

"Smoke less" she said "drink less, brood less."

"Brood?" He was shocked to hear it called that.

"You brood" she said "like a sick hen."

And herself, he would have the courteous impertinence to be interested to know en passant, before effecting a breach into a subject . . .

"Oh, me" in the comfortable tone of one delivered from hope *"my soul has no use for an anchor."*

. . . a subject that happened for once to be rather near and dear to him. He stormed it, he battered in.

"I do no brood" he said resentfully. "My mind goes blank. It is no brooding, it is no reflecting. It is the abdication of the daily mind, it is hush and gloom ousting the workaday glare . . ."

He let her have the whole saga, it came gushing out like the Bhagavad-Gîtâ of a co-operative Cincinnatus. Sewerly the Alba was too intelligent to associate silence, a somatic silence and accidental tension of countenance, with the sulks or sorrows of the mind pouting over a grievance, poring over its stock of woe. Sewerly . . .

"Like a sick hen." The Alba stuck quite rightly to at least one of her barrels. He could talk and talk. He would not invalidate her thesis. The pith of her thesis, simile included, would stand.

But the important thing was that he again in his youth had stiffened against her. Scraps of German played in his mind in the silence that ensued; grand, old, plastic words. As for her, she adjusted herself for her greater comfort of body, she was a sensible girl, and quietly delivered herself up to the place and the hour, pleased, not that she had had the last word, that was not her genre, that was too easy, but that she had pricked him into elucidating, i.e. defending, a position.

It was strange how this expression of themselves at odds, the surface ruffled, if they had known (she may have), of the profound antagonism latent in the neutral space that between victims of real needs is as irreducible as the zone of evaporation between damp and incandescence (We stole that one. Guess where.), a wedge of Ophir if they only knew it between them, prising them apart, the key of the relation that cannot do more than couple them, set them side by side, if they are of any consequence: it was strange how the bubbles of this essential incompatibility seemed always to introduce a passage of something like real intimacy. No, not strange, simply so. It is possible that she, knowing what those bubbles betrayed, thanks to the abundant legacy of her failures to annul in real encounter the bed from which they rose and to the fine filter of her great désœuvrement, provoked them. What wisdom she had acquired, from which she had distilled a *savoir ne pas faire* that was seldom abashed, she had, in common with her consœurs, acquired empirically. It was of merely human scope. It was valid only up to a point. This also, instinctively, she seemed to know. This core of awareness, a greater treasure than any extract of experience, set her apart, separated her from the few women he had met and the few more he was ever likely to meet. *Savoir ne pas faire* was a jewel of great price in man or woman: the delicacy, on the spiritual plane, that has a sense of distance, and does not lose smell of the fact that what is breath of balm for one may very well be halitosis for another. But the further inner awareness, the recognition of a plane on which noses had something better to do than be turned up, and surety of abstention, free nilling, was of as little use as elegant participation, and was from the uttermost coasts, as rare as heavenly bodies colliding. Do we exaggerate her credit? But she had said: *my soul has no use for an anchor.* She had said that.

He wondered could she lend him a book on hens.

"There is a long poem" he said "waiting to be written about hens and eggs. There is a great subject there, waiting to be written."

The Alba thought that having waited so long . . .
"They have fleas" she said "I can't relish them."
Christ, she thought, he is a literary man.

One more brief evisceration (or, perhaps better, decortication) of the Alba, and thenceforward we keep our hands off her, we let her speak for herself, we state her dearworthy cuticle and hair if we state her at all, and leave it at that.

She could just manage to appreciate Belacqua's stand-offishness, his shrinking away from contact with the frail dust of her body. She could even contrive on occasions to be flattered that she for him remained a climate that did not comfort and a dream that did not serve. Had he not made it clear that he did not propose to Blake her, did not propose to Hieronymus Bosch her? She was to remain quite useless and beautiful, like the very best music that could be had.

"You are white music" he had given her indirectly to understand, he seemed to say something of this kind, "shall I plaster you with cuckoos and tempests?"

Her mind was flexible enough to wheedle a few drops of pleasure from the ineffable reverberations of this attitude. A rather despairing pleasure, for she was full of lassitude and pain, her soul had no use for an anchor. She played up to him when she felt like it, the way one tip of a tweezers plays up to its vis-à-vis. She mirrored his oscillations when she felt like it. When he sheered off, she on her side sheered off. When he bent a little towards her she activated the rather despairing, full that she was of lassitude and pain, sympathy that would bend her a little towards him. Is not that abominably clear?

But: it would not do. It could not go on. She was beyond the puerile graciousness of such a relation. She had got over the salt-marsh phase, the pretty-pretty noli-me-tangere love-wound phase, while she was yet a child, before she put up her hair or sheared it off or did with it whatever was done when she was ceasing to be a child. All this pallor and umbilicism à deux might be the very thing for a certain class of gémisseur, it might be the very thing for him, permanent and pertinent and all the rest of it for him. But it was fundamentally all my eye for her. It might, like a new game, entertain her for a time, but it would never be anything more than light entertainment, a piece of mildly amusing, and, for a soul whose drifting was not distress, on the contrary, rather tragic codology. She used to say affectionately that he would get over this and that, she bestowed "niño!"'s and "mamon"'s on him when she felt like it, but her real opinion the whole time was that there was little hope for him, that he was too irremissibly naive for her altogether, too permanently selfish, faithful to himself, trying to be like himself as he fancied himself all the time, an irretrievable stickler for his own wretched standard, and wretched was what she thought, and wretched was what she meant. He lay coiled up in the shadow, always the shadow, of the dread of leze-personality, at his own hands or another's. Personality! That old bugbear bastard of hell! She thought that he would not get over it, that he did not want to get over it, that he thought of getting over it as the sin against the Belacqua third person. And that he thought of her, at times, as being, in spite of her satisfactory mirror and tweezer work up to date, if anything rather too willing to give him a leg over it. When she would make up her mind finally that all that was so, that he was inextricably Limbese, then that was where she stepped off. He could rot away in his darling gloom if that was what he wanted, she would not be there to listen. *Nolle consolari*

ab aliqua creatura . . . ! The filthy blague! To hell with
purity, fake purity, to hell with it and to hell with it.

How far she was right and how far wrong belong to
another story, a far far better one.

The distinction between her impatience with this
heir of a penny heaven and the Smeraldina-Rima's purely
technical chagrin is too plain to require comment.

Now we really must be getting on.

Followed upon her strangulation of the hen motiv
an immense nebulous conversation obiter that only our
fever to have done refrains us from recording in its en-
tirety, we nearly made the grave blunder of saying in toto,
so witty and revelative was it in parts: all in overtones and
a fairly good standard of obscenity. They enjoyed themselves very much. When he forgot himself so far as to utter
she found him less of a crab. Uttering here to be opposed
advantageously to the ghastly incontinence of his interior
poliloquy, hors d'œuvre of colostrum never to be suivis,
and not worthy to amuse an infant in arms. But when he
forgot himself he could hold his own with the best in the
bandying of gross and subtle futilities, and that was what
she liked best, since it was a question here below of talking
most of the time.

So engrossed were they in this agreeable banter
that the hours slipped by unbeknown to them and the
shore grew cold and dark. When he (for she, like a woman
of Spain, would have been quite happy to sit on till the
cows of the dawn) was astonished to see how the day declining had stolen a retreat on them:

"Before we rise to go" he said, pompously, "for go, willy-
nilly, now we must, and call this happy afternoon off for
ever, may I enquire do you know a . . . a girl called Frica?"

"Both mare and filly" said the Alba, organising herself

sullenly for departure, "for my sins. You're in a great hurry."

"But it will be black night" he exclaimed "before we know where we are."

"And then?" said the Alba. "Are we birds?"

"The Frica . . ." he hesitated to predicate the Frica.

"Offered herself" suggested the Alba.

"Oh" he said "in holocaust to heaven, that daily, like a P.R.B. belch. Not to me."

"Well then?"

"She asked me to a party . . ."

"Well?"

"She said she asked you."

The Alba, clearly, did not know what he was talking about.

"Needless to say" needlessly he said "I wouldn't be seen there."

My God, she thought, you most likely would not.

She was genuinely at a loss. She beseeched him to let her know in as few words as possible what all this had to do with the tide coming in, to get it off his chest and pull her quick out of the sand seeing that they had, apparently, to go.

"Your going" he bent towards her a little "would put a different complexion on the proposition."

Hah! Now he was beginning to talk!

"Hah!" she clapped her hands like a child "hah! the great greedy wild free human heart of him!"

This transfixed Belacqua.

"You extraordinary girl!" he exclaimed. "What's that?" The great, greedy.

She pointed out that if he had already regretted to be

unable he could not suddenly turn round now and discover great pleasure in accepting.

"I swooned" he explained "into my reserve of slush, leaving the door open."

She exhorted him to slam it rudely at once.

"Ah."

"I want to go and be the belle of the ball. And how can I be that with you there mourning your mace in your little black corner?" Let him make what he chose of that.

"The belle of the ball?"

"Of the ball" she said "and of the party. What else?"

"The idea" said Belacqua, not one whit abashed by the cruel gird she had just administered, "I had in the back of my mind in asking was that if you were there we might crowd into a little private shade together beside the basin of cup. They have announced cup. So far" he said bitterly "as far as I am concerned, they have announced cup and you."

She was white and still and Hermioned all of a sudden. Now she would make a definite statement.

"I hate Omar" she said "and your fake penumbra. Haven't we had enough of that in this festering country. Haven't we had enough Deirdreeing of Hobson's weirds and Kawthleens in the gloaming hissing up petticoats of sororarrhœa? Haven't we had enough withered pontiffs of chiarinoscurissimo. 'The mist' " she sneered " 'an' it rollin' home UP the glen and the mist agin an' it rollin' home DOWN the glen.' Up, down, hans arown . . . Merde. Give me noon. Give me Racine."

"Help yourself" he said, mollifying her with a betrayal of annoyance, "but Racine is all twilight."

"All brightness" she said.

"Well anyhow" for it was too late to go into that "I can take it you'll be there."

"You can take it from me" she said "that I'll be there in my scarletest robe."

Here ends the Silver Strand episode, unless it be worth while to add: one, that the wooing engaged there that afternoon with such good auguries, though it broke in no love storm after all, was pursued apace, its main features as they have appeared developed, but not there, elsewhere, in the city vaguely, here and there, far into the night and the following morning, neither party having previous engagement; and, two, that brusquely as, turning their backs on the sea that we let off the epithet just this once, they made to leave the place, and he, taking her gingerly by the arm, urging her unhangable person up the bank of shelving sand that clove the foreshore from the shingle, a phrase to the effect that life taken in the gross, as seemingly it ought to be taken, is but an Irish Sea, floated up in his desolate mind, and on its heels the banal nostalgia for the hour empowering him to rise from siesta on its shore, for none would dispute that his being was in the marge, he had chosen the marginal part, as now at the threat of nightfall he had risen.

We thought it might be wiser to mention that, one and two, before bringing down the curtain on this episode.

Next: two little haply elephantine dreams in brackets for jolly youngsters. Alba speaking.

1. *Mild Form.*

I was all set in a long white silk gown that became me to marry a man in a bowler whom I had never seen and did not want to, for somehow he was not worth seeing. Suddenly I thought: My God, I can't be married in white, off with this bloody thing. Then I saw that it was not white silk, but rather écru. Still I thought: can't possibly be married in this bloody thing. So I tore it off in handfuls, I ripped it away in tufts, it seemed to be coming *up* rather than *off*, from my hips, breasts and shoulders. Grandmother was there and I regretted having to destroy the gown.

2. *Mild Form.*

My father must have been a butcher. I was coming home from some dance or ball or other, because I wore a superb evening gown that became me and satin shoes. I crossed the road and went into the house. It was a big bare room, in a lather of blood. Afraid of staining the gown I caught it up, like Nicolette in the dew, and tiptoed over to the foot of the stair. I was surprised how easily and gracefully I was able to avoid the red puddles. Upstairs just a bare skivvy's cell: wash-hand stand, dresser, stretcher, cracked mirror. Suddenly it seemed that everything, I, my body, my clothes, the party, the whole content of the evening, was a result of the blood I had come through on my way up.

At last the plot looks as if it might begin to thicken, the storm-clouds to gather. The season of festivity and goodwill is upon them. Shopping is in full swing, the streets are thronged with revellers, the Corporation has offered a substantial reward for the best window-dressing, Hyam's trousers are down yet again.

Mistinguett, were she an Empress Wu, would abolish chalets of necessity. She does not think they are necessary. Not so Belacqua. Emerging happy body from the hot bowels of McLouglin's it struck him again how just exactly right was Tom Moore's bull neck, not a whit too short, as most critics maintained. Bright and cheery above the strom of the College Green, as though coached by the Star of Bethlehem, the Bovril sign danced and danced through its seven phases.

The lemon of faith jaundiced, annunciating the series, was in a fungus of hopeless green reduced to shingles and abolished. Next, in reverence for the slain, the light went out. A sly ooze of gules, carmine of solicitation, lifting the skirts of green that the prophesy might be fulfilled, shocking Gabriel into cherry, annexed the sign. But the long skirts rattled down, darkness covered their shame, and the cycle was at an end. Da capo.

Bovril into Salome, thought Belacqua, and Tommy Moore there with his head on his shoulders. Doubt, Despair and Scrounging, shall I hitch my bathchair to the greatest of these? Across the way, under the arcades of the Bank, the blind paralytic was in his place, he was well tucked up in his coverings, he was eating his dinner like any working man. A friend, not even a friend, a hireling, would come for him at the appointed hour and wheel him home through the dark streets. He would be put to bed. He would be called for punctually and wheeled gently, for he was a power in the Coombe. At cockcrow in the morning he would be shaved and wheeled swiftly to his post. And no man had ever seen him come or go. He went and he returned. When you scrounge you go and you return. That was the first great article of scrounging. Out of his own country no man could scrounge, not properly. The Wanderjahre were a sleep and a forgetting, the proud dead point. You came back wise and staked your beat in some sheltered place. Pennies came dribbling steadily in and you were looked up to in an alley.

Belacqua had been proffered a sign. Of what avail is it to flog a dead cow. Let attention be drawn simply to the fact: Bovril had made a sign.

Wohin now? To what public? To where the bottled was well up, first; and the solitary shawly like a cloud of the latter rain after the sands of poets and politicians, second; and he neither knew nor was known, third. A lowly house dear to shawlies where the stout was up and he could sit himself to himself on a high stool with a high round and feign to be immersed in the Moscow notes of the Twilight Herald. They were very piquant.

Of the two houses that appealed to these exigencies the one, in Merrion Row, was a home from home for jarveys. That was a point very much in its disfavour. As the Alba hens, so Belacqua could not relish a jarvey. Rough, gritty men. And to Merrion Row from McLouglin's underground was a long perilous way, alive at this hour with poets and peasants and politicians. The other house lay in Lincoln Place. He could go gently by Pearse St, there was nothing to stop him. Long straight Pearse St, it permitted of a simple cantilena in his mind, its footpaths peopled with the tranquil and detached in tiredness and its highway dehumanised in a tumult of buses. Trams were monstrous, moaning along under the wild gesture of the trolley. But buses were simple, tyres and glass and noise. To pass by the Queens, the home of tragedy, was a pleasure at this hour, to pass between the old theatre and the long line of the poor and lowly queued up for thruppence worth of pictures. For there Florence would slip into the cantilena, the Piazza della Signoria and the No 1 tram and the festival

201

of St John there with the torches of resin ensconced in the niches of every tower flickering all night long and children with the rockets at the fall of night over the Cascine still flagrant in their memory opened the little cages to the glutted cicadæ that had survived the long confinement and sat on with their irresponsible parents long after their usual bedtime. Then he walked slowly in his mind down the sinister Uffizi to the parapets of the Arno etc. This pleasure was bestowed by the knowledge of the Fire Station across the way that had apparently been copied here and there from the Palazzo Vecchio. In homage to Savonarola? Hee! Hee! Anyway, no matter how you looked at it, it was a toleramble ramble in the gloaming, and all the more so as he had a great thirst towards the lowly house that would snatch him in off the street in the end through the door of the grocery department if by good fortune that were still open.

Painfully then under the College ramparts, past the smart taxis, he set off, winding up the cerebro-musical-box. The Fire Station worked like the trusty fetish it was, and all was going as well as could be expected considering what lay before him later in the evening when a terrible thing happened. He ran plump into Chas. It was Chas who could not or would not leave well alone, Belacqua being absorbed in his poor feet and the line of the tune in his mind. It was all Chas's fault.

"Halte-là" exclaimed the pirate "whither so gay?"

Under the overhead railway Belacqua was obliged to halt and face this machine. It carried butter and loaf bought at the dairy. There is only one dairy of any real consequence in Pearse St proper—though a multitude of fine little general groceries in the lanes that lie between it and the river—and it is close to the tomb-stone man-ufactory. It is of great consequence. Chas bought his fuel there. Every evening he called round for re-fills. Belac-qua, however, was giving nothing away.

"Ramble" he said vaguely "in the twilight."

"Just a song" said his dear friend "at twilight. Hein?"

Belacqua fidgeted in the gloom cast by the viaduct. Had he been blocked on his way and violated in the quiet of his mind to listen to this clockwork fiend? Apparently.

"How's the world" he said, however, in spite of every-thing, "and what's the news of the great world?"

"Fair" said Chas, cautiously, "fair to meedling. The poem moves, eppure."

"Ah."

"Yes."

"Well" said Belacqua, drawing away, "au plaisir."

"But this very evening" cried Chas "chez the Frica? Hein?"

"Alas" said Bel, well adrift.

And she. In her scarletest robe. And her broad bored pale face. The belle of the ball. Aïe!

But never one without two, and sure enough behold now from out the Grosvenor sprang the homespun poet wiping his mouth and a little macaco of an anonymous politico-ploughboy setting him off. The Poet sucked his teeth over this unexpected pleasure. The golden Eastern lay of his bullet head was mitigated by no covering. Be-neath the Wally Whitmaneen of his Donegal tweeds his body was to be presumed. He gave the impression of hav-ing lost a harrow and found a figure of speech. He struck terror into the heart of our hero.

He issued a word of command.

"Drink."

Belacqua slunk at his heels into the Grosvenor, the bright gimlet eyes of the macaco probed his loins.

"Now" proclaimed the Poet, as though he had just brought an army across the Beresina, "give it a name."

"Excuse me" stammered Belacqua "just an instant, will you have the kindness?"

He waddled out of the bar and out into the street and up the street at all speed and into the lowly public through the door of its grocery department. That was a rude thing to do. When intimidated he was rude beyond measure, not timidly insolent like Stendhal's Comte de Thaler, but finally rude on the sly. Timidly insolent when, as by Chas, exasperated; definitely rude on the sly when intimidated, outrageously rude behind the back of his oppressor. That was Belacqua. Do we begin to know him?

He bought a paper from a charming little sloven, no, but a positively exquisite little Stoebli, he would not menace him, a freelance clearly, he slipped in on his dirty bare feet with only three or four under his arm for sale. Belacqua gave him a threepenny bit and a cigarette picture. He sat on a stool to himself in the central leaf of the main triptych, his feet on a round so high that his knees topped the curb of the counter—a most comfortable seat— and drank stout scarcely at half-mast (but he durst not stir) and made a show of reading the paper.

'A woman' he read with appreciation 'is either: a short-below-the-waist, a big-hip, a sway-back, a big-abdomen or an average. If the bust be too cogently controlled, then shall fat roll from scapula to scapula. If it be made passable and slight, then shall the diaphragm bulge and be unsightly. Why not invest therefore chez a reputable corset-builder in the brassière-cum-corset décolleté, made from the finest Brochés, Coutils and Elastics, quintuple stitched in wearing parts, fitted with unbreakable spiral steels. It bestows glorious diaphragm and hip support, it enhances the sleeveless backless evening gown . . .'

Very good! Would the scarletest robe be backless? Was she a short-below-the-waist or a sway-back. She had no waist. If she swayed at all it was forward. She was not to be classified. Not to be corseted. Not a woman. *Grock ad libitum inquit.*

He began now to be harrassed by dread less the robe should turn out, by God, to be backless. Not but that he thought the back thus bared would not be good. The omoplates would be well marked, they would have a fine free ball-and-socket motion. In repose they would be the blades of an anchor, the fine furrow of the spine its stem. His mind pored over this back that he hoped devoutly not to see. He saw it in his mind as an anchor, a flower-de-luce, a spatulate leaf with segments, like the wings of a butterfly at work on a flower, angled back slightly from the common hinge; then, fetching from further afield, as an obelisk, a cross-potent, pain and death, still death, a bird crucified on a wall. This flesh and bones swathed in scarlet, this heart of washed flesh draped in scarlet.

Unable any longer to bear his uncertainty as to the rig of the robe he passed through the counter and got her house on the telephone.

"Dressing" said the Venerilla "and raging."

No, she couldn't be got down. She'd been up in her room cursing and swearing for the last hour.

"I'm afraid of me gizzard" said the voice "to go near her."

"Is it closed at the back" demanded Belacqua "or is it open?"

"Is what closed?"

"The dress" cried Belacqua "what do you think? The dress she is wearing. Is it closed?"

The Venerilla said to hold on while she called it to the eye of the mind.

"Is it the red one?" she said, after a pause.

"The scarlet bloody dress of course" he cried out of his torment "do you not know?"

"Hold on now . . . It buttons . . ."

"Buttons? How—buttons?"

"It buttons up behind, sir, with the help of God."

"Again" said Belacqua.

"Amn't I after telling" moaned the Venerilla down the instrument "that it buttons up on her!"

"Praise be to God" said Belacqua "and his Blissful Mother."

Now they get themselves ready, the men, women and children that the Frica's mother through the Frica had bidden. From divers points of the cities and suburbs, the nursery, the public-house, the solicitude of the family circle, the bachelor from his cosy and the student from his dirty quarters, they converged now upon her. Who—her? The Frica. Some were on their way, others on the threshold, the threshold of departure, yet others putting the finishing touches to their toilet, or, having done so, chafing to be on the road. But all, one and sundry, whatever their status and wherever their dwelling, however great their impatience or reluctance to be off, would be at more pains to respect the ten or fifteen minutes that etiquette required should intercalate the hush of their proud dead calm between the opening of the door and the first application for admission than would at first thought seem compatible, except the enormous importance in the cerebellum of fashionable Dublin of so grotesque a function as that now to be held be fully appreciated, with their complete indifference, on the occasion of an orchestral concert, as to whether they reached their seats before the conductor his pulpit, or inversely. To set out to make those pains consistent with this nonchalance would be to do the fashional psyche at all times and in all places, and a fortiori the Dublin specimen, the injury of supposing it to partake of the nature of a fixed gear. Our constant concern for the necks, and more particularly when they threaten to turn out to be wry, of our figures, will not tolerate anything more persuasive on this head than a bald blunt pronunciamento, to wit: that the fashionable psyche disposes of a more restless clutch and a more copious gamut of ratios than any engine ever contrived by the bottom speed ingenuity of man. That is why it is more charming than any engine.

There is yet time, before the masks get together and join issue, for a quick razzia of eavesdropping, a few pothooks and hangers of peeping and creeping and instantaneity.

Calm now and sullen the Alba, dressed insidiously up to the nines, bides her time in the sunken kitchen, paying no heed to her fool and foil the Venerilla. She is in pain, her brandy is at hand, mulling in the big glass on the range. We have seen her absented and distracted in mind, we have been privileged to see her, in a manner of speaking, sheathed. But now we are expected to suppose, behind this façade abandoned in elegance, sagging in its elegance and clouded in its native sorrow that her thought for the moment is at no pains to dissemble, a more anxious rite than luxury of meditation. The truth of the matter is that her mind is at prayer-stool before a perhaps futile purpose, she is loading the spring of her mind for a perhaps unimportant undertaking. Letting her outside rip for the moment she is screwing herself up and up, she is winding up the weights of her mind, to being the belle of the ball. Any less bountiful girl would have scorned such a performance and considered this class of absorption at the service of so simple an occasion unwarranted and, what was worse, a sad give away. Here am I, a less bountiful would have said, the belle, and yonder is the ball. It is only a question of bringing these two items together and the thing is done. Are we then expected to insinuate, with such a simplist, that the Alba questioned the virtue of her appearance? Not for a moment. She had merely to unleash her eyes, she had merely to unseel them, and well she knew it, and she could have mercy on whom she would. That was all right. Everything was in order as far as that went. But what she did question, and this ought to do to explain her demeanour to the puzzled, was the fitness of a distinction that was hers for the wanting. She only had to open her eyes and take it. That the very simplicity of the gest turned her in the first place against it, relegating it among the many things that were not her genre, cannot be denied. But there we have only a minute aspect of her position. It is with the disparagement attaching to the quality of the exploit in the thought of Belacqua, and in hers tending to, that she now wrestles. It is with its no doubt unworthiness that she has now to do. Sullen and still, aware of the brandy at hand but not thirsting for it, she cranks herself up to a reality of preference, slowly and surely she gilds her option, she exalts it into realms of choice. She will do this thing, she will, she will be the belle, gladly, gravely and carefully, humiliter, simpliciter, fideliter, and not merely because she might just as well. Is she, who *knows,* to be equilibrated in Buridan's marasmus? Shall she founder in a strait of two wills? By hanging in suspense be the more killed? She who *knows?* Soon she will chafe to be off. And now she dare, until it be time, the clock strike, delegate a portion of her attention for the purpose of re-organising her features, hands, shoulders, back, hang of robe, general bearing, outside in a word. The inside is fixed up. At once she is thirsty for the Hennessy. She sings to herself, for her own pleasure, stressing all the words that should be stressed, like Dan the first to warble like a turdus:

> No me jodas en el suelo
> como se fuera una perra,
> que con esos cojonazos
> me echas en el cono tierra . . .

The Polar Bear was on his way, speeding along the dark country roads in a big honest slob of a clanging bus, engaging with the effervescent distinction of a Renaissance cardinal in rather indolent tongue-play an acquaintance of long standing, a Jesuit with no or but little nonsense about him.

"The Lebensbahn" he was saying "of the Galilean is the tragedy of an individualism that will not capitulate. The humilities and renunciations are on a par with the miracles, arrogance and egoism. He is the first great self-contained man. The *crytic* abasement before the woman taken red-handed is as great a piece of megalomaniacal impertinence as his interference in the affairs of his friend Lazarus. He opens the series of fashionable suicides. He is responsible for the wretched Nemo and his co-ratés, bleeding in paroxysms of dépit on an unimpressed public."

The Polar Bear coughed up a plump cud of mucus, spun it round the avid bowl of his palate and stowed it away for future degustation.

The Jesuit with no or but little nonsense about him was grateful for the opportunity of making it clear that this kind of thing tired him.

"If you knew" he said "how you bore me with your twice two is four."

The P.B. failed to appreciate the application . . .

"You bore me" said the S.J. "the way an infant prodigy does . . ." He paused. "In his hairless voice" he continued "preferring the chemist Borodine to Mozart."

"Mozart" said the P.B. "was, I understand, an infant prodigy."

That was a nasty one. Let him make what he chose of that one.

"Our Lord . . ."

The Polar Bear, nettled, requested him rudely to speak for himself.

"Our Lord was not."

"By some accounts" said the Polar Bear "he had a prodigious birth."

"When you grow up to be a big boy" said the Jesuit "and are old enough to understand the humility that is beyond masochism, come and talk to me again. Not cis-, but ultra-masochistic. Beyond pain and service."

"But precisely" exclaimed the P.B. "he did not serve, the late lamented. What else am I saying? A valet does not have big ideas. He let down the central agency."

"The humility" murmured the dissociable sociétaire "of a love too great for skivvying and too real for the tonic of urtication."

The infant prodigy sneered, at this comfortable variety. "You make things pleasant for yourselves" he sneered "I must say."

"The best reason" said the Jesuit "that can be given for believing is that it is more amusing. Disbelief" said this soldier of Xist, preparing to arise "is a bore. We do not count our change. We simply cannot bear to be bored."

"Say that from the pulpit" said the P.B. "and you'll be drummed into the wilderness."

The Jesuit laughed profusely. Was it possible to conceive of a more artless impostor of a mathematician than this fellow!

"What I say" he laughed "is strictly orthodox. I could justify it on my head before any Council, though I cannot imagine the Council naive enough to take exception to it. And would you" he begged, buttoning across his coat, "would you, my dear fellow, have the goodness to bear in mind that I am not a P.P."

"I won't forget" said the P.B. "that you don't scavenge. Your love is too great for skivvying."

"Egg-sactly" said the S.J. "But they are excellent men. A shade on the assiduous side. A shade too anxious to balance accounts. Otherwise . . ." He stood up. "Observe" he said "I desire to get down, I pull this cord and the bus stops and lets me down."

"Well?"

"In just such a Gehenna of links" said this remarkable man, with one foot on the pavement, "I forged my vocation."

With these words he was gone and the burden of his fare had fallen on the Polar Bear.

211

*   *   *

Chas had promised to pick up the Shetland Shawly, and now, cinched beyond reproach in his smoking, he paused on his way to catch the tram in order to explain the world to a group of students.

"The difference, if I may say so . . ."

"Oh" cried the students, una voce, "oh please!"

"The difference, then I say, between Bergson and Einstein, the essential difference, is the difference between a philosopher and a sociologist . . ."

"Oh!" cried the students.

"Yes" said Chas, casting up what was the longest phrase that could be placed before his tram, that had hove into view, would draw abreast.

"And if it is the smart thing nowadays to speak of Bergson as a bit of a cod" he edged away "it is that the trend of our modern vulgarity is from the object" he made a dive for the tram "and the idea to sense" he cried from the step "and REASON."

"Sense" echoed the students "and reason!"

The difficulty was to know what exactly he meant by *sense*.

"He must mean *senses*" said a first "smell, you know, and so on."

"Nay" said a second "he must mean *common sense*."

"I think" said a third "that he meant *instinct*, intuition, don't you know, and that kind of thing."

A fourth was curious to know what instinct there was in Einstein, a fifth what absolute in Bergson, a sixth what either had to do with the world.

"We must ask him" said a seventh "that is all. We must

not confuse ourselves with inexpert speculation. Then we shall see who is right."

"We must ask him" cried the students "then we shall see . . ."

On that understanding, that the first to see him again would be sure and ask him, they went on their not so very different ways.

The hair of the homespun Poet did not lend itself kindly to striking effects of dressing, so closely was it cropped. Here again, in his plumping for the austerity of a rat's-back, he proclaimed himself in reaction against the nineties. But the little there was to do he had done, with a lotion he had given alertness to the stubble. And he had changed his tie. Now, though alone and unobserved, he paced up and down. He was making up his piece, almost an occasional one, whose main features he had established one recent gusty afternoon on the summit of the Hill of Allen. He would deliver it when his hostess came with her petition, he would not hum and haw like an amateur pianist nor yet as good as spit in her eye like a professional one. No, he would stand up at once and say—not declaim, state with gravity—with that penetrating Middle West melancholy like an ogleful of tears:

CALVARY BY NIGHT

the water
the waste of water

in the womb of water
an pansy leaps

rocket of bloom flare flower of night wilt for me
on the breasts of the water it has closed it has made
an act of floral presence on the water
the tranquil act of its cycle on the waste
from the spouting forth
to the re-enwombing
an untroubled bow of petal and fragrance
kingfisher abated
drowned for me
Lamb of my insustenance
till the clamour of a blue flower
beat on the walls of the womb of
the waste of
the water

Determined to put across this strong composition and
make something of a stir, he was anxious that there
should be no fault or flaw in the mode of presentation
that he had adopted as being the best suited to his Hill
of Allen manner. He must have it pat, so as to be able to
not say it pat, so as to give the impression that in the
travail of its exteriorisation he was torn asunder. Taking
his cue from the humblest juggler who charms us by failing once, twice, and then the third time, in a positive
lather of willing, bringing it off, he deemed that this little
turn, if it were to go down at all, required stress to be
laid not so much on the content of the performance as on
the ordeal of spiritual evisceration endured by the performer. So he paced to and fro, making a habit of the
words and effects of *Calvary by Night.*

*   *   *

The Frica combed her hair, back and back she raked her tresses till to close her eyes became a problem. The effect was throttled gazelle, more appropriate to evening wear than foal at foot. The Smeraldina-Rima, in the early stages of her campaign, when her face would still stand it, had favoured the same taut Sabine coiffure. Until Mammy, by dint of protesting that it made her little face look like a sucked lozenge, had persuaded her to fluff things a bit and crimp them. Alas! nimbed she was altogether too big dolly that opens and shuts her eyes. Nor indeed was lozenge, sucked or bucked, by any means the most ignoble office that the face of woman might discharge. For here at hand, saving us our fare to Derbyshire, we have the Frica, looking something horrid.

Throttled gazelle gives no idea. Her features, as though the hand of an unattractive ravisher were knotted in her chevelure, were all set at half-cock and locked in a rictus. She had frowned to pencil her eyebrows, so now she had four. The dazzled iris was domed in a white agony of entreaty. The upper-lip snarled away to the untented nostrils. Would she bite her tongue off?—that was the interesting question. The tilted chin betrayed a patent clot of thyroid gristle. It was impossible to put aside the dreadful suspicion that her flattened mammæ, in sympathy with this tormented eructation of countenance, had been exalted into two cutwaters and were rowelling her brassière. But the face was beyond suspicion, a flagrant seat of injury. She had only to extend the fingers of both hands so that the palm and fingers of the one touched the palm and fingers of the other and hold them thus joined before the breast with a slight upward inclination to look like a briefless martyress in rut.

Nevertheless the arty Countess of Parabimbi, backing through the press, would dangle into the mauve presence of the crone-mother, and "My dear" she would be positively obliged to ejaculate "naver have I seen your Caleken *quite* so striking. Quite Sistine!"

What would Madame be pleased to mean? The Cumaean Sibyl on a bearing-rein, sniffing the breeze for the Grimm brothers? Oh, she did not care to be so infernally finical and nice, that would be like working out how many pebbles in Tom Thumb's pocket, it was just a vague impression, it was just that she looked, with that strange limy hobnailed texture of complexion, so *frescosa,* from the waist up, my dear, with that distempered cobalt modesty-piece, a positive gem of ravished Quattrocento, a positive jewel, my dear, of sweaty Big Tom. Upon which the vidual virgin, well aware after all these years that all things in heaven, the earth and the waters were as they were taken, would return thanks to the Countess of Parabimbi for her erudite and gracious appreciations.

This may be premature. We have set it down too soon, perhaps. Still, let it stand.

It would be nice to go on sneering at the Frica, the long afternoon would slip over like a dream of water. What more agreeable way of getting through the hours of siesta than with itching point and graver to overcharge her with the stipplings and hatching of a fabricated indignation? Not sæva, fabricated. Alas, not at all sæva. If only it were possible to be genuinely annoyed with the girl. But it is not. Not for any length of time. No doubt she has her faults. Who has not? No doubt also she is someone's darling. Neither shall we, however that may be, condemn the damn girl further. She is dull, she is stale, she is not worthy of our steel. And anyhow there is the bell at last, pealing down her Fallopian pipettes, galvanising her away from the

216

mirror as though her navel had been pressed in annunciation.

The Student, whose name we shall never know, was the first to arrive. A foul little brute he was, with a brow.

"Gracious goodness!" he exclaimed, for the benefit of the two Fricas, on the threshold of the mauve drawingroom "don't tell me I am the first!"

"Only" said Caleken, who could smell a poet against the wind, "by a short gaffe. Don't" she said coldly "distress yourself. You are not the only one."

Hard on the heels of the Poet came a gaggle of nondescripts, then a young pastoralist, then a Gael, an Irish one, then the Shawly with her Chas. Him the Student, mindful of his vow, buttonholed.

"In what sense" he demanded, without exordium, "did you use *sense* when you said . . ."

"He said that?" exclaimed the pastoralist.

"Chas" said the Frica, as though she were announcing a score.

"Adsum" said Chas.

A plum of phlegm burst in the vestibule.

"What I want to know" complained the Student "what we all want to know, is in what sense he was using *sense* when he said . . ."

The Gael was endeavouring to transmit Camden Street's thought for the day to the Freudlose Witwe for the benefit of the nondescripts.

"Owen . . ." he began, when an anonymous ignoramus anxious to come into the picture as early on in the proceedings as possible said rashly:

"What Owen?"

"Good-evening" gushed the Polar Bear "good-evening good-evening good-evening. Wat a night, Madame" he addressed himself vehemently, out of sheer politeness, directly to his hostess, "God, *wat* a night."

Now she had great gradh for him.

"And you so far to come!" She was sorry she could not croon it frankly, nor lay her claw tenderly on his shabby sleeve. He was a shabby man, and often moody. "So good of you to come" as fondly as she durst "so good of you."

The Man of Law was next, accompanied by the Countess of Parabimbi and three tarts dressed for the back-stairs.

"I met him" whispered Chas "staggering down Pearse Street, Brunswick Street you know, that was."

"En route ?" said the Frica.

"Hein?"

"On his way here?"

"Well" said Chas "my dear Miss Frica, I fear that he did not make clear to me if he is coming or not."

The Gael said to the P.B. in an injured voice:

"Here's a man who wants to know what Owen!"

"Not possible!" said the P.B. "you astonish me."

"Is it of the sweet mouth?" said a sandy son of Han.

Now the prong of the Polar Bear's judgement was keen and bright.

"That emmerdeur!" he jeered. "The strange sweet mouth!"

The Countess of Parabimbi started back.

"You said?" she said.

The Frica emerged from the ruck, she came to the fore.

"What can be keeping the girls" she said. It was not exactly a question.

"And your sister" enquired the pastoralist "your charming sister, where can she be, I wonder."

218

"Unfortunately" said the Beldam, precipitately, "in bed, unwell. A great disappointment for us all."

"Nothing serious, Madame," said the Man of Law "let us hope?"

"Thank you, no. Happily not. A slight indisposition. Poor little Pissabed!"

Madame passed a heavy sigh.

The Polar Bear looked significantly at the Gael.

"What girls?" he said.

"Pansy"—the Poet's heart went pit-a-pat—"Lilly Neary, Olga, Miriam, Alga, Ariana, tall Tib, slender Sib, Katty, Alba . . ." they were too numerous for the harried Frica to name.

"Alba!" ejaculated the P.B. "Alba! She!"

"And why" interposed the Countess "not Alba, whoever she may be, rather than, say, the Wife of Bath?"

A nondescript came up with the good tidings. The girls had arrived.

"They are girls" said the pastoralist "beyond any doubt. But are they *the* girls?"

By God, they were girls, he was quite right. But were they *the* girls.

"I suppose we can start now" said Frica the younger and, the elder being aware of no let or hindrance, up on to the estrade smartly she stepped and unveiled the refreshments. Then, turning her back on the high dumb-waiter, with a great winged gesture of lapidated piety, she instituted the following variety:

"Claret-cup! Lemon-squash! Tea! Coffee! Cocoa! Ovaltine! Force!"

"Great cry" said the pastoralist "and little wool."

The more famished faithful surged towards her.

Two novelists, a bibliomaniac and his mistress, a paleographer, a violist d'amore with his instrument in a bag, a popular parodist with his sister and six daughters, a still more popular professor of Bullscrit and Comparative Ovoidology, the macaco the worse for drink, an incontinent native speaker, a prostated arithmomaniac, a communist decorator just back from the Moscow reserves, a merchant, two grave Jews, a rising whore, three more poets with Lauras to match, a disaffected cicisbeo, the inevitable envoy of the Fourth Estate, a phalanx of Grafton Street Stürmers and Jem Higgins arrived now in a body. No sooner had they been assimilated than the Parabimbi, very much the lone bird on this occasion in the absence of her husband the Count who had been unable to escort her on account of his being b--- if he would, got in her attributions of the Frica for which, as has been shown, she was carefully thanked by the beldam.

"I do no more" said the Countess "than constate."

She held the saucer under her chin like a communion-card. She lowered the cup into its socket without a sound.

"Excellent" she said "most excellent Force."

Madame Frica smiled from the teeth outward.

"So glad" she said "so glad."

The Professor of Bullscrit and Comparative Ovoidology was not to be seen. But that did not matter, that was not his business, that was not what he was paid for. His business was to be heard. He was widely and clearly heard.

"When the immortal Byron" he bombled "was about to leave Ravenna, to sail in search of some distant shore where a hero's death might end his immortal spleen . . ."

"Ravenna!" exclaimed the Countess, memory tugging at her carefully cultivated heart-strings, "Did I hear someone say Ravenna?"

"Allow me" said the rising whore "a sandwich. Egg, to-mato, cucumber."

"Did you know" blundered the Man at Law "that the Swedes have no fewer than seventy varieties of Smörrbröd?"

The voice of the arithmomaniac was heard:

"The arc" he said, stooping to all in the great plainness of his words, "is longer than its chord."

"Madame knows Ravenna?" said the paleographer.

"Do I know Ravenna!" exclaimed the Parabimbi "Sure I know Ravenna. A sweet and noble city."

"You know of course" said the Man of Law "that 'twas there that Dante died?"

"To be sure" said the Parabimbi "so he did."

"You know of course" said the paleographer "that his tomb is in the Piazza Byron? I translated his epitaph into heroic couplets."

"You know of course" said the Man of Law "that under Belisarius . . ."

"My dear" said the Parabimbi to the beldam "how well it goes! What a happy party and how at home they all seem. I declare" she declared "I envy you your flair for making people feel at their ease."

The beldam disclaimed faintly any such faculty. It was Calaken's party really. It was Calaken who had arranged everything really. She had had very little to do with the arrangements. She just sat there and looked mauve and exhausted. She was just a weary exhausted old Norn.

"To my mind" boomed presumptuously the ovoidologist "the greatest triumph of human thought was the calcula-tion of Neptune from the observed vagaries of the orbit of Uranus."

"And yours" said the P.B. That was an apple of gold and a picture of silver if you like.

The Parabimbi waxed stiff.

"Who's that?" she cried. "What does he say?"

A terrible hush fell upon the assembly. The macaco had slapped the communist decorator.

Supported by Mr Higgins the Frica was on the scene of the disturbance at once.

"Go" she said to the macaco "and let there be no scene."

Mr Higgins led him away. The Frica now addressed herself to the decorator. "I do not propose" she said "to tolerate any political brawls at any party of mine."

"He called me a bloody Bolshy" protested the decorator "and he a labour man himself."

"Let there be no more of it" said the Frica "let there be no more of it."

She was very optative. "I beg of you" she said, and stepped back fleetly to the altar.

"You heard what she said" said the Gael.

"Let there be no more of it" said the native speaker.

"I beg of you" said the Polar Bear.

But now the lady cometh that all this may disdain, the Alba, dauntless daughter of desires. She made her entry just on the turn of the hush, she advanced like a midinette to pay her respects to the beldam, and voices sprang up in her wake. She suffered herself to be presented to the Parabimbi and then, without further ado, she mounted the estrade and there, in profile to the assistance, silent and still before the elements of refreshment, she cast her gravitational nets.

The rising whore studied how to do it. The daughters of the parodist passed on to such as were curious the little they knew. She was much spoken of in certain circles to which they had access. But how much of what one heard was true and how much mere gossip they were really not in a position to say. However, for what it was worth, it appeared . . .

The Gael, the incontinent native speaker, the reporter and the violist d'amore got together as though by magic.

"Well?" invited the reporter.

"Pret-ty good" said the Gael.

"Dee-licious" said the violist d'amore.

The incontinent native speaker said nothing.

"Well?" repeated the reporter "Larry?"

Larry turned his eyes away from the estrade at last and said, drawing his palms slowly up the thighs of his trousers:

"Jaysus!"

"Meaning?" said the reporter.

Larry turned his wild gaze back upon the estrade.

"You don't happen to know" he said finally "does she do it?"

"They all do" said the violist d'amore.

"Like hell they do" said the Gael.

"What I want to know" said the Student "what we all want to know . . ."

"Some do abstain" said the reporter "our friend here is right, through bashfulness from Venery. It is a pity, but it is so."

From widely divergent points the Polar Bear and Mr Higgins approached the estrade.

"You look pale" said the Frica "and ill, my dear."

The Alba raised her big head from the board and looked longly at the Frica.

"Pale" she repeated "and ill. Then keep them away."

"Keep them away!" echoed the Frica "keep whom away?"

"Who is here?"

"Chas, Jem, the Polar Bear . . ."

The Frica was anxious to calm her. Such stories were related of the Alba. It was always to be feared that she would make a scene. Tricks and turns and games were food and drink to the Frica. The party, as far as she was concerned, did not begin to be a party until the tricks and turns and games started. Scenes only held up things, besides risking to frighten people away. One on whom she might count, Chas or a willing poet or musician, for a little contribution if all were going quietly and smoothly, might well be frightened away by the unpleasantness of a scene.

"We go through the world" said the Alba "like sunbeams through cracks."

"The Polar Bear" said the Frica, thoroughly alarmed, "you know, and Jem of course I know you know. Take a little cup, dear, it will do you good."

"Keep them away!" cried the Alba, clenching the altar, "keep them away."

But the P.B. and Jem were on the estrade. They closed in upon her.

"All right" said the Alba "make it a strong one."

Phew! the Frica was inexpressibly relieved.

Half-nine. The guests, led by the rising whore and the cicisbeo, began to scatter through the house. The Frica let them go. In half-an-hour she would visit the alcoves, she would round them all up for the party proper to begin. Had not Chas promised a piece of old French? She had seen the viol d'amore in its bag in the hall. So they would have a little music.

*   *   *

224

Half-nine. Belacqua stood in the mizzle in Lincoln Place, taking his bearings. But he had bought a bottle. He set off unsteadily by the Dental Hospital. He hated the red of the Dental Hospital. Suddenly he felt clammy. He leaned against the little gate set in the College wall and looked at J. M. & O'B.'s clock. Had he any sense of his responsibilities as an epic liŭ he would favour us now with an incondite meditation on time. He has none and he does not. To his vague dismay it looks like a quarter to ten by the clock, and he scarcely able to stand, let alone walk. And the rain. He lifted his hands and held them close to his face, so close that even in the dark he could discern the lines. Then he pressed them over his eyes, he pressed the heels viciously against the eyeballs, he let himself sag heavily against the gate and the sill of the wall fitted into the groove of his nape. Stupefied and all as he was he could feel the pressure crushing little quirts of pain out of the baby anthrax that he always wore just above his collar. He forced his neck hard back against the stone sill.

The next he knew was his hands torn roughly away from his eyes. He opened them on a large red hostile face. For a moment it was still, a plush gargoyle. Then it moved, it was convulsed. This, he thought, must be the face of somebody talking. It was. It was the face of a Civic Guard abusing him. Belacqua closed his eyes, there was no other way of ceasing to see it. He felt a great desire to lie down on the pavement. He was sick quietly and abundantly, mainly on the boots and trousers of the Guard. The Guard struck him fiercely on the breast and Belacqua dropped hip and thigh into his vomit. He felt weak, but not hurt in any way. On the contrary, he felt calm and lucid and well and anxious to be on his way. It must be after ten. He bore no

225

animosity to the Guard, though now he could hear what he was saying. He knelt before him in the vomit, he heard every word he was saying in the recreation of his duty, and bore him no ill will of any kind. He reached up for a purchase on the Guard's coat and pulled himself to his feet. The apology he made when firmly established on his feet for what had occurred was profusely rejected. He furnished his name and address, where he was coming from and where he was going to, and why, his profession and immediate business, and why. He was sorry to hear that the Guard had a good mind to bring him to the Station, but he appreciated the Guard's position.

"Wipe them boots" said the Guard.

Belacqua was only too happy. He made two loose balls of the Twilight Herald and stooped down and cleaned the boots and trouser ends as best he might. Then he stood up, clutching the two soiled swabs of newspaper, and looked timidly at the Guard, who seemed rather at a loss as to how his advantage might be best pressed home.

"I trust" said Belacqua "that you can see your way to overlooking this regrettable incident."

The Guard said nothing. Belacqua wiped his right hand on his coat and extended it. The Guard spat. Belacqua strangled a shrug and moved away in a tentative manner.

"Hold on there" said the Guard.

Belacqua halted and waited.

"Move on" said the Guard.

Belacqua walked away, holding tightly on to the two swabs of newspaper. Once safe round the corner of Kildare Street he let them fall. Then, after a few paces forward, he stopped, turned and hastened back to where they were fidgeting on the pavement. He picked them up and threw them into an area. Now he felt extraordinarily light and active and hæres cœli. He followed briskly through the mizzle the way he had chosen, exalted, fashioning intricate festoons of words. It occurred to him, and he took great pleasure in working out this little figure, that the locus of his fall from the vague grace of the drink must have intersected with that of his climb to that grace at its most agreeable point. That was certainly what must have happened. Sometimes the line of the drink graph looped back on itself like an eight, and if you had got, what you were looking for on the way up you got it again on the way down. The bumless eight of the drink figure. You did not end up where you started, but coming down you met yourself going up. Sometimes, as now, you were glad; other times you were sorry, and you hastened on to your new home.

Suddenly walking through the rain was not enough, striding along smartly, well muffled up, in the cold and the wet was an inadequate thing to be doing. He halted on the crown of Baggot Street Bridge, took off his reefer and hat, laid them on the parapet and sat down beside them. The Guard was forgotten. Stooping forward there where he sat and flexing his leg until the knee was against his ear and the heel rested on the parapet he took off his shoe and set it down beside the coat and the hat. Then he let down that leg and did the same with the other. Next, in order that he might get full value from the bitter northwester that was blowing, he slewed himself round on his chilled soaked bottom. His legs dangled over the canal and he could see the trams hiccuping across the remote hump of Leeson Street Bridge. Distant lights on a dirty night, how he loved them, the dirty low-church Protestant! He felt very cold. He took off his jacket and belt and laid them down beside the other garments on the parapet. He unbuttoned the top of his filthy old trousers and pulled out the German shirt.

227

Then, bundling the skirt of the shirt under the fringe of his pullover, he rolled them up clockwise together until they were hooped fast across his thorax. It was not worth his while taking them off altogether, and the less so as there was collar and studs and tie and cufflinks to complicate the operation. The rain beat against his chest and belly and trickled down. It was even more agreeable than he had hoped, but very cold. It was now, beating his bosom thus bared to the mean storm vaguely with marble palms, that he parted company with himself and felt wretched and sorry for what he had done. He had done wrong, he realised that, and he was heartily sorry. Still, uncertain as to how best he might be comforted, he sat on, drumming his stockinged heels irritably against the stone. Suddenly the thought of the bottle he had bought pierced through his gloomy condition like a beacon. It was still there in his pocket, in the breast of his reefer. He dried himself as best he might with his Paris pochette and adjusted his clothes. When he was more or less in order, but not before, well muffled up once more in his reefer and with the shoes back on his feet, then he took a stiff pull on the bottle. That did him the hell of a lot of good. It sent what is called a warm glow what is called coursing through his veins. He repeated the dose and felt better again. Heartened, he squelched off down the street at a trot, resolved to make it, in so far as in him lay, a non-stop run as far as the Frica's. The rain had abated, and he saw no reason why it should be remarked that there was anything amiss with his appearance. With his elbows well up he jogged along. Some hundred yards short of the house he drew up and lit a cigarette for malas and maxillas, lit it to put himself into countenance.

228

Why did the Smeraldina-Rima elect to rise before him at this precise moment, and in a posture suggestive of reproach what was more, the little head bowed and the arms dangling and the tall stout body still? That was what he could not make out. He called to mind the calamitous Silvester: how he had offended her in the first instance by wanting to languish on quietly in the Wohnung, with the candle-light and a sanies of music from Mammy and the wine of music, Rhine wine; how then he had all but swooned with joy at the spectacle of his to all intents and purposes betrothed prancing off angrily in the embrace of the glider-champion; how then, having delivered her over to the unbridled desires of the Belshazzar and Herr Sauerwein the portraitist, of whom it may perhaps be now the moment to say that he did away with himself in the Seine, he jumped from a bridge, like all suicides, never from the bank, in consideration of his being too modern to live, he had sought, found, and lost, accompanied by the Mandarin, Abraham's bosom in a house of ill fame.

It was with this phrase, the ut sharpened, quantified and sustained to a degree that had never been intended by the Swan of Bonn, moaning in his memory, that he rang hell out of the Frica's door.

His mind, in the ups and downs of the past half-hour, coming now to a head in such a stress of remembrance, had not had leisure to pore over what was in pickle for him. Even the Alba's scarletest gown or robe—for the qualified assurance of the Venerilla, that it buttoned up *with the help of God,* had not been of a nature to purge it altogether of misgiving—had ceased to torment it. But now, standing in the hall, the full seriousness of his position burst upon him. When the Frica pattered out of the mauve salon, where all her guests were rounded up, to greet this late arrival, he was shocked and sobered by her appearance and general rig-out.

"There you are" she bugled "at long last."

"Here" he said rudely "I float."

She recoiled, clapped a hand to her teeth, and goggled. *Where* had he been? *Wat* had he been doing? Had he, oh was it possible he had, been trying to drown himself? To be sure, the wet dripped off him as he stood aghast before her and gathered in a little pool at his feet. How dilated her nostrils were!

"You must get out of those wet things" she declared "this very moment. I declare to goodness you are drenched to the . . . skin." There was no nonsense about the Frica. When she meant skin, she said skin. "Every stitch" she gloated "must come off at once, this very instant."

From the taut cock of her face viewed as a whole, and in particular from the horripilating detail of the upper-lip writhing up and away in a kind of a duck or a cobra sneer to the quivering snout, he supposed her to be in a state of more than usual excitement. This he was conceited enough to ascribe to the prospect she appeared to entertain of his divesting himself instantly of every stitch. Nor was he entirely at fault. A condition of the highest mettle and fettle had followed hard upon her asinine dumbfusion. For here indeed was an unexpected little bit of excitement! In a moment she would break into a caracole. Belacqua thought it might be wiser to take this disposition in time.

"No" he said composedly "if I might have a towel . . ."

"A towel!" The scoff was so shocked that she had to blow her nose headlongly before him.

"It would take off the rough wet" he said.

The rough wet! How too utterly absurd to speak of rough wet when it was clear to be seen that he was soaked through and through.

"Through and through!" she cried.

"No" he said "if I might just have a towel "

She was profoundly chagrined, but realised that there was no shaking his resolve to accept no more thorough comfort at her hands than that which a towel could provide. And in the salon they were waiting for her, her absence was beginning to make itself felt in the salon. So off she canterered with the best grace she could muster, and was back in no time with a bath-towel.

"Really!" she said, and left him for her guests.

Chas, conversing in low tones with the Shawly, was waiting nervously to be called on for his contribution. This was the famous occasion on which Chas, as though he had suddenly taken leave of his senses, closed his perfectly respectable recitation with the iniquitous quatrain:

Toutes êtes, serez ou fûtes,
De fait ou de volonté, putes,
Et qui bien vous chercheroit
Toutes putes vous trouveroit.

The Alba, whom in order to rescue Belacqua we were obliged to abandon just as with characteristic impetuosity she made up her mind to see things through come what might, had opened her campaign by sending Jem Higgins and the Polar Bear flying, there is no other word for it, about their business. Upon which, not deigning to have any share in the sinister kiss-me-Charley hugger-mugger that had spread like wild-fire through the house, till it raged from attic to basement, under the ægis of the rising whore and the disaffected cicisbeo, she proceeded quietly, on her own, in her own quiet way, to bewitch those who, in ordinary circumstances, would have partic-ipated joyfully in the vile necking, but who had remained on expressly to see what could be made of this little pale person so self-possessed and urbane in the best sense in the scarlet costume. The parodist, notably, she had strongly affected. So that, from a certain point of view, she was quite a little power for good that evening.

Fond as she was, really very, very fond in her own rather stealthy and sinuous fashion, of Belacqua, it did not occur to her to miss him or think of him at all unless it were as a rather distinguished spectator whose eyes behind his glasses upon her and vernier of appreciation might have salted her fun. Among the many hounded by the implaca-ble Frica from their shabby joys she had marked down for her own one of the grave Jews, him with the bile-tinged conjunctivae, and the merchant prince. Then she supposed Jem could drive her home. She addressed herself to the Jew, but too slackly, as to an insipid dish, and was re-pulsed. Politely repulsed. This was a set-back that she had been far from expecting. Scarcely had she reloaded and trained her charms more nicely upon this interesting mis-creant, of whom she proposed, her mind full of hands rub-bing, to make a most salutary example, than the Frica, still smarting under the disappointment inflicted on her by Bel-acqua, announced in a venomous tone of voice that Mon-sieur Jean du Chas, too well known to them all for what he was, a most talentuous young Parisian, to require any in-

232

troduction, had kindly consented to set the ball a-rolling. In spite of the satisfaction that would have accrued to the Alba had Chas there and then been torn limb from limb before her eyes, she made no attempt to restrain her merriment, in which of course she was joined by the Polar Bear, when he concluded his recitation with the cynical aphorism quoted above, and the less so as she observed with what an aigre-douceur the paleographer and Parabimbi, who had been surprised by the Frica being a little naughty together, dissociated themselves from the applause that greeted his descent from the estrade. *Je hais les tours de Saint-Sulpice* could have caused her scarce more amusement at that particular moment, though in a less stale run of events she would certainly have found the one as banal as the other.

This, roughly speaking, was the position when Belacqua appeared in the doorway.

Watching him closely as he stood bedraggled in the doorway, clutching his glasses in his fist (a precautionary measure that he never neglected when there was any danger of his *appearing* embarrassed), bothered seriously in his mind by a neat little point that had presented itself to him in the hall, waiting no doubt for some kind person to offer him a chair, the Alba thought that she had seldom seen anybody looking more sovereignly ridiculous. Seeking to be God, she thought, in the slavish arrogance of a piffling evil.

"Like something" she said to the P.B. "that a dog would bring in."

The P.B. played up, he overbid.

"Like something" he said "that, upon reflection, he would not."

He cackled and snuffled over this sottish mot as though

233

it were his own. In an unsubduable movement of misericord she started out of her chair.

"Niño" she called, without ceremony or shame.

The cry came like a drink of water to drink in prison to the ear of Belacqua. He stumbled towards it.

"Move up in the bed" she said to the P.B. "and make room."

Everybody in the row had to move up one.

"Niño" she came again, thumping the place thus freed, "here."

Belacqua collapsed heavily into the chair by her side. You see, now they are side by side. She placed her hand on his sleeve. He sat not looking, his head lowered, plucking vaguely at his filthy old trousers. When she shook him he lifted his head and looked at her. To her disgust he was crying.

"You've been drinking" she said.

The Parabimbi snatched at the paleographer, she craned her neck at the same time.

"What's that?" she demanded in a general way. "What's going on there. Who's that? Are they promessi?"

She was not alone in her impertinent curiosity.

"Who is the young man?" said the parodist, and, "Who might that be, do you suppose" in the whisky contralto of the bibliomaniac's light of love.

"I was astonished" said a voice "really astounded, to find that Sheffield was more hilly than Rome."

Belacqua made a stupendous effort to acknowledge the cordial greeting of the Polar Bear, but he could not. He felt an enormous desire to slip down on the floor and lay his head against the slight madder thigh of the Alba.

"The bicuspid" from the professor "monotheistic fiction

torn by the sophists, Christ and Plato, from the violated matrix of pure reason."

Oh, who shall silence them, at last? Who shall circumcise their lips from talking, at last?

The Frica insisted on the fact that she trod the estrade.

"Maestro Gormely" she announced "will now play."

Maestro Gormerly executed Scarlatti's Capriccio, without accompaniment, on the viol d'amore. This met with no success to speak of.

"Plato!" sneered the P.B. "Did I hear the name Plato? That dirty little Borstal Bœhme!" That was a sockdologer for someone if you like.

"Mr Larry O'Murcahaodha" said the Frica "will now sing for us."

Mr Larry O'Murcahaodha tore a greater quantity than seemed quite fair of his native speech-material to flat tatters.

"I can't bear it" said Belacqua "I can't bear it."

The Frica threw the Poet into the breach. She informed the assistance that it was privileged:

"I think I am accurate in saying" she paused to be given the lie "one of his most recent compositions."

"Vinegar" moaned Belacqua "on nitre."

"Don't try" said the Alba, with forced heartiness, for she did not like the look of Belacqua the least bit, "to put across the Mrs Gummidge before the coucherie on me."

He had no desire, none at all, to put across the Mrs Gummidge at any moment of her life or anything whatever on her or anyone else. His distress was profound, it was unaffected. And two needs stood like stone out of his dereliction: to backslide quietly down on the parquet and fit his nape against the Alba's thigh, and to be delivered from

235

the ravening wolf whose ears his mind in self-defence was grasping. He leaned across to the Polar Bear:

"I wonder" he said "could you possibly . . ."

"Lotus!" screamed the bibliomaniac, from the back row.

The P.B. turned a little yellow, as well he might.

"Let the man say his lines" he hissed "can't you."

"Merde" said Belacqua, in a loud despairing voice. He would understand that. He fell back into his place. There was no God in heaven.

"What is it?" whispered the Alba.

He was green, he fluttered a hand helplessly.

"Curse you" said the Alba "what is it?"

"Let the man say his lines" he mumbled "why don't you let the man say his lines?"

An outburst of applause unprecedented in the annals of the mauve salon suggested that he had done so at last.

"Now" said the Alba.

After a moment's hesitation he stated his absurd dilemma as follows:

"When with indifference I remember my past sorrow, my mind has indifference, my memory has sorrow. The mind, upon the indifference which is in it, is indifferent; yet the memory, upon the sadness which is in it, is not sad."

"Da capo" said the Alba.

"When with indifference I remember my past sorrow, the content of my mind is indifference, the content of my memory sorrow. The mind, upon the indifference which it contains, is indifferent; yet . . ."

"Basta" said the Alba.

The early birds were making a move already. Suddenly the Alba had an idea.

"Will you see me home?" she said.

236

"Have you got it" said Belacqua "because I haven't."

She covered his hand with her hand.

"Will you?" she repeated.

"What I want to know" said the Student.

"I see" said the Man of Law agreeably to Chas "by the paper that sailors are painting the Eiffel Tower with no less than forty tons of yellow."

The Frica had taken a cold farewell of the renegades. To her mind they were neither better nor worse than renegades. Now she was making as though to regain the estrade.

"Quick" said Belacqua "before they start."

He stood up and disengaged himself from the row. He stood back for her to pass and followed her out through the door of the torture-chamber into the vestibule. The Frica plunged after them. Torrents of spleen came gushing out of her. Belacqua opened the street-door and stood by it. Seeing the Alba inclined to do the polite, he said, in a loud outrageous voice (he was not afraid) that carried, as he learned later, even to the ears of the hard of hearing:

"Will you come on, for the love of God, away out of this?"

They taxied in silence to her home. Je t'adore à l'égal . . .

"Can you pay this man" he said, when they arrived, "because I spent my last make on a bottle."

She took the money out of her bag and handed it to him and he payed the man off. They stood, side by side, on the asphalt in front of the gate. The rain had ceased.

"Well" he said, intending at the most to clap a chaste kiss on her hand and take himself off on his ruined feet, and let it go at that. But she shrank away from the gesture and unlatched the gate.

Tire la chevillette, la bobinette cherra.

"Come in" she said "there's a fire and a bottle."

He went in. She would fill two glasses and poke up the fire and sit down in the chair and he would sit down on the floor with his back turned to her.

Voice of Grock . . .

AND

It began to rain again and now it would rain on through the night until morning. It was to be feared that the morning would have a fatigued appearance, and that the air, after its broken sleep, would be inclined to take the light of day sullenly. Even for Dublin, where seasonable weather is the exception rather than the rule, it was a rainy Xmas. A Leipzig prostitute, to whom Belacqua had occasion some weeks later to quote our rainfall for the month of December, exclaimed:

"Himmisacrakrüzidirkenjesusmariaundjosefundblütigeskreuz!"

All in one word. The things people come out with sometimes!

But the wind had fallen, as it so often does with us after midnight, a negligence on the part of Æolus alluded to in the most bitter terms by mariners of yore, as can be read in any of the old sea-journals that constitute so important a fund of our civic records, and the rain fell in a uniform untroubled manner. It fell upon the bay, the champaign-land and the mountains, and notably upon the central bog it fell with a rather desolate uniformity.

What would Ireland be, though, without this rain of hers. Rain is part of her charm. The impression one enjoys before landscape in Ireland, even on the clearest of days, of seeing it through a veil of tears, the mitigation of contour, to quote Chas's felicitous expression, in the compresses of our national visibility, to what source can this benefit be ascribed if not to our incontinent skies? Standing on the Big Sugarloaf, it may well be objected, or Douce, or even a low eminence like the Three Rock, the Welsh Hills are frequently plainly to be discerned. Don't cod yourselves. Those are clouds that you see, or your own nostalgia.

Consequently when Belacqua came out (you didn't suppose, it is to be hoped, that we were going to allow him to spend the night there), no moon was to be seen nor stars of any kind. He stood well out in the midst of the tramlines and established this circumstance beyond appeal. There was no light in the sky whatsoever. At least he could not discover any (and after all it is to his system, and none other, that we are obliged to refer for this passage), though he took off his glasses and wiped them carefully and inspected every available inch of the firmament before giving it up as a bad job. There was *some* light, of course there was, it being well known that perfect black is simply not to be had. But he was in no state of mind to be concerned with any such punctilio. The heavens, he said to himself, are darkened, absolutely, beyond any possibility of error.

Not having any money in his pocket the absence of city-bound conveyances caused him no chagrin to speak of. He had walked before, and now he could walk again. But so stiff and aching were his bones after his wetting, so raw and sore his feet, that he was reduced to a snail's pace. To make matters if possible more disagreeable, he developed an enormous pain in his stomach as he went along, and this bowed him more and more towards the ground till by the time he reached Ballsbridge he was positively doubled in two and unable to proceed. Marooned on the bridge and far from shelter, he had no choice but to sit down on the streaming pavement. What else was he to do? There was a more comfortable seat within striking distance, it is true, but he was in such a panic of discomfort that he never knew. He leaned back against the parapet and waited for the pain to get better. Gradually it got better.

What was that in his lap? He shook off his glasses and bent down his head to see. That was his hands. Now who would have thought that! He turned them this way and that, he clenched and unclenched them, keeping them on the move for the wonder of his weak eyes that were down now almost on top of them, because he was anxious to see the details. He opened them in unison at last, finger by finger together, till there they were, wide open, face upward, rancid, an inch from his squint, which however slowly righted itself as he began to lose interest in them as a spectacle. Scarcely had he made to employ them on his face when a voice, slightly more in sorrow than in anger this time, enjoined him to move on, which, the pain being so much better, he was only too happy to do.

END

Dear Parent:
Your child's love of reading starts here!

Every child learns to read in a different way and at his or her own speed. Some go back and forth between reading levels and read favorite books again and again. Others read through each level in order. You can help your young reader improve and become more confident by encouraging his or her own interests and abilities. From books your child reads with you to the first books he or she reads alone, there are I Can Read Books for every stage of reading:

SHARED READING
Basic language, word repetition, and whimsical illustrations, ideal for sharing with your emergent reader

BEGINNING READING
Short sentences, familiar words, and simple concepts for children eager to read on their own

READING WITH HELP
Engaging stories, longer sentences, and language play for developing readers

READING ALONE
Complex plots, challenging vocabulary, and high-interest topics for the independent reader

ADVANCED READING
Short paragraphs, chapters, and exciting themes for the perfect bridge to chapter books

I Can Read Books have introduced children to the joy of reading since 1957. Featuring award-winning authors and illustrators and a fabulous cast of beloved characters, I Can Read Books set the standard for beginning readers.

A lifetime of discovery begins with the magical words **"I Can Read!"**

Visit www.icanread.com for information
on enriching your child's reading experience.

For Margaret,
who hates 'cary masks
—H. P.

To Kevin, Sara, and Ian
—L. S.

HarperCollins®, 🐻®, and I Can Read Book® are trademarks of HarperCollins Publishers Inc.

Happy Haunting, Amelia Bedelia Text copyright © 2004 by Herman S. Parish III Illustrations copyright © 2004 by Lynn Sweat All rights reserved. No part of this book may be used or reproduced in any manner whatsoever without written permission except in the case of brief quotations embodied in critical articles and reviews. Manufactured in China. For information address HarperCollins Children's Books, a division of HarperCollins Publishers, 195 Broadway, New York, NY 10007. www.harperchildrens.com

Library of Congress Cataloging-in-Publication Data
Parish, Herman.
Happy haunting, Amelia Bedelia / by Herman Parish ; pictures by Lynn Sweat.
    p.   cm.
"Greenwillow Books."
Summary: Amelia Bedelia tries to help Mr. and Mrs. Rogers with their Halloween party.
ISBN-10: 0-06-051893-6 (trade bdg.) — ISBN-13: 978-0-06-051893-6 (trade bdg.)
ISBN-10: 0-06-051894-4 (lib. bdg.) — ISBN-13: 978-0-06-051894-3 (lib. bdg.)
ISBN-10: 0-06-051895-2 (pbk.) — ISBN-13: 978-0-06-051895-0 (pbk.)
    [1. Halloween—Fiction. 2. Humorous stories.] I. Sweat, Lynn, ill. II. Title.
PZ7.P2185Ha 2004
[E]—dc22   2003013788
          15 16 SCP 20 19 18 17 16 15 14 13 12
                                    ❖
Originally published by Greenwillow Books, an imprint of HarperCollinsPublishers, in 2004.

I Can Read!

READING
2
WITH HELP

HAPPY HAUNTING, AMELIA BEDELIA

story by Herman Parish
pictures by Lynn Sweat

HarperCollins*Publishers*

When Amelia Bedelia arrived for work,
she could not believe her eyes.
"Oh my gosh," said Amelia Bedelia.
"What has happened to the house?"

"This is terrible," said Amelia Bedelia.

"Mr. and Mrs. Rogers must need me.

Someone has ruined their house."

She ran to the front door.

"Aghhh!" yelled Amelia Bedelia. "Help!"

Mr. and Mrs. Rogers rushed outside.

"Hold still," said Mrs. Rogers.

"I will get the bats out of your belfry."

"Ha!" said Mr. Rogers.

"That would be a full-time job.

She has made me bats for years."

"You are untangled, Amelia Bedelia,"

said Mrs. Rogers.

"Come inside and relax."

"Wow," said Amelia Bedelia.

"Who wrecked your house?"

"We did," said Mrs. Rogers.

"We are getting ready for Halloween."

"Is that tonight?" said Amelia Bedelia.

"How did you forget?" said Mr. Rogers.

"Those bats on the front porch
must have made you batty."

"Sorry," said Amelia Bedelia.

"I have been very busy.

I was at school helping children

make their costumes."

"Good for you," said Mrs. Rogers.

"We invited all of our neighbors

for a Halloween party. And you, too.

Tonight, the best costume wins a prize."

"Gosh," said Amelia Bedelia.

"Your house looks so spooky."

"Thank you," said Mrs. Rogers.

"The spookier the better."

"That is the idea," said Mr. Rogers.

"What fun," said Amelia Bedelia.

"I will help you clean up."

"No you won't," said Mr. Rogers.

"I worked hard

to get this place to look shabby."

"Then I will help you mess up,"

said Amelia Bedelia.

"What should I do first?"

"Hand me that hammer,"

said Mr. Rogers.

"But first, crack a window.

It has gotten very warm in here."

15

"Uh-oh," said Amelia Bedelia.
"I tried to just crack it,
but it broke instead."

"Amelia Bedelia!" said Mr. Rogers.

"I meant, open the window a bit."

"It is open," said Amelia Bedelia.

"There are lots of bits . . . and pieces."

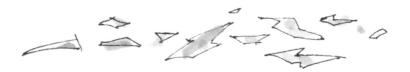

"It's not your fault, dear,"
said Mrs. Rogers.
"Besides, that broken window
makes our house
look truly haunted."
Mr. Rogers shook his head.
"I think you both
have gone batty,"
he said.

"What is next?"
asked Amelia Bedelia.

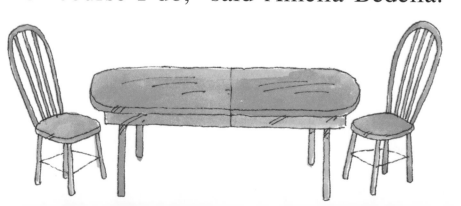

"Let's see," said Mrs. Rogers.

"A lot of people are coming tonight.

We should add a leaf to the table."

"A leaf?" said Amelia Bedelia.

"Yes, of course," said Mrs. Rogers.

"A leaf or two makes the table larger.

Do you know

where to find the leaves?"

"Of course I do," said Amelia Bedelia.

"Before you go,"
said Mr. Rogers,
"please hand me that witch."
"That which what?"
said Amelia Bedelia.
"Not what," said Mr. Rogers.
"Witch."
"Which what?" said Amelia Bedelia.
"Not which what," said Mr. Rogers.
"That witch there,
with the pointy hat."

Amelia Bedelia held up two witches.

"They both have pointy hats," she said.

"Which witch do you want?"

"Whichever," said Mr. Rogers.

"No, I mean, whatever witch,

which . . . oh, skip it!

Just get those leaves."

Amelia Bedelia skipped away.

"Good thing it is fall,"
said Amelia Bedelia.
"I can get lots of leaves for the table."
She saw something wriggle
under a leaf.
"Sorry, Mister Worm, but back you go,"
she said.
"Yoo-hoo," called Mrs. Rogers
from the kitchen window.
"There is no time to do yard work.
I need your help."

Amelia Bedelia went inside.

"There we go," said Amelia Bedelia.

"Now the table looks smaller to me,

but it is so much prettier.

Mrs. Rogers always has great ideas."

Amelia Bedelia went into the kitchen.

"There you are," said Mrs. Rogers.

"You are so creative with food.

Let's cook up some gruesome goodies."

"Goody," said Amelia Bedelia.

THIS WORM CASSEROLE NEEDS MORE SPAGHETTI.

Mmmmm! CRANBERRY JUICE MAKES A TASTY VAMPIRE PUNCH.

CRUMBLE UP COOKIES FOR THE KITTY LITTER CAKE.

WE NEED MORE EYEBALLS.

I'LL PEEL ANOTHER BUNCH OF GRAPES.

DRIED APRICOTS MAKE DELICIOUS EARS.

There was a knock at the kitchen door.

"Trick or treat," said Cousin Alcolu.

"I do not know any tricks,"
said Amelia Bedelia.

"But you can sample some treats."

"Thank you," said Cousin Alcolu.

Mr. Rogers walked into the kitchen.

"Something smells good," he said.

"Well, it sure isn't me,"

said Cousin Alcolu.

"I have been working very hard.

I harvested a load of pumpkins

for the party tonight."

"How generous," said Mr. Rogers.

"Do you know how to carve

jack-o'-lanterns?"

"I did one," said Cousin Alcolu.

He showed them his pumpkin.

"That face looks very familiar,"

said Amelia Bedelia.

Mrs. Rogers tried not to laugh.

"Very funny," said Mr. Rogers.

"But that pumpkin is too handsome.

Have you got anything scarier?"

"Wait here," said Cousin Alcolu.

He went out to his truck.

Cousin Alcolu returned
with the scariest scarecrow ever.
"Meet Oswald," said Cousin Alcolu.
"He scares away birds for miles."
"Ooooooh!" said Mrs. Rogers.
"He sends shivers down my spine.
Oswald can sit here for tonight."

"He doesn't scare me," said Mr. Rogers.

"I do not know the meaning

of the word fear."

"You don't?" said Amelia Bedelia.

"The word 'fear' is in the dictionary.

I will look it up for you."

"Show me later," said Mr. Rogers.

"I must get my costume ready.

I am going to be

a circus strongman."

"And I am going to be

a queen," said Mrs. Rogers.

"Amelia Bedelia, what is

your costume going to be?"

31

"Gee," said Amelia Bedelia.

"I do not have a costume."

"Sure you do," said Mr. Rogers.

"You wear a costume

every day."

Mrs. Rogers glared at her husband.

"What do you mean?"

said Amelia Bedelia.

"These are my clothes, not a costume.

I have always dressed like this."

Mr. Rogers felt bad about

what he had said.

He was too embarrassed

to say anything.

"Come along, Amelia Bedelia,"

said Mrs. Rogers.

"I have an idea for you . . .

and for Cousin Alcolu."

"See you tonight?" said Mr. Rogers.

Amelia Bedelia did not reply.

That night, as darkness fell,

the house really did look haunted.

Spooky music with scary sounds

made it even more fun.

Floorboards creaked.

Chains rattled.

Moans and groans

filled the air.

CLANTY. CLANK. KLUNK

AI-YEEEEEE

The doorbell rang.

"Our first trick-or-treaters,"

said Mrs. Rogers.

"Would you get the front door, dear?"

"Yes, Your Majesty," said Mr. Rogers.

As soon as he was out of sight,

Mrs. Rogers ran to the back door.

While Mr. Rogers
handed out treats
at the front door . . .

Mrs. Rogers
let in a trick
at the back door.

"Right this way," said Mr. Rogers.

"Thank you," said a skeleton.

"I was dying to come in."

The party food was a big hit.

"Care for an eyeball?"

said a girl to her dad.

"Yuck!" he said.

"Yum," she said.

"They are good and disgusting."

"Try some finger food,"

said Mr. Rogers.

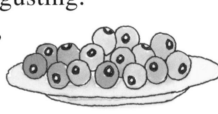

"Oh, cool!" said the boy.

"These cookies have little fingers."

"They were Amelia Bedelia's idea,"

said Mr. Rogers.

"Where is she?"

asked the boy.

"Good question," said Mr. Rogers.

"May I have two cups of blood?"
asked a girl.

"My pleasure," said Mrs. Rogers.

"I love your costumes."

"Amelia Bedelia helped us,"
said a little boy.

"Wonderful," said Mrs. Rogers.

"Maybe you will win the prize."

"Have you seen Amelia Bedelia?"
asked Mr. Rogers.

"Not yet," said Mrs. Rogers.

"She might not come,

thanks to you."

"What did I do wrong?"
said Mr. Rogers.

"You know," said Mrs. Rogers.

"You made fun of her clothes."

"I feel terrible," said Mr. Rogers.

"I will apologize when I see her."

Just then Mr. Rogers shuddered.

"What is wrong?" said Mrs. Rogers.

"It sounds silly," said Mr. Rogers.

"That scarecrow gives me the creeps."

"Scaredy-cat," said Mrs. Rogers.

"It looks alive," said Mr. Rogers.

"I feel like it is watching me."

Ding-dong!

Mr. Rogers jumped.

"Relax," said Mrs. Rogers.

"You are imagining things.

Go and see who is at the door."

Mr. Rogers opened the door.

He smiled a big smile.

"Well, well," he said.

"I have never been so glad
to see a ghost. Do come in,
Amelia . . . uh, Miss Ghost."

"WOOOOOOOO!" said the ghost
as it floated into the house.

Mr. Rogers was a perfect host.

"Care for refreshments?"

he asked.

The ghost shook its head no.

"Well," said Mr. Rogers,

"would you like to judge

our costume contest?"

The ghost nodded yes.

"Attention, everyone," said Mrs. Rogers.
"It is time for our Halloween contest.
Anyone who wishes to compete
for the prize, step right this way."

"I am Sonny Day,

your T.V. weatherman.

I forecast that I will win!"

"You can't beat peace and love. This hippie has the grooviest 'tea' shirt and 'bell' bottoms."

"If I win, I will still be in a pickle!"

"I am all eyes."   "I am all ears."

"And I am
right under your nose."

"Bravo!" said Mrs. Rogers.

"Yes," said Mr. Rogers.

"I can tell that Amelia Bedelia
helped them a lot. Too bad
she could not be here tonight."

He winked at Mrs. Rogers.

Just then the clock struck ten.

"Okay, everyone," said Mrs. Rogers.

"Time to take off your masks."

"Uh-oh!" said the ghost.

It tried to slip away.

"Whoa there," said Mr. Rogers.

"It's time I put my foot down."

Mr. Rogers stepped on the sheet.

As the ghost kept walking,

the sheet was pulled off to reveal . . .

"Cousin Alcolu!" said Mr. Rogers.

"Where is Amelia Bedelia?"

Cousin Alcolu looked very afraid.

He pointed behind Mr. Rogers.

He opened his mouth to speak,

but he was scared speechless.

Mr. Rogers wheeled around.

"BOO!" screamed the scarecrow.

"Yiiiiii!" yelled Mr. Rogers.

He threw his barbell up in the air.

Mr. Rogers turned around

and ran right into Cousin Alcolu.

They both fell in a heap.

"Happy Halloween!"
said Amelia Bedelia.
"Amelia Bedelia!"
said Mr. Rogers.
"Ha-ha," said Cousin Alcolu.
"I think you should call her
Amelia *Boo*delia."

"As your queen," said Mrs. Rogers,
"I declare Amelia Bedelia the winner
for the best costume."

The next day Amelia Bedelia

and Cousin Alcolu

came to help clean up.

"Great party," said Cousin Alcolu.

"Thank you," said Mrs. Rogers.

"We will do it again next year.

Start planning your costume now."

"I will," said Amelia Bedelia.

"But you have the best ideas."

"Those trick-or-treaters!" said Mr. Rogers.

"Somebody piled leaves on our table."

"That was me," said Amelia Bedelia.

"That was lovely," said Mrs. Rogers.

"They made a beautiful centerpiece."

Mrs. Rogers showed Amelia Bedelia
how to add a leaf to the table.
"There we go," said Mrs. Rogers.
"Now let's set the table for lunch."

"Amelia Bedelia," said Mr. Rogers.

"I apologize for what I said yesterday."

"Apology accepted,"

said Amelia Bedelia.

"Try some leftover

Worm Casserole."

Mr. Rogers took a huge portion.

"It is very tasty," he said.

"Glad you like it," said Amelia Bedelia.

"I got worried yesterday

when I ran out of spaghetti."

"You ran out?" asked Mr. Rogers.

He took a closer look at his food.

"Then what is this?" said Mr. Rogers.

"Lucky me," said Amelia Bedelia.

"Every leaf I picked up in your yard

had a fat, juicy worm under it."

Mr. Rogers turned as green as a witch.

"Trick or treat!" said Amelia Bedelia,
laughing.